"Her Unexpected Mistletoe Kiss"

Bulbs, Blossoms and Bouquets #9

By Laura Ann

This is a work of fiction. Similarities to real people, places, or events are entirely coincidental.

HER UNEXPECTED MISTLETOE KISS

First edition. November 15, 2021.

Copyright © 2021 Laura Ann.

Written by Laura Ann.

DEDICATION

To my Dad.
Your quiet support is never ending.
Thank you for all you've done.
I'm who I am because of you.

ACKNOWLEDGEMENTS

No author works alone. Thank you, Tami.
You make it Christmas every time
I get a new cover. And thank you to my Beta Team.
Truly, your help with my stories is immeasurable.

Prologue

(From the back of "Her Unexpected Protector")

Carson whistled as he walked to grab his mail. Life was going pretty good at the moment. Work was plugging away, there seemed to be no end to people who hated other people and wanted justice in court, giving him a hefty paycheck and too many tasks for daylight hours.

He paused at the thought. Really, if he broke it down, that wasn't a very good way to look at his life's work, especially because he enjoyed what he did. But still...

He shrugged. Who cared how he broke down his work? He paid his bills, had enough extra to have fun with, and he was enjoying almost every minute of it.

He grabbed the mail and slowly walked back inside his townhome as he thumbed through the envelopes.

"Hey, Carson."

With his hand on the knob, Carson turned to smile at his neighbor. "Emme!" He took in her stylish outfit of white shorts with a baby blue sweater hanging off her shoulder. "Don't you look nice."

Emme smiled enticingly and stuck out her hip. "Maybe one of these days you'll think I look good enough to have dinner with."

Carson winked. "I don't think that's the issue," he said. "I think you're already too far ahead for me to ever catch up." With a quick wave, he ducked inside and closed the door.

Emme was a beautiful woman, Carson would have to be blind to not see it. The problem? Like so many of the other women he met, they all knew he was related to Grayson Cordova; Hollywood heartthrob, action hero and recently turned director. His change in career, however, didn't change the thousands of women who wanted to meet Gray.

Despite Carson's earlier thoughts about how well life was going, if there was one thing Carson would change, it would be the fact that he couldn't seem to meet a woman who actually wanted to know him for him. They either enjoyed his money, or they wanted a crack at his brother.

"Stupid fame," he grumbled, tossing the mail on the counter. A bright red envelope caught his eye and Carson paused before pulling it out of the stack. "Speaking of..."

The letter was from Gray and Brook. Brooklyn was Grayson's lovely wife that he'd met while hiding up in Oregon during a time when Gray was recuperating from an onset injury.

Carson ripped open the card and frowned when he read the invitation. Apparently, his brother and sister-in-law were holding a Christmas party next month. A week-long Christmas party.

"You've got to be kidding me," Carson grumbled. He pulled out his phone and quickly dialed Jude.

Jude was Grayson's personal physical therapist, but with Grayson married and moving from house to house as he worked on different projects, Carson and Jude had become closer without Gray playing mediator between them.

"Hey man," Jude answered.

"Jude, the dude," Carson responded, knowing his friend hated the nickname. "What's up?"

Jude sighed. "Really? You're over thirty years old now, don't you think the dumb nicknames have gotten a little old?"

Carson chuckled. "Ticking you off never gets old," he responded. Really, Carson enjoyed playing devil's advocate in every part of life, not just in teasing his friends. It was part of what made him such a good lawyer.

"You're impossible," Jude grumbled. "Did you have a point for this call?"

"Did you get today's mail?"

"You too, huh?" Jude said. "I was just looking at the invite and deciding how to politely decline."

"What?" Carson cried. "You can't decline!"

"Why not?"

"Because then I'll be left without a wingman!" Carson explained.

"You're a grown man," Jude said. "I have no doubt you can handle it. Besides, aren't you friends with a lot of Brook's buddies up in Seaside Bay?"

"Aren't you?" Carson shot back.

"I really only got to know Brook while I was there," Jude said. "Though I met the rest once at a bonfire...and at the wedding. They're all nice."

"They are, but they're also all very married."

"Why do you think I was trying to get out of it?" Jude said with a laugh. "Like I want to walk around Gray's coastal mansion for a week being a third wheel to every person I meet."

"Which is exactly why you need to come," Carson groaned. "Otherwise, I'm the one walking around like that."

"Yeah, but you're family."

"Which is why *I* can't say no. Gray won't let me." Carson fell onto his couch. This was not how he had planned to enjoy his holiday break. A week in Oregon? In the winter? The people were nice enough, but geez. What the heck was he going to do for a week? Especially as possibly the only single man in the group.

Jude sighed. "Car, I really don't want to go."

"Me either," Carson grumbled. "Please...I'm begging. Don't leave me alone like this."

There was silence on the other line for a few seconds and hope shot into Carson's chest. If he could at least have Jude there, then Carson would have someone to play pool with or cover for him if he escaped out the back door to get away from all the happily hitched folks.

"I have to work…" Jude hedged.

"I'll pay you twice your normal salary."

"Really?"

Carson nodded. "Yep. Scout's honor."

"I didn't even know you were a Scout, but I just might take you up on that. I might need to get a new car, so if you richy lawyer types are passing out money just for spending time with friends, then that might be a good deal. Torture. But a good deal."

Carson grinned. "And people say money doesn't talk."

"It doesn't," Jude replied. "We just let it lead us by the nose." He huffed. "Alright. I'll come, but you have to promise not to throw me under the bus."

"Scout's honor," Carson said for the second time.

"Again, I have no idea if you were a scout."

"I plead the fifth," Carson answered with a grin.

"You would." Jude took a deep breath. "Fine. I'll confirm. But if I regret this, then next time you ask me to work on your back, I'm totally going to throw something out of alignment."

Carson winced at the thought, but smiled at his victory. "So noted." He calculated things in his head. "We've only got three weeks. Better let your boss know."

"Yeah, yeah. I'll make sure things are fine on my end. You just worry about getting your own butt there."

"Yes sir!" Carson saluted the phone. "I owe you one!"

"You owe me a new car!" Jude called out before the line went dead.

Carson flipped the invite onto the coffee table. He wasn't exactly thrilled at the idea of going, but having Jude there would make things better. And if Jude was naive enough to think that Carson wouldn't throw him under the bus if it meant avoiding the matchmaking of his family? Then it would only make Carson's escape easier.

CHAPTER 1

Isabel, or Belle, Kerr rubbed her upper arms. The wind blowing in off the ocean was icy. Much colder than Belle would have expected for a place that rarely saw snow. Shivering, she slammed her car door, then winced, hoping the whole thing didn't fall apart from the impact. The hinges didn't move well, so she had to give it a good boost, but with the way the small sedan shook each time, Belle was certain that one of these days it would simply crumple to the ground in a heap of dust and rust, just like in the cartoons she had watched growing up.

She debated about getting her luggage out of the back and ended up leaving it. Her brother could help bring it in later. Right now, Belle was desperate for a little heat. Rubbing her hands together, she sprinted up the driveway of her brother's small Oregon coast cottage and knocked on the door.

It sprang open almost immediately, letting her know her family had been waiting for her.

"Look what the cat drug in," Richard drawled with a smug grin.

"I don't know why I let you talk me into this," Belle said through her chattering teeth. "I'm freezing my tail off."

Richard laughed and opened the door wider. "Hurry in before you let out all the warm air."

As soon as Belle had crossed the threshold, the door shut behind her and she found herself enveloped in a bear hug that took her breath away. "Too tight," she squeaked as her brother practically lifted her off her feet.

He chuckled low and dropped her back to the ground. After letting go, he kept ahold of her upper arms and held her away from him, studying her from head to toe. His bearded, friendly smile dropped and he frowned. "You've lost weight."

Belle rolled her eyes. "I'm a starving college student. Of course I lost weight."

"You told me you had enough to get through that last semester," he argued. Letting go of her completely, he put his hands on his hips. "You were studying culinary arts, for heaven's sake, Belle. How in the world could you be going hungry?"

Her cheeks heated up and Belle tucked a stray piece of hair behind her ear. "It's not that hard when you barely sleep because of finals," she said back. She chose to leave out the fact that by the end of graduation, her bank account held an entire twenty dollars. Besides, she'd always had plenty of curves. A few pounds here and there wouldn't be missed.

Rich reached up and cupped her cold cheek, rubbing under her eye. "I guess that explains the half moons here. For a second there, I thought you'd joined a fight club."

Belle pushed his hand away. "It's not like you got through college without being in the exact same position."

Richard sighed. "Maybe not, but still...you're my kid sister. I don't like seeing you one step away from collapsing."

The indignation in Belle melted. Rich really was the best big brother, almost too good, actually. Ever since their parents had decided they wanted to see the U.S. from the back of a motorcycle, it had been Rich that Belle had turned to whenever she needed help or advice.

She had tried, of course, not to call on him too often, but sometimes, even an independent woman needed a shoulder to lean on.

Another shiver ran through her and Rich laughed while scratching his beard. "Welcome to Seaside Bay," he said, ushering her farther into the house. "It's only going to get worse."

"Great," Belle muttered as they walked farther into the house interior. "Just what I wanted."

"You'll have to get over your California wimpiness quickly, or this will be a miserable winter," Rich said with a grin.

"Belle!" Sofia, Rich's wife, was standing at the stove when they walked into the kitchen. Wiping her hands on her jeans, she rushed over and engulfed Belle in a much less tight, but just as comforting, hug. "We're so glad you're here," Sofia whispered.

Belle smiled and melted a little bit more. Her annoying brother had somehow managed to snag the heart of the sweetest woman Belle had ever met. They might joke that women are full of sugar and spice, but Sofia had somehow missed the memo. She was nothing but pure sugar and Belle loved it.

"Thank you so much for being willing to put up with me for the winter," Belle said, smiling at her sister-in-law. "Until I get a real job, I'm not quite sure where I'm going to end up."

Sofia waved a hand through the air. "We're happy to have you any time. And if it takes longer than the winter to figure out your plan, then that's fine too." She spun on her heel. "I made clam chowder for dinner," she threw over her shoulder. "And homemade bread. I hope that's okay."

"Sounds delicious," Belle offered. "And warm."

Sofia laughed softly. "That wind has teeth, huh?"

Belle nodded. "I didn't realize there were piranhas in Oregon."

"We don't. But there are great white sharks." Rich came up behind Belle and snapped his teeth.

Belle jerked away and pushed his shoulder. "On second thought, I might not even make it the whole winter."

Rich only grinned wider while Sofia sighed. "Rich, don't you dare drive off your sister on her first day here. At least let her warm up a bit before she decides you're too much to live with."

Rich came up behind his wife and wrapped his arms around her. "Are you saying you don't like living with me?" he whispered in her ear.

Belle spun as Sofia's giggle echoed through the kitchen. She was happy for her brother in his wonderful marriage, but in no way did Belle want to watch them be lovey all day long.

"Cole should be awake," Sofia called as Belle wandered into the family room. "Second door on the left upstairs if you want to go get him."

Belle grinned. "On it!" She practically raced up the stairs. Her brother might be a dork, but he had produced the cutest nephew this side of the Mississippi. At fourteen months, Cole was proving to be just as stubborn and active as his father. The videos Sofia had kept Belle supplied with while she was in college were adorable and sweet justice for all the pranks Rich had pulled on Belle when she and her brother were young.

Babbling and a thumping sound could be heard as Belle got closer to Cole's door. She turned the handle and slowly peeked inside. "Where's my favorite boy?" Belle said in a silly voice.

The thumping and baby speak stopped as Cole looked wide eyed at his visitor.

Belle stepped in the rest of the way and held up her arms. "Cole! Did you miss Aunt Belle?"

It took a moment, but finally a wide smile spread across the toddler's face and he held out his arms. "Beh! Beh!"

"That's what I like to hear!" Belle teased, walking over to lift him out of his crib. "Ugh! Good gracious, little man," she said as she settled her nephew on her hip. "You've gotten huge! Little man isn't going to work for you anymore."

Belle nuzzled his neck, enjoying Cole's giggles as they walked back downstairs. "Dada!"

Belle sighed and gave her brother a look when she got back to the kitchen. "Figures," she grumbled.

Rich chuckled and took his son, who practically knocked Belle over in his hurry to get to his father. "The boy has good taste. What can I say?"

Belle shook her head, but the smile never left her face. She had never planned to be jobless when she graduated college, nor had she expected to have a bank account so small it barely existed. But right here, right now, she was grateful for her family, including her annoying brother. Maybe the winter wouldn't be quite so bad if it included the warm scene unfolding in front of her. Smiles, laughter, and love... Yeah...she could definitely have ended up somewhere far worse.

*****

Carson Cordova groaned as he let his front door slam behind him. His briefcase felt especially heavy this evening and he didn't even bother trying to put it on the usual table, letting it fall to the floor instead.

Walking toward the couch, he let himself fall face first into the cushy pillows. Without looking up, he kicked off his shoes and then let out a long breath, deflating every muscle in his body.

His phone buzzed in his briefcase and Carson let out another groan. "What now?" he muttered.

The noise came again and reluctantly he pushed himself upright and stomped back to where he'd left his work load. After digging around, he finally found the infernal device and it took a whole ten seconds of holding his breath to keep from chucking it across the room.

Forcing himself to look at the screen, he bit back a curse. "Two days," he grumbled. "How the heck am I supposed to have everything wrapped up in two days?"

The notification had been a reminder that he was leaving for Oregon soon. Sometimes Carson's work made it impossible for him to keep track of time, and he had come to know over the years that if he didn't have a reminder set, he would more than likely work through whatever event he was supposed to attend.

This year he was attending his brother's Christmas party up in Oregon. This time, Carson wished he hadn't remembered to put down a reminder. Working through a party full of in-love couples didn't sound too bad.

Not that Carson was against relationships... He just didn't like being the only single guy in the group. Talk about awkward.

He pulled up Jude's name and punched the call button.

"Jude Lisbon," the baritone voice on the other end of the line said.

"Dude, don't you check your caller ID?" Carson asked. He shuffled back to the couch and fell backward this time. Right now he was extremely grateful that he hadn't listened to the designer about what furniture to pick. Carson might not have the biggest house in Hollywood, but he at least had a comfortable one. His couch wasn't as pretty as the one the woman had tried to foist on him, but he could sleep on it without getting a crick in his neck and that had to count for something.

Jude sighed. "I was busy and didn't bother looking." His voice perked up. "Are you calling to cancel the trip?"

Carson rubbed his forehead. "I wish. Brook called me last week to tell me how excited she was that I was coming. I can't back out now."

Jude grumbled something unintelligible. "I shouldn't have listened to you," he snapped. "This is going to be a disaster."

"It's not going to be a disaster," Carson argued. "Just a...semi-disaster."

"Why do you always have to have the last word?"

Carson grinned. "Because I'm a lawyer. Speaking last is the best place to be. I can refute anything the other counsellor said and then give an ending statement that sticks in a jury's mind longer."

"Well, bully for you, sunshine," Jude muttered.

"Wow, must have been a great day at work," Carson said.

Jude sighed again. "Sorry," he said in a contrite voice. "I'll get control of myself."

"Are you that upset about the party?" Carson asked, suddenly feeling bad that he'd talked Jude into being his wingman. At the time a few weeks ago, it had been the only way Carson could think of to keep from being the only single person at the party. But now he wondered if maybe he'd pushed Jude too far.

"No," Jude responded. "I just...nevermind. It really doesn't matter."

"Are you sure? Do you need legal advice?" Carson grinned. "I'm pretty good at giving advice."

"It's your advice that got me in this mess in the first place," Jude retorted.

"Touché." Carson squished his lips to the side. "How much do you think we'll have to hang around the house?"

"Uh..."

"I mean...what if we're there for the important bits, but the rest of the time we make sure we have somewhere else to be?"

"Like where?" Jude asked.

Carson shrugged. "I don't know. Don't they have pretty good fishing up there?"

"Are you crazy? It's cold up there. Getting out on the ocean is asking to be turned into an icicle."

"Careful. Your Cali roots are showing," Carson teased.

"There's a reason I've lived here since becoming an adult," Jude said. "I hate cold weather. And it's not like you have thick skin either. You're just as wimpy as I am when it comes to the cold."

"I go skiing every year," Carson reminded his friend. "I know how to handle the weather."

"Still...being out in the middle of the ocean has got to be far from pleasant."

Carson shrugged again. "But it's something to do. Better than sticking around the house all day."

"True..." Jude paused. "Okay, sign me up. If I have to watch a bunch of people kiss under the mistletoe, the least I can do is come home with a freezer full of salmon."

"I think the sturgeon run during the winter," Carson offered.

"Aren't those catch and release?"

Carson frowned. "I don't know. Guess I'll have to check." He shook his head. "But it doesn't matter. We'll get it figured out. One of Brook's friends has a boat and I have no doubt that he'll be willing to set us up."

"Sounds good," Jude said. "Did you wanna carpool to the airport?"

"Yeah..." Carson scratched his chin. "Might as well. There's no reason we should pay for two parking spots."

"True. I'll swing by Thursday morning, then."

"Perfect. Thanks, man!" Carson said.

"Yep. See ya then."

Carson hung up the phone and tossed it the next cushion over. He felt a little better after chatting with Jude, but the party was still a weight on his shoulders. It stunk being the last single person in his family. Jude was a good friend of the family, but Carson knew full well that his happily married brother and sister would both use the Christmas party as a way to try and set him up with a woman, which was the absolute worst way for anyone to meet somebody else.

The pressure, the expectation, the subsequent disappointment, it was the recipe for that disaster Jude was talking about earlier.

Picking his phone back up, Carson decided maybe one fishing trip wasn't going to be quite enough. If he was going to avoid having his siblings play matchmaker, he needed to be too busy for them to pin down. Looked like it was time for him to find out all that Seaside Bay had to offer.

CHAPTER 2

"Your resume is fine," the woman across the desk said, pulling off her glasses. "But I have a few questions." She leaned back, her gray hair pulled so tightly it tugged at the sides of her eyes slightly. She toyed with her glasses. "What brings you to Seaside Bay? I'm not fond of hiring workers every few months and had hoped to receive a few more applicants that would be long term."

Belle swallowed. That was a harder question than she'd expected. She wasn't sure how long she planned to be in Seaside Bay. It was a fine enough place, but Belle didn't have a particular attachment to it. Not to mention, her hope was to eventually open her own bakery. She definitely wasn't looking at this catering gig as a career option. Its purpose was to give her an income and give her food experience that would look good when she wanted a loan to open her shop, wherever that ended up being.

"I'll be honest," Belle started.

"Please do," Mrs. Stallings inserted, her eyebrows raised.

Belle hesitated at the interruption. Mrs. Stallings was a formidable woman, and a little intimidating. She hadn't been cruel during the interview or overly demanding, but she didn't give off any warm and fuzzy vibes either. "I don't know how long I'm here for." Belle paused to see if the other woman planned to speak. When she didn't, Rose continued. "As you can see from my resume, I just graduated a week ago. My plans right now are very fluid. I hope to open my own bakery and want to do it sooner rather than later."

"Do you plan to open it here in Seaside?"

Belle shrugged. "I'm not sure. If I find a good reason to stay and can find a spot, then sure. My brother mentioned that you don't have a bread shop here, so I'm sure that the competition would be workable." Belle had an entire binder full of recipes that she had created during her time in culinary school and she guarded them with her life. She knew that no matter where she ended up, she could have something unique, but looking at similar businesses was always a good idea.

"We have a chocolate and cookie store, run by a married couple," Mrs. Stallings mused, chewing on the earpiece of her glasses. "We have a saltwater taffy shop that has all the usual coastal candies the tourists are looking for. And there's my catering company, of course, but as far as I know, there are no homemade bread shops within twenty miles of us."

Belle smiled. "Be that as it may, only time will tell if Seaside becomes my home." She folded her hands together and laid them in her lap. "I'm sorry I can't give you more than that. I'm here until I'm not. The only thing I can say for sure is that it will be through the major holidays."

Mrs. Stallings pursed her lips. "That's not exactly what I was hoping for, but right now I don't have enough applications to fill positions." She sighed. "I always need more help during the holiday season, so I suppose taking you on as a seasonal worker is fine." She pierced Belle with a dark look. "But seasonal or not, I don't tolerate inefficiency. You will work just as hard as the long term employees or I will make do without you."

Belle nodded, though she felt the rebuke was slightly undeserved. "I understand. And I won't let you down."

"See that you don't." Mrs. Stallings stood and offered her hand over the desk. "We have a few office parties coming up. They're always the first ones to be catered for Christmas. After that I have a very large party at the Cordova home."

Belle choked. "Cordova? As in, Grayson and Brook Cordova?"

Mrs. Stallings rolled her eyes. "All you young people and your obsession with celebrities."

Bell scowled. "You caught me off guard," she said to her new boss. "I'll maintain professional decorum no matter who we serve. I just hadn't expected to find such famous people in this small town."

Mrs. Stallings nodded. "Mrs. Cordova—Brook—grew up here and still has friends here. She and her husband come back quite often to visit. This year they're hosting a week-long Christmas party and we're providing most of the food."

Belle whistled low. "A week. Wow. That's impressive."

"Which is exactly why we're not going to mess it up." She raised an eyebrow at Belle. "Tomorrow, eight a.m. sharp, I want you here in my kitchen. I don't have anyone who specializes in breads, and I'd like to see yours. Specifically croissants and dinner rolls."

Belle tilted her head to the side. "You don't want me to serve?"

"In a company as small as ours, you'll do that too, but being able to offer more specialties will be a boon to us."

Belle nodded. "You'll have all the ingredients, I presume."

"I'll have the basics, but if you want something special, I'd suggest you grab it yourself."

"Then I'll plan on seeing you then." Belle shook Mrs. Stallings hand one more time, then let herself out.

Once out in the cool wintery air, she blew out a long breath and broke into a smile. Her boss was a tough cookie, but Belle felt sure the woman was fair. She finally had her first real job in the food industry, she was going to get a chance to share her work with others, and she had a place to sleep for the whole holiday season.

Life was looking up.

Belle climbed into her rust bucket of a car and quickly dialed Sofia.

"Belle! How'd it go?" Sofia asked loudly over the crying of little Cole.

"Ah, geez, Sof. What's he mad about?" Belle held the phone away from her ear.

"I wouldn't let him put the scissors in his mouth," Sofia drawled. "It's amazing how well the human race has survived when our first instincts as children are to impale ourselves with sharp objects."

Belle laughed, then relaxed as the crying calmed down.

"So..." Sofia pressed. "What happened?"

Belle waited just a second more, drawing out the suspense. "I got the job!"

"Oh, sweetie, that's wonderful!" Sofia cried. "I *knew* that would be a good fit for you. You're so talented in the kitchen. Mrs. Stallings couldn't have chosen better."

Belle laughed a little. "I think it was her lack of applicants that gave me a boost, not my sourdough."

"Doesn't matter. Once she sees what you can do, she'll never let you go."

Belle laughed again and shook her head. "Thanks for the ego boost."

"Any time. Now...I'm not trying to hurry you, but what are your plans for the day? Should I count on you for dinner or do you already have some kind of cute date for the evening?"

Belle groaned and threw her head back. "Are we seriously going there? I've only been in town a few weeks, if I was even interested in looking for a guy, which I'm not. I mean, do you even have any single cute guys in this tiny place?"

"I'm sure there are a few," Sofia trailed off. "I can't think of any off the top of my head, but we can't be all out. That would be impossible. And I think meeting someone new would be good for you. It'll help you forget the jerk who shall not be named."

"I'm coming for dinner," Belle said, determined to change the subject. "But I'm gonna run a couple of errands first, okay?"

"Gotcha. Take your time! We'll see you in a bit."

Belle hung up and turned on the car, cranking the heater as high as it would go. Getting a job on her first interview required a celebration even if there wasn't much to do in Seaside Bay. Mrs. Stallings, however, had inadvertently mentioned something that was right up Belle's alley.

After glancing at her GPS, she pulled onto the street and headed for Main Street. Some authentic saltwater taffy sounded just right about now and Belle wasn't the least bit upset that she would be eating them alone. She had tried the family thing and it had ended up being a disaster. Belle was in no mood for another go. Her brother, sister-in-law, and nephew were enough to fill that family bucket for quite a while yet.

*****

"Ah..." Carson drawled, sticking his nose in the air as he and Jude walked off the plane. "Smell that sea air."

"We came from sea air," Jude grumbled. "And it doesn't smell like the ocean inside an airport." He took a tentative sniff. "It smells like people. And it's not a good thing."

"You really are crabby," Carson said, frowning at his hand. "What's going on?"

Jude shook his head. "Nothing."

"Is this like one of those girl moments where they say they're fine, but they're really not fine...and men are expected to know that fine means not fine, even though they say they're fine?"

Jude looked sideways at Carson. "I'm not sure that made any sense."

Carson shrugged. "Women never do," he said with a shake of his head.

Jude deflated a little as they walked across the airport to the baggage claim. "I'm sorry. I'll try to lighten up."

"So there really is something wrong," Carson responded. "What's going on?"

Jude's jaw tightened and Carson recognized the stubborn look. It was one he'd seen on himself and his brother from time to time. There wouldn't be any more information coming from Jude the Dude.

"Looking like we're in baggage claim 4," Carson said, changing the subject. If Jude wanted to talk, he would. "To the right."

Jude followed obediently, the two of them going quiet.

The problem with quiet was it meant Carson was left to his own thoughts. He hated that. Inevitably, he would wrap around to the lonely, work-filled hours of his life, where the only social life he had were people who wanted to use him as a stepping stone to meet his brother. That mess didn't exactly put him in the holiday mood that he'd need to get through the next ten days at his brother's.

"Isn't that one yours?" Jude asked, nudging Carson.

Carson allowed himself to be pulled from the dreariness of his own mind and locked in on the rotating belt. "Yep. On it." He left his carry-on at Jude's feet and walked up to grab his larger suitcase. He waited just a second before pointing to one coming around the corner. "Yours?"

Jude nodded.

Carson grabbed it as well and then wheeled them back to his friend.

"Thanks."

Carson nodded. "Let's head to rental and then we'll settle in for a nice drive down to Seaside Bay."

Forty minutes later, the two men were on the freeway and Carson was allowing himself to enjoy the engine in his rental. He'd decided to treat himself for the holiday, and rented a sports car.

"This thing is sleek," Jude said, looking around the car.

"Yeah. Merry Christmas to me," Carson said with a grin. Jude didn't laugh as expected and Carson began to worry that he was going to have to do something. This wasn't like Jude at all. He was the good guy. He and Grayson had become friends, even though they were often complete opposites. Ying and yang. Uptight and casual.

Jude was known for making friends with anybody and everybody no matter their gender, race, or age.

The angry, grumpy, uptight man to Carson's left was unrecognizable.

"So I've got a couple of ideas for entertainment," Carson said as they drove.

"Yeah? Something besides fishing?"

Carson nodded. "Yep. I mean, I still plan to fish, but there's an aquarium not far from Seaside Bay. There are, like, a dozen sweets shops within twenty miles. There are some hiking trails, if we want to freeze our backsides off."

Jude chuckled. "I'm starting to think I'll hunker down near Gray's fireplace with a cup of hot chocolate, the remote, and leave you to the rest."

"Wimp," Carson said through a fake cough.

Jude punched his arm. "Just because I'm not built like a boulder like you Cordovas doesn't mean I'm weak."

"If you say so," Carson hedged. He grinned when Jude continued to argue. This was more like it. Maybe his bud had had a bad morning. Surely getting away from work and taking a few days off would be enough to help Jude get back on his feet.

The two men bantered back and forth while Carson drove, enjoying the sights and the company. When they were nearly within city limits, Carson's phone chimed.

"Don't you dare look at that," Jude warned. "No texting and driving."

"Then you see who it is," Carson offered.

"Aren't you afraid I'll see something from a case I shouldn't?" Jude asked, picking up Carson's phone.

Carson scoffed. "Uh, no. We don't just leave messages like that out in the open. If there's something dire, they'll ask me to call. But just see if it's Gray or Brook. I'd hate for them to change plans just as we were getting into town."

Jude grinned. "Oh, ho! Not a case at all."

Carson frowned. "What? Who was it?"

"You never said you were dating anyone," Jude continued.

Carson gave his friend a look. "I'm not."

Jude's smile fell. "Really? You're not dating her?"

"Who in the world are you talking about?" Carson demanded, his mind trying to piece together the conversation. Who the heck could have texted that would have Jude thinking Carson had a girlfriend? It made absolutely no sense.

"And I quote," Jude said, holding up the phone. "Car. I miss you already. Be sure and let me know when you land."

"What the—?" Carson shook his head, completely baffled. "Who wrote that?"

"Emme?" Jude said, the name sounding more like a question than a statement.

Carson rolled his eyes. "You've got to be kidding me," he grumbled.

"So, not a girlfriend, then."

Carson shook his head and rested his elbow against the door. "Definitely not. She's my neighbor and only interested in me as a means to an end."

"Let me guess," Jude said wryly. "You can get her closer to Grayson."

Carson tapped the side of his nose. "Exactly."

Jude sighed and shook his head. "Women are crazy."

"That one is," Carson grumbled. "I barely even speak to her. I'm not sure how she even knew I was leaving." The thought bothered him, but he pushed it away when he saw a sign for Seaside. "Winner, winner, chicken dinner!"

"Speaking of...I'm starving," Jude said.

"Me too, but Brook'll probably skin us alive if we eat first."

"What she doesn't know won't hurt her," Jude said in an enticing manner.

Carson glanced at his friend and raised an eyebrow. "Are you thinking what I'm thinking?"

"They can't be closed yet, right?"

Carson pursed his lips and shook his head. "I wouldn't think so."

Jude rubbed his hands together. "I haven't had one of Jack's cookies since last year."

"And Brook can't blame us if we accidentally filled up on airplane pretzels, right?"

Jude laughed. "Nope. And she wouldn't anyways. She's too nice."

"Which we are going to take full advantage of," Carson said as he took the off ramp. "Cookies Up! Here we come!"

CHAPTER 3

Belle was working hard to hide it, but she was beyond excited this morning. Only two days ago, she had managed to see Grayson Cordova from a distance as she drove away from purchasing her candy and today, she was invited to be a part of a planning meeting with Brook Cordova, Grayson's wife.

Gotta play it cool, Belle reminded herself as she parked her car behind Mrs. Stallings. The only reason Belle had even been invited to the planning meeting was because Mrs. Stallings had been so impressed with Belle's croissants yesterday.

It had been completely nerve-wracking to work on such a delicate pastry while Mrs. Stallings stood by watching Belle's every move. It was almost as bad as her finals at college, but somehow, Belle had made it through and the croissants had turned out perfectly. Crisp, flaky, and oh so buttery. Just the way they were meant to be.

And they had earned Belle the chance to present herself to Mrs. Cordova and offer to make some specialty breads for the upcoming parties.

"Are you coming?" Mrs. Stallings snapped, her white eyebrow raised high.

Belle scurried out of her door and slammed it shut, wincing as usual. "Yeah. Sorry." She straightened her jacket, smoothed the front of her slacks, and then hurried to keep up with her boss.

The seaside mansion was stunning and Belle couldn't help but gawp a little. She could feel that her eyes were wide and at one point, she wondered if she should double check for drool, but instead, she snapped her mouth shut and forced her mind back to the present.

Who cared if the ocean was only a few feet away and soft sand stretched as far as Belle could see in every direction? The four stories of the home shouldn't have been impressive at all, nor the stunning landscaping around the home that almost made it feel tropical even though it was placed in the Pacific Northwest.

The door began to open and Belle straightened her shoulders. She could daydream later. And if she caught another glimpse of Grayson, Belle knew she'd have plenty of daydream material.

She had no intention of trying to catch Grayson's attention—he was married after all—but there was no harm in enjoying the view, was there? The man was stunningly handsome and built like a bull. What not blind female wouldn't enjoy taking a peek from a distance?

"Gloria, you made it!" a beautiful brunette said, reaching out to gather Mrs. Stallings into a tight hug. She stepped back and locked eyes with Belle. "You must be Ms. Kerr." The woman held out her hand. "Brook Cordova. Nice to meet you."

Belle kept her shaky smile on her face and tried not to look as awestruck as she felt. This stunning woman was far more gracious and warm than Belle had expected. The wife of a world famous movie star and producer didn't seem like the type of person who would be hugging caterers or even opening her own door. It was against everything Belle had ever imagined from the movie portrayals of the wealthy elite.

"Nice to meet you as well," Belle managed to say without too much of a wobble in her voice. She made a point of glancing around. "Your home is lovely."

Mrs. Cordova beamed. "Thank you! We haven't had it very long, but it's one of my favorites." She stepped back and opened the door wider. "Come on in. We can chat in the sitting room."

Belle tried to wrap her head around the idea of having enough homes that she actually had a favorite, but since she technically didn't have a home at all at the moment, and previous to now had been living in a tiny, rundown apartment, it was a completely foreign thought.

As they walked inside, Belle kept thinking a large bodyguard type man was going to walk up with a checklist, asking for her name, but none of that happened. Instead, Belle barely managed to keep her feet from stumbling as her eyes couldn't seem to tear themselves away from the festive and amazing Christmas decor that filled the already beautiful home.

It was like something out of a magazine and Belle was positive she had entered some kind of alternative dimension. Did people really live like this? Like they were on a movie set? She had always assumed it was just for show or for the paparazzi, but as Brook casually led Belle and her new boss to a seating of couches that probably cost more than Belle's first car...Belle quickly became a believer.

"Please, have a seat," Brook said, waving to the large sofa as she, herself, sat so that she was facing Mrs. Stallings and Belle. "I'm so excited for us to get this menu finalized." Her smile was wide. "I've been looking forward to hosting this Christmas party for over a year!"

Mrs. Stallings nodded and gave a small smile of her own. "I heard you haven't been able to have Christmas in town with your friends yet. I'm sure it's good to be back."

Brook laughed. "I don't know if I can get used to you treating me like this, Gloria." She scrunched her nose. "Of course, calling you Gloria is weird enough." Her eyes drifted to Belle. "Mrs. Stallings was my middle school home ec teacher before she started her catering business. It's hard to break old habits, no matter how old we are."

Belle smiled, but didn't speak. She was feeling more and more out of place in this setting. Her boss and Mrs. Cordova were obviously friends, which put Belle at a decided disadvantage, but Belle was also feeling more and more like she simply wasn't good enough. Her baking skills might be, but Belle herself was like a burnt pot next to a shiny stainless steel pan.

"What do you think, Belle?"

Belle snapped out of her self pity and tuned back in to the conversation. *Great. Just what I needed.* Mrs. Stalling was giving her a look, letting Belle know she wasn't doing her part. Her second day on the job and Belle was already struggling. So much for hoping for a better situation.

"I'm sorry," she said sincerely. "I was so caught up in looking at your Christmas decorations, I completely spaced from the conversation. Can you remind me what you were talking about?"

Brook laughed. "Actually, that's a wonderful compliment. I did the decorating myself, so thank you."

Belle's eyes nearly bugged out of her head. "You did?"

Brook nodded. "I used to run a fashion boutique in town. I ended up closing it down since I traveled so much with my husband and it just wasn't feasible to keep it going, but I've always loved creating outfits, so creating a mood in my house wasn't that difficult."

"Well, it's amazing," Belle gushed.

Mrs. Stallings cleared her throat.

"Right." Belle forced her back to straighten. "I'm sorry. Back to the menu."

Brook tapped the binder lying between them on the coffee table. "I was thinking it might be nice to try a chocolate croissant on Christmas Eve, and Gloria said that's your area of expertise."

Belle nodded, the familiar topic helping her feel a little more comfortable. "Would you like them to be red and green? We make them look holiday-ish as well as taste like dessert."

"Really? That would be amazing," Brook said.

Belle let out a long breath. "I can do just about anything you want with them."

Brook grinned. "Girl, you and I are going to get along just fine." She laughed and went back to the binder. "So, let's chat appetizers."

*****

Carson breathed a sigh of relief as he got into his rental and headed down the road. Brook had planned a meeting that morning with the caterer and he was terrified he was going to get stuck in the house, going over menu plans about things he didn't care about at all.

As long as it tasted good and there was enough so that he wasn't hungry, Carson was good to go. He'd eaten food from the extremely fancy to the meals made in a dive on a back alley. In his experience, the fancy food was often the less edible of the bunch, though there were a few things Carson enjoyed.

But give him a greasy hamburger slathered in American cheese and he was just as happy as the movie star holding a chip full of beluga caviar.

Brook had been working hard during the last couple of days to make Carson and Jude feel welcome, and was trying to include them in the planning of the upcoming party, but it was just as horrible as Carson had feared. Which was exactly why he'd snuck out this morning to avoid the caterers and all the drama that would eventually ensue.

He pulled into the marina and parked the car, clicking the lock button as he got out and walked to a large boat tied against the dock.

"Felix, my man!" Carson's smile was wide as he boarded the *Morwenna.*

Felix, Brook's captain friend who ran fishing charters, put out his hand. "Welcome aboard."

After following through with the greeting, Carson put his hands on his hips and looked around. "You sure you're okay taking me out today? It looks pretty dead around here."

Felix grunted. "Not a lot of people enjoy cold weather fishing." He grinned. "But lucky for you, I'll fish anytime, anywhere." Felix looked back toward the dock. "Wasn't Jude coming up from Cali with you?"

Carson rolled his eyes. "Yes, but the guy is a wimp. He refused to come along. Something about being allergic to cold air."

Felix chuckled. "You California folks are ridiculous."

Carson put a hand on his chest. "And yet I'm the one out here."

"Do I need to get you a drink? Or are you manly enough to handle the temps?"

Carson gave Felix an unimpressed look. "Just sail, Captain. I think that's what you're being hired for."

Felix was still grinning as he gave Carson a mock salute. "You're the boss." He turned to look out the door of the wheelhouse. "Julian! Let's get this show on the water!"

"On it, Captain!" Julian, Felix's first mate, untied the boat and gave it a push before leaping aboard. He rushed around for a few minutes, moving things and preparing for them to get out of the marina.

Carson folded his arms over his chest and leaned his shoulder against the window of the wheelhouse. It was fascinating to watch the process of getting them out to sea. Maybe one day he'd make the splurge to own a boat of his own. Probably not one as big as this one, but still...

"Hoping to catch anything in particular today?" Felix asked over the sound of the motor coming to life.

"Whatever's biting," Carson responded.

Felix grinned. "That makes my job easier."

"Do you even have room for more fish? Last time I was in town, Charli was positive that you would need another freezer before you had room for more fish."

Felix shrugged. "We've eaten some. I give some away during the holidays, and plus...there's always room for more."

"Do you even have a grocery bill?" Carson said with a laugh.

"I don't, but my wife does." Felix made a face. "She says we have to have produce in order to eat a balanced diet."

"Regretting the old ball and chain?"

Felix shook his head. "Never. She's the best thing that ever happened to me." He immediately patted the wheel in front of him. "Except for you, baby. You know that."

Carson rolled his eyes. Even in the middle of the ocean, he was going to have to be careful about the topic of conversation. Felix, the broody one of Brook's friends, was just as sappy about his relationship as Grayson was.

"Speaking of..." Felix sent a look over his shoulder. "I have to admit I found it odd that you wanted to go on the water when we're so close to Brook's party."

Carson gave his friend a bland smile.

Felix's responding chuckle said a bookload of words. "That bad, huh?"

"I'm pretty sure she's planning to set me up with someone."

Felix snorted. "Families. Can't live with 'em, can't live without 'em." He paused for a moment. "Have you tried just telling her you don't want to be tied down right now?"

Carson didn't have an answer to that. It was a complicated question, and this conversation was definitely headed in a direction he didn't want it to go.

"Brook can be stubborn, but all you have to do is say no," Felix insisted again.

"It's not that simple," Carson grumbled.

Felix frowned and stared for a second before understanding blossomed across his face. "So it's not the idea of having a girlfriend, it's the idea of someone pushing one on you."

Carson shrugged. "Sort of. That's part of it anyway."

"What's the rest of it?"

Carson gave Felix a look. "Really? I thought we came out here to fish."

"Brook is family," Felix said with an unapologetic shrug. "I can't help protect you from her if I'm not sure why I'm doing it."

"I didn't ask for your help." Carson immediately clamped his jaw shut. He hadn't meant to be quite so rude. Felix wasn't a bad guy, but was it so bad to just wish that everyone would butt out of his life? Why couldn't people understand that Carson wanted to live according to his own terms, not those everyone else thought were important.

He was a well-known lawyer, who was actually quite good at his job. He was cool under pressure, most of the time anyways. He knew how to keep the attention of a crowd and how to shape words to persuade people to his side of an argument. He also had a quick mind, enjoyed playing devil's advocate, and didn't mind researching inane topics if they were a means to an end.

What was it about that description that made people think that he was completely unprepared to find himself a companion?

"True enough," Felix said, turning back to the front. "Forget I asked."

Carson pinched the bridge of his nose. So much for being cool under pressure. "Sorry, man," Carson finally managed after taking a few deep breaths. This trip had him more uptight than usual. It wasn't the most pleasant of feelings. And definitely not the one he normally would have hoped for around the holidays.

"It's fine," Felix responded, turning the wheel to pull them farther away from the shore. "I get it. It's your life. I'm sure you can handle it."

Carson decided to let it drop. He could continue hashing out his apology and eventually give in, telling Felix all his woes, but despite not wanting to be at odds with the ship captain, Carson still didn't want to talk about his situation.

Someday, a woman would come into his life who wasn't obsessed with his brother, and when that day happened, Carson planned to take full advantage of it. But until that happened, he'd keep dodging matchmaking attempts, ignoring stupid texts from neighbors who couldn't take hints and booking fishing trips to keep him away from his sister-in-law.

Just another day in the life of Carson Cordova.

CHAPTER 4

Belle glanced at her list once again, though she really had the ingredients memorized. But for some reason, walking through a new grocery store messed with her confidence and instead of walking around filling her cart, she found herself stopping every two seconds to double check what she had come to buy.

"Irish butter," she reminded herself for the thousandth time. She turned her stiff cart—seriously, why did she always end up with the three-wheeled cart—toward the dairy section. Scanning over the displays, Belle couldn't find what she was looking for. She huffed and looked around. Maybe there was a worker nearby who could tell her whether it was out of stock or if they just never carried it to begin with.

With as small as this store and town were, Belle was more than a little afraid of what the answer was going to be.

"Excuse me!" she said as a teenage boy walked past with an apron and name tag on.

"Yes, ma'am?" he asked, looking at her with wide eyes.

Belle forced herself not to bristle at the title. It wasn't like she was that much older than this kid...right? She immediately wanted to smack herself. The fact that she had mentally called him a kid told her all she needed to know. "I was wondering if you ever carry Irish butter?" she asked.

The teenager blinked at her.

"You know...butter made in Ireland?" Belle pressed. "From Irish cows?"

"Uh..." He gave her a weird look. "Is that a thing?"

Belle smiled with a calm she didn't feel. "It is," she answered. "It has a higher butterfat content than American butter does," she began. "Making it richer and creamier, which is better for baking..."

Belle trailed off as she noticed the young man's eyes glaze over. "Nevermind," she said quickly. "I guess that answers my question."

The worker shrugged and walked away.

Belle rubbed her forehead as she tried to figure out how she was going to get the ingredients she needed for that pain au chocolat. It just wouldn't be as flaky or rich if she changed her ingredients. Every baker knew that, and this was for a client that Belle needed to impress! Not only was she brand new in her position at the caterer's, but she also couldn't afford to start her career in Seaside Bay with limp, non-flaky croissants.

A choked bit of laughter caught her attention and Belle turned, freezing in place as she realized who had overheard her conversation. *You've got to be kidding me...*

None other than Grayson Cordova stood a few yards from Belle, laughing behind a fist. His smile was swoon-worthy and his eyes filled with tears of mirth. "Sorry," he choked out. "But I think you're in the wrong place if you're looking for the finer things in life."

Belle forced her frozen muscles into action and gave him a small smile. "You're probably right, but it didn't hurt to ask, right?" She gripped her cart and began to move forward, but Mr. Cordova grabbed the end of her cart as she went to pass him.

She could see the muscles in his arm, even from that slight movement, and her heart skipped a beat. Part of her wished she was the fangirling type, who could gush and squeal and ask for a selfie. After all, how many times would she have the chance to speak to a famous movie producer in person? When she worked his Christmas party, she was going to be part of the serving class, so there would be no mingling there. But right now, with her hair in a messy bun, a pencil stuck in the depths of it somewhere, and having him witness her situation with the store worker, Belle found herself unwilling to act the part. And most of all...the man was married to one of the sweetest women Belle had ever met. Even if their encounter here was completely unplanned, she wasn't about to drool over another woman's husband. It just wasn't right.

"Want me to take a look at your list?" Grayson teased. "I might be able to save you some time."

Belle frowned. Here she was, just reminding herself not to look at another woman's husband that way, and he was flirting with her! Disgust roiled through her stomach. How dare that man treat his wife that way. Belle didn't care if he was famous, that was no excuse for behaving that way with another woman.

"I'm fine, thank you," she said tightly, pulling her cart out of his hands. "Now if you'll excuse me."

Grayson stepped back, his hands in the air, the basket he was holding dangling. "My mistake," he said.

Sticking her nose in the air, Belle marched on. She was glad she hadn't met the man at the meeting the other day, or he would know she was part of the catering gig. In fact, snubbing him the way she just had could have dire consequences if he ever found out.

Scowling, Belle made a mental note to herself to make sure she stayed out of sight when she was serving. Not only did she not want to be around a guy who flirted with other women, but she also didn't want to get her boss, or herself, fired.

She headed to the baking aisle, perusing the different flours. She needed some unbleached flour if she was going to have a chance of saving her non-Irish-butter-croissants. "Bingo." Belle bent down and gathered a couple of the five-pound bags, then stood to put them in her cart. She froze again when she saw none other than Mr. Movie Star walking down her aisle.

He was studying the cake mixes a little too studiously for Belle to believe his actions.

Rolling her eyes, she went back for more of the flour.

"There's not going to be any left for the rest of us at that rate."

The deep voice could only belong to one person. Gritting her teeth, Belle stood and gave him a sarcastic smile. "I'm sure they'll get more in soon." This time she didn't bother to excuse herself before marching her cart away.

The man had some nerve! All these years she had thought he was one of the good guys! The kind of person other men should look up to and emulate because the media always portrayed him as someone good and loyal.

There was a pinch in her heart that Belle had to be the one to discover just how wrong the reporters were. She still remembered when he got married. Brook had been stunning in her designer gown and artfully swept updo. There had been a media frenzy, since the Cordovas had managed to hold the ceremony secretly, without any of the paparazzi there. The only photos were ones the family had put out themselves.

They looked like such a happy and in love couple. There had been nothing in either of their faces to indicate that they weren't totally and completely dedicated to each other.

Belle sighed as she glanced at her list yet again. Another dream...shattered. Why did life have to be so hard? Why couldn't people stay true to their word? Why couldn't men keep their attention on one person and one person only?

She was starting to feel like she knew more people who broke their vows than kept them, and the picture that created was more bleak than Belle wanted to think about.

Unfortunately, she would have to add Mr. Cordova to her growing list of stupid men. And people wondered why Belle hadn't remarried. She could give a two hour presentation on the subject without any preparation at this point.

She shook her head. "Let it go," she whispered to herself. "It's not worth it." Forcing her mind out of darkness and back to a poorly stocked grocery store, she worked her way down yet another aisle that probably didn't contain everything she needed. But as long as she didn't run into Mr. Cordova again, Belle would make do.

*****

Carson couldn't help but chuckle as the pretty, brown-haired woman stormed past him. He wasn't sure what he'd said that was so offensive, but it had been so long since someone had treated him this way, rather than schmoozing, that Carson found he couldn't get himself to leave her alone.

The second time he'd tried to speak to her had been even better. She'd actually rolled her eyes! He wasn't sure what to think at this point. Should he back off and leave her be, or continue seeing if he could break past that prickly exterior?

She couldn't be a local to the area, or she would have known from the start that a place like The Corner Grocery didn't carry luxurious items such as Irish butter. But she also didn't have a ring on, which meant she wasn't married.

Was she just passing through? Was she a tourist or a guest? Was she visiting a boyfriend and that's why she rebuffed his small attempts at flirting? But why would a guy bring a girl who bought that kind of food to a place like Seaside Bay? It wasn't exactly a hub of fancy cuisine. Their fanciest restaurant was called The Crab Pot. And while it had good food, it definitely couldn't compare with a place like California or New York. Both of which were the exact type of place where people ate things like Irish butter.

He couldn't seem to help himself. Carson walked to the end of the aisle and slowly peeked around the corner. He didn't see the stranger at first, but the grocery store wasn't very large. Surely he could *happen* to run into her again without it being a big deal.

Taking a chance, he chose right and headed toward the meat section. His eyes flitted over the deli meats and ground beef, all while his peripheral vision waited for the appearance of a beautiful woman. "Shoot," he muttered a couple minutes later. He'd chosen wrong.

Backtracking, he walked toward the produce, only picking up his pace slightly. He didn't want to appear too eager. After all, he didn't even know the woman's first name.

He stopped. There she was, bent over the apples. She picked each one up, felt it and smelled it before either putting it back or putting it in her bag. Before Carson had given his feet permission, he was striding to her side. "Fancy meeting you here," he said as he set down his basket and ripped a plastic bag off the display.

The woman closed her eyes and took in a deep breath, as if praying for patience.

"Do you always handle each and every piece of produce you buy?"

The woman refused to look at him. "Only when I find the quality of it questionable," she said snippily.

She began to move away from him again and Carson jumped into action. "If you don't like the food here, why come? You could always drive down the coast a ways to get whatever it is you need for that vegan, no carb, high protein whatever you call it diet you're on." Oooh...if eyes were lasers, Carson knew he'd be a puddle.

"Don't you have something better to do than bother women?"

"Don't you have better manners?" Carson shot back. A muscle ticked in her jaw and Carson was sure he was going to hear the squeal of her grinding her teeth at any moment.

"Go home to your wife," she said in a tone of steel, then promptly swung around and disappeared.

Carson didn't move for a moment, trying to process what she had just said. "My wife?" he said. "Where did she get the idea I have a wife?" He glanced down at his bare finger. It wasn't like there was an indentation or a tan line. Maybe she just was using the line to discourage him in general. He had to know. This was the most fun he'd had in ages. A little bit of a fight always got him excited and he loved the fact that she didn't seem the least bit interested in him, which meant she also wasn't interested in his brother. Add in the fact that the woman was easy on the eyes and Brook had had nothing to do with setting them up? Well, that made things just about perfect.

"Excuse me," he said, chasing her down. "But where did you get the idea that I have a wife?"

The woman rolled those chocolatey brown eyes. "I'm not that naive, Mr. Cordova."

He stuttered to a stop. How did she know who he was? Carson was absolutely sure he had never seen her before. He let his eyes study her for a moment, trying to place her in his memory. Her hair was haphazardly thrown on top of her head, with tendrils dripping every which way. It was messy, but endearing at the same time. Her sunglasses were pushed into her hair, keeping her face free from strands, allowing him to see those brown eyes, which were darker than her hair, creating a lovely contrast.

Her skin was smooth, with a small sprinkling of freckles across the bridge of her nose, and her chin came to a point, which gave her an almost elfin look. But it was her curves that caught his attention the most. She was definitely not the thin as a reed type of woman who graced the front of every magazine down in Cali. She looked healthy and feminine, and it was a wonderful change.

But despite the growing attraction, he still didn't remember her.

"Where did we meet?" he asked, coming up behind her.

"We haven't," she said curtly.

"Then how do you know who I am?"

The woman stopped and spun to face him, her hand going to her hip. "Really? *Really?* The whole world knows who you are! Or at least anyone who's seen a movie in the last ten years." Shaking her head, she turned back to her cart. "And to think they call you a gentleman."

Carson was rooted to the spot as she rushed to the check out counters. He could see her putting her food on the conveyor belt and his eyes stayed glued the whole time she bagged and paid for her load.

He probably should have gone after her. Probably should have offered to load her groceries in her car. Probably should have cleared up the little misunderstanding they were having. But instead, he stood and watched.

A short, curvy brunette in a podunk grocery store thought that Carson was his brother.

And she didn't want anything to do with me.

A slow smile crept across his face. He'd done it. In Seaside Bay, Oregon, of all places. He'd finally found a woman who wasn't the least bit interested in getting to know his brother or in using Carson as a way to reach his brother.

"Man." A teenage boy came up beside Carson and whistled. "That lady has a bite."

"She thought I was someone else," Carson clarified, his eyes still stuck on the front doors.

"Wonder what the other guy did," the grocery store employee mused.

"Apparently, all he had to do was exist," Carson said with a laugh. He had no idea who the woman was, but Carson decided then and there he was going to find out. This was too perfect. No more fishing long hours in the icy cold ocean wind. No more driving an hour to go through a history museum on Maritime laws. No more dodging every activity Brook tried to rope him into.

Carson had found an activity that not only was going to be interesting but fun. He was going to find the one woman in the entire world who didn't want Grayson Cordova...and then he was going to take her on a date.

And if all went well, he might even steal a kiss...or two.

CHAPTER 5

"I'm telling you he was full on flirting," Belle said as she stirred her pate choux. She threw her body into the movement, tensing every muscle from head to toe. Maybe if she stirred hard enough, she could get rid of all the bitter and angry feelings she'd been dealing with since getting home from the store, very few of which had to do with the lack of selection.

Sofia shrugged and fed Cole another bite of sweet potato. "Maybe that's just his style? You know, some guys are natural born flirts, even if they don't really mean anything by it."

"But he's married," Belle ground out. "Whether it's a natural reaction or not, it's rude to his wife to speak to other women that way." She could hear Sofia sigh behind her, but Belle's mind couldn't be changed. Unfortunately, she had personal experience with this exact matter and she knew how much it hurt to be the wife stuck at home while the husband went off to play.

Once again, Belle swore to herself that she would never put herself in that position again. It was exactly why she'd gone back to school. She was going to stand on her own two feet. She would never again rely on a man or trust one, and meeting people like Grayson Cordova just solidified her resolve.

"I'm sorry," Sofia said softly. "It must have been so disappointing to meet someone you've looked up to, only to discover they're a fraud."

Belle slowed down her rapid beating and looked over her shoulder. "Thank you," she said softly. "That means a lot."

Sofia's saintly halo was glowing again. It made Belle question for the thousandth time why Sofia had married Belle's brother. A small smile tugged at her lips. *Maybe it's because he struck her as a work in progress.*

"But I feel like whenever you see someone similar to Dale, you come to the conclusion that all men are like that, and it's just not true," Sofia continued.

Belle went back to her pastry dough. She didn't want to talk about her ex-husband. She didn't want to *think* about him either. He was a cheat and a charmer and basically everything that Belle had come to hate about men. They thought they owned the world, but Belle now knew better. She refused to let herself be part of the masses that fell at a handsome man's feet and did his bidding.

"Piping bags," she muttered as she looked through the drawers. "Do you have any piping bags?"

Sofia stood and came over, pointing out a small packet of plastic bags.

Belle only hesitated slightly. She wasn't particularly fond of that style, but she had no excuse for complaining. Her brother and sister-in-law were going above and beyond at the moment, the least Belle could do was be grateful. "Thanks."

Sofa nodded and went back to the table, unstrapping her son. "Looks like bath time for you," she cooed.

"Thanks, but I prefer a shower," Belle quipped, glancing up to grin when Sofia gave her a look.

"Hardy, har, har," Sofia said sarcastically, carrying Cole out of the kitchen. "Be back in a bit."

"Yep!" Belle filled her bag and began to pipe the cream puffs. She wanted to try out a new filling and maybe after the holidays were over, Belle could present it to Mrs. Stallings. *If I'm around that long,* she reminded herself.

Belle did her best to lose herself in her work. She loved baking and had been grateful she'd received enough in her divorce settlement to be able to afford school. She might not have had as much to eat as she wanted, but she came out with a degree and no student loans. That had to count for something.

No matter how hard she tried to focus, however, she found her mind wandering back to the grocery store. The mere fact that her self discipline couldn't get the handsome actor out of her head was enough to have Belle gnashing her teeth.

"He wasn't that handsome," she grumbled to herself, trying to dissuade her hormones from bringing up his picture over and over again.

"Who wasn't that handsome?"

Belle whipped around with a gasp and then bent over, breathing heavily. "Geez, Rich. Was that necessary?"

He scowled as he stepped farther into the kitchen. "Who wasn't that handsome? Have you already met some guy?"

Belle shook her head. "No, don't worry about it." She straightened and went back to her piping.

"Isabelle," Rich growled. "What's going on?"

"She met Grayson Cordova in town and he flirted with her, and now Belle's teenage crush has been ruined because she didn't realize he was such a sleazeball," Sofia said casually as she swept into the room, a newly clean Cole on her hip. "Hey, honey." Raising up on tiptoe, Sofia gave Rich a welcome kiss.

"Since when do you talk to celebrities?" Rich asked, after greeting his wife.

Belle rolled her eyes. "Richard..." She drew out his name the same way he had done to hers only moments earlier. "I don't speak to celebrities," she said. "I was buying groceries...so was he...he tried to strike up a conversation." She turned to look over her shoulder. "I made it clear I wasn't interested in one. And you should be proud of me. I didn't even ask for a selfie."

Rich frowned harder and shook his head. "You don't need a selfie with someone like that. Isn't he married?"

"Yes," Belle responded. "Which is exactly why I didn't appreciate his flirting." She glared at Sofia. "And just for the record, girl talk is supposed to stay among girls."

Sofia smiled. "I don't keep anything from him."

"Good to know," Belle grumbled. She opened the oven and put her treats inside, then wiped her hands on her apron. "Apparently there's still some loyalty left in the world."

"Belle," Rich said softly. He walked across the kitchen and wrapped Belle in a tight hug.

"What are you doing?" Belle tried to squirm away, but Rich was way too big for her to get away from. Finally, she admitted defeat and let herself relax in his hold. If she was being honest with herself, it was kind of nice. She rarely had anyone hold her anymore. An occasional hug from a friend, and the hug Rich had given her when she'd arrived, were about it. Belle had forgotten how something so simple could feel so good.

Slowly, Rich pulled away. "Not all guys are like Dale," he said softly. "Or this Cordova guy." He gave her a small smile. "Believe it or not, there are still a few good people in the world." He tweaked her nose. "Like yourself. So don't give up just yet."

Belle rolled her eyes, but her heart wasn't in the sarcastic response. "I suppose you'll say you're an example of a good guy next."

Rich grinned smugly. "I don't have to say it. It's a given." He chuckled when Sofia hit the side of his arm.

"Here, good guy," Sofia said, handing over Cole. "You can watch your son for a while and give my back a break."

Rich picked up Cole and immediately began making funny noises, causing the toddler to laugh.

Belle watched them walk out of the room, her heart breaking slightly, though she didn't want to admit it. She had always hoped to have children, and had entered into her marriage with high hopes of a family. But all that had come crashing down when Dale had decided to build a family somewhere else.

"He's right," Sofia said from Belle's left.

Belle looked over at her sister-in-law.

"There are still good guys out there. I know you've had some bad experiences, but don't give up." Sofia put an arm around Belle's back and squeezed. "You're too wonderful to never give it another try someday."

Belle rested her head against Sofia's. She had no reassuring words or assurances right now. Belle, herself, wasn't sure what she was hoping for in the future, only that she wanted it to include a bakery. She could admit that doing it all alone sounded lonely and long, but the thought of marrying another guy like Dale made her nauseous. Was there some kind of middle ground or happy medium? If so, Belle had yet to experience it and little hope in something she couldn't see.

*****

Carson stuffed his snacks in his room, making sure no one casually walking around would find them. He loved Brook and his brother, but man...they kept way too much healthy stuff around the house. What was wrong with keeping a few cookies or chips in the cupboard? Or even something as simple as a pretzel?

Grayson took his muscles way too seriously since their fridge was eighty percent protein drinks and twenty percent fruits and vegetables.

Once he was satisfied, Carson headed downstairs. He really shouldn't ignore his family quite so much, and he should probably figure out where Jude was hiding as well. Not to mention, he wanted to know who the woman was in the grocery store, and the only way to find out answers was to ask questions.

He just needed to be able to do it in a way that no one suspected what he was up to.

"Car!" Grayson hollered. He limped Carson's direction. Grayson had come a long way in his recovery from the accident that brought him to Brook. He'd gone from not being able to sit down, to walking with a cane and now he could walk by himself, though doctors were unsure if the limp would ever completely go away.

Knowing how determined his brother was, however, Carson was sure that Grayson would eventually be one hundred percent normal. The disciplined movie star simply wouldn't accept anything less.

"What's up?" Carson asked, meeting his brother halfway.

"Where have you been? Brook's been searching for you everywhere." Grayson punched Carson's shoulder playfully.

Carson stilled. "For what?"

Gray's eyes sparkled just a little too much with humor. "She was trying to plan dinner tonight."

One eyebrow rose high on Carson's forehead. "And?"

"And she was hoping you would join us."

Carson folded his arms over his chest. He wasn't as thickly built as his brother, but he worked out. He knew the stance showed it off too, though the intimidating technique would be lost on Gray. "And who else was she hoping would come?"

Grayson's cheeks tinged with pink and he rubbed the back of his neck. "I'm not sure what you mean."

"I think I have plans tonight," Carson said, walking around his brother.

"Come on, Car," Grayson said as he hurried to catch up. "All she wants is to see you happy."

"Yeah, well, it won't make me happy to have her set me up on some blind date," Carson shot back.

Grayson stopped his brother by grabbing his arm. "It's just one dinner. What can it hurt?"

Carson shook his head. "You wouldn't understand."

All hints of teasing left Grayson's face and he narrowed his gaze. "You're serious." It wasn't a question.

Carson nodded. "I am."

"It would really make you that upset?"

Carson nodded again. "Look. I get that you two are happy, and I'm happy for you. But I don't need or want any interference in my own life." He slapped the back of his hand against Grayson's chest. "You can't tell me that you would have been okay with someone trying to set you up," he pressed. "You hated that kind of thing."

Grayson sighed. "Yeah...you're right." He made a face and glanced down the hall. "Brook is gonna give me trouble though."

"Brook has too much time on her hands," Carson grumbled. Grayson shot him a look and Carson put his hands in the air. "Sorry. But seriously, can't she find a different pasttime than my love life?"

Grayson huffed. "When we're in the middle of a movie, she's almost too busy, but the downtimes are hard sometimes." He scratched the back of his head. "I'll figure something out though."

"Thanks, man, I owe you." Carson began to walk away, but paused. "So...I was wondering...have I met all of Brook's friends? I mean, the group she hung out with, they're all married, right?"

This time it was Grayson's eyebrows that shot up. "Are you telling me you're interested in someone? Already? I thought you've been spending your time with Felix and the salmon."

Carson gave his brother an unimpressed look. "I didn't say that. I was just trying to figure out who all would be coming to the party. If Brook is trying to set me up with someone, I want to know who to avoid." *Or not avoid as the case may be.*

"Right." Grayson pinched his lips as he thought. "All her friends are married, at least the inner circle. I think Brook was planning to set you up with Grandma Nan's granddaughter."

"Who the whatta?"

Grayson chuckled. "Grandma Nan runs the small motel down on Main. If I remember Brook's explanation well enough, her granddaughter is here helping for the next little while. I'm not sure what it was all about now that I think about it." He shrugged. "But if Brook gave her seal of approval, I'm sure she's a lovely girl."

"What does she look like?" Carson wanted to smack himself as soon as he said it. He'd managed to fend off the first round of questioning, but asking about her looks definitely made him sound interested...which he wasn't...unless it was his mysterious fancy shopper.

Grayson put his hands on his hips. "Are you sure we shouldn't invite her to dinner tonight?"

"I'm sure." Carson waved a hand through the air. "Like I said earlier, I was just figuring out who I should avoid."

Gray's hands fell. "Oh, well...I think she's blonde. Just like all those California girls you're used to."

Carson held back a wince. He wasn't the least bit interested in a stereotypical California girl. Right now he was looking for curvy brunettes. "Okay...well...good to know. Thanks." He turned and continued toward the main part of the house.

He wasn't even sure where he was going at this point, but at least he had dodged a bullet when it came to dinner. Maybe if Brook wasn't constantly trying to set him up, Carson would have a chance at finding his brunette. And if he could find a way of asking Brook without giving away his interest, he might even be able to finagle a way to get her to the party.

"All I need to do is order some of that Irish butter and she'll come running," he murmured with a grin.

CHAPTER 6

"You just have to try it," Sofia gushed as she wiped Cole's sticky fingers. "Sassy Sweets has some of the best treats in town."

Belle chewed on her bottom lip. She had started to think that maybe staying in Seaside Bay would be an enjoyable thing. The town was small and sweet...for the most part anyway. It wasn't as if Carson Cordova lived here regularly.

But everyone else she had met was kind and the pace was much slower than the big cities Belle had lived in before. There was something appealing about a less hectic way of life. The ocean was right there anytime she needed a break and she had thought that her bakery would fit in well. But if there was already a baked goods store, maybe Belle's business plan wasn't as good as she thought. She tried to remember what Mrs. Stallings had said about it, but she couldn't quite bring up the conversation.

"What kinds of things do they bake?" she asked.

Sofia pursed her lips. "Well, it's a husband and wife team. Jack makes cookies and they are *divine*!" Sofia moaned. "Oh my gosh, I've never tasted anything like them."

Belle leaned her hips into the kitchen counter and folded her arms over her chest. "That good, huh? Should I tell Rich he's got competition?"

Sofia made a face as she set her toddler on the ground, who immediately rushed off into mischief unknown. "Like I'd choose cookies over Richard."

Belle laughed softly and turned to grab a glass.

"Caro is Jack's wife and she works in chocolate." Sofia dumped the soiled rag in the kitchen sink. "She's every bit as good as her husband, but in a different medium." Sofia shook her head. "I'd be so heavy if I worked over there. I'd never stop eating."

Belle finished draining the glass of water. "I guess maybe I will have to check it out. It certainly sounds destination-worthy."

Sofia glanced at her watch. "Do it now. They're still open, and dinner's in the crockpot. You don't have a project you're working on." She grinned. "And you can bring home cookies for dessert tonight."

"Oh, ho!" Belle crowed. "Now I see how it goes. You don't care if I try it. You just want me to run errands and bring home the goods!"

Sofia shrugged. "Guilty. But you'll be thanking me when you're done."

"We'll see," Belle said ominously before breaking into laughter. "Let me grab my purse and I'll head over."

After getting in the car, Belle turned on the radio, enjoying the holiday music that managed to squeak out of her speakers. She really was going to have to replace her vehicle at some point. There was no telling when it would break down, though it had gotten her through a lot of long drives and early morning commutes.

She patted the front dash. "You've been good to me," Belle crooned. "But I think our time together is almost at an end."

She pulled into a parking spot off Main Street, right in front of a pink awning. It was only a few doors down from the taffy shop Belle had gone in the other day. The theming of the store was adorable and definitely had to be from the wife's creativity. Belle couldn't imagine a man choosing pink stripes as their go-to appearance.

She wrapped her coat tighter around her, ducked her head against the icy wind, and rushed inside, after slamming her car door and hoping it didn't rattle all the glass windows at the front of the shop.

Inside was just as Belle pictured. Warm, cutesy, and smelled like heaven. The only smell better than a baked treat was the indulgence of yeasty bread.

"Hi!" a voice chirped from behind the counter. "How can I help ya?"

The woman's Southern twang caught Belle off guard. She definitely hadn't expected to find that in Oregon. "Uh, hello." Belle smiled. "I was sent on an errand to bring cookies for dessert tonight."

The blonde put her hands on her curvy hips, which only accented the very pregnant stomach she was toting. "Well, someone sent you on the wrong mission. It's the truffles you want."

Belle laughed. "You wouldn't happen to be the one who made them, would you?"

The shop clerk narrowed her eyes. "I guess that depends on who's asking."

Belle opened her mouth to answer, but the door blasting open caught both of their attention. Belle blinked against the wind, then scowled when she saw who had entered.

"Well, well, well...if it isn't Irish Butter Lady!" Grayson Cordova stood in all his glory, looking like he had just stepped off the set of a GQ photo shoot. His peacoat fit him perfectly, emphasizing his broad shoulders and smaller waist. The medium gray color brought out his eyes, making them look more gray than blue, but it was still a stunning combination with his dark hair and brown skin.

There was another man just behind him, who was also quite handsome, but couldn't quite compare to the A-list actor. The stranger was lean with medium brown hair that was windswept in a very attractive way. His coat had a slightly more athletic vibe to it, which looked perfect on his runner's frame.

"Mr. Cordova," Belle said tightly. She turned back to the counter. "Can I get a box to go?"

The woman nodded, looking curious, but didn't press anything. Instead, she gathered a pink box and got it ready. Her blue eyes kept darting between Belle and the actor in the doorway.

Belle couldn't blame her. Grayson was beyond attractive. But he needed to save it for his wife! What was it about fame and fortune that made men think they didn't have to be faithful?

The shopkeeper's eyes stayed on Grayson for a moment and she made a face, causing Belle to turn to see what was going on.

Grayson scratched at his chin and gave her an overly cheesy smile. "Finding anything good? You could always ask if she uses the right kind of butter."

Belle whipped around. She had the distinct feeling that she was missing something, but she had no idea what it was.

"What is he talking about?" the woman on the other side of the counter muttered.

"Beats me," Belle said briskly. "I'd love half a dozen truffles and the same of the cookies. What do you recommend?"

There was some heavy whispering going on behind Belle, but she studiously ignored it. Her helper, however, couldn't seem to keep her attention on the task at hand.

"Let's see," the petite blonde said in a distracted tone. "My cookies and creams are a crowd favorite."

"Great. I'll take two of those," Belle said, praying the woman would hurry up. She could practically feel Grayson's presence behind her, and she didn't like how it made her stomach flip and her heart pick up speed. She absolutely would *not* allow herself to be attracted to a man who was married.

"The orange and raspberry flavors are also popular."

"Perfect. One of each, please," Belle continued. *Almost done, almost done,* she chanted mentally, willing herself to be composed and cool. She hadn't noticed that the whispering had stopped until a deep voice sounded in her ear, scaring her into nearly jumping out of her skin.

*****

"The mint are my personal favorites," Carson said in a low tone, just behind the beauty's ear.

She jumped so high that Carson had to back up to keep from being smacked in the face. Her skin turned an alarming shade of red as she slowly turned to face him. "I don't know what type of manners you've been taught, Mr. Cordova, but you have no right to get that close to me."

Carson raised his eyebrows. Wow. She was really ticked off. Part of him wanted to spill the beans that he wasn't his brother, but the side of him that enjoyed a little stimulating argument once in a while was rubbing his hands in glee. He had the upper hand in this situation, knowing he could identify himself at any time. But he also loved the fact that she appeared to want nothing to do with Grayson. Just how far would she go in order to keep him at bay?

"I don't care who you are or what kind of reputation you have in the media. I have a set of personal boundaries, and I'm not afraid to ask for them to be respected." The woman turned back to Caro, who was staring slack-jawed at the escalating situation. "I'm sorry," Irish Butter Woman said in a polite tone. "It looks like you're busy right now. I'll come back another time."

Without another word, or bothering to look back, the mysterious stranger swept from the shop, leaving the heat of her anger in her wake.

Carson watched her leave, knowing he had a weird smile on his face, but he couldn't help it. This was only the second time he'd seen her, but he was even more intrigued than the first time. His determination to get to know her before he left doubled. *Maybe Caro knows her.* He quickly turned back to the counter, but paused.

Caro stood to her full five-foot-two and was glaring at him as if he'd kicked a puppy. "All righty, Mister Fancy Pants," she snapped in that Southern twang. A red manicured fingernail bounced back and forth between Carson and Jude. "One of you idiots better explain what just happened and why in the world you allowed that poor woman to think you're Grayson, before I hunt her down and help her deflate your tires."

Carson put on his best innocent face, the one he used in court a little too often. "I don't know what you're talking about."

"Jude?" Caro snapped.

Jude put his hands in the air. "I have no idea," he defended himself. "This is the first I've seen or heard anything."

Caro's bright blue eyes came back to Carson. "Don't make me call Brook."

Carson threw his head back and groaned. "Cruel and unusual, beautiful Caro. That's cruel and unusual."

Caro pursed her lips and looked smug. "I work my resources, Carson. You have plenty of experience with that."

He laughed. "Too true." He stuffed his hands in his pockets and sauntered up to the counter. "Tell me," he said, bringing his tone down. He jerked his head toward the door. "Who was she?"

Caro gave him a look. "You called her Irish Butter Woman and you don't know who she was?"

"I saw her in the grocery store asking about Irish butter." Carson shrugged. "That's all I got before she stormed away from me."

"Well, it's no wonder!" Caro cried. "Although I'm not sure why she's so mad at you. What does she have against Grayson?"

Carson shrugged and shook his head. "No idea. I made a couple of comments to her at the grocery store, she nearly bit my head off, and later I figured out she thought I was my brother." Carson looked back at Jude, who was a little too amused.

"Are you telling me the golden boy has an enemy?" Jude rubbed his chin. "I never thought I'd see the day."

"Now you know why I want her name," Carson said, waving his hand at Jude.

"Wait, wait, wait." Caro put her hand in the air. "You want to get to know her because she hates your brother?" The blonde made a face and laid her hand on her swollen belly. "What kind of cockamamie excuse is that?"

The kitchen door opened and Jack walked out. He came to a quick stop. "Jude! Car! Hey!" Jack reached over the counter and shook hands with the two men. "What brings you here?"

Carson chuckled. "We came early for Grayson's party."

"You mean Brook's party," Jude grumbled.

Carson nodded in agreement while Jack laughed.

"You boys leave her alone," Caro argued. "Brook has worked her tail off to have this thing be as wonderful as possible. She hasn't been able to visit much since she and Grayson got married, and this is her chance to get together."

Jack came up behind his wife and wrapped his arms around her. "No one is complaining about Brook," he said. "And no getting upset. It'll make the baby angry."

Carson bit back a laugh when Caro sent laser eyes at her husband.

"Then perhaps you shouldn't do things that upset me," she said in a saccharinely sweet tone.

Jude covered a laugh with his fist and a cough.

"Come on, sweetie," Jack crooned, holding out his hands. "You know I only want what's best for you."

"Don't you dare talk to me like I'm a small puppy," Caro shot back. She picked up the box of truffles and threatened to throw them. "Back away or you're gonna be a mess."

"I'm already a mess," Jack said, putting his hand over his heart. "A mess over you."

"Ugh," Jude muttered. "I think I just threw up in my mouth."

"Little too much sugar," Carson said loudly, getting his friend's attention. He waved at the display case. "Care if we take some of it off your hands?"

Caro huffed and straightened her shirt, then fluffed her hair. "You better, after you just drove away a lifelong customer."

Carson frowned. "Lifelong? I thought you said you didn't know who she was?"

"I don't," Caro responded. "But after eating my truffles, she definitely would have been a lifelong customer."

"You're about to lose a customer if I don't get one of those cookie and creams right now," Jude argued, stepping up to the counter. He raised his eyebrows. "Maybe I'll just take the box that lady abandoned."

"Not a chance," Carson argued before he could think better of it. He mentally smacked himself. He didn't care if people knew he found the beautiful woman intriguing, but he didn't want them to think it was anything more than an enjoyment of a good fight. Buying the treats she had left behind showed a little more serious interest and Carson wasn't ready for people to know that.

When he saw Jude's eyes widen, Carson knew it was too late.

"Oh, right," Jude drawled, his eyes darting to Caro, then back. "I forgot you were going to apologize to her." He nodded. "Good thinking. Taking a gift always gives you a better chance of forgiveness."

Caro looked between the two men like they were insane. "I thought you didn't know who she was."

Jude kept nodding, but didn't look away from Carson. He was sending a message and Carson was reading it loud and clear, and he wasn't happy about it. *Stupid friends who see too much.* "Thanks, buddy," Carson said sarcastically. "Your idea sure is a good one."

Caro slapped the counter. "What the heck is going on here?"

"Babe," Jack said, putting his hand on his wife's shoulder. "They're just helping each other out. Why don't you wrap the box up all pretty?"

Caro glared at each of them in turn, then grabbed the box and turned back to the wrapping station.

Jack winked, Jude looked like he was holding back laughter, and Carson did his best to keep a blush at bay.

This was definitely *not* how he had planned for this to go.

CHAPTER 7

A week passed and Belle grew more and more nervous about the party at the Cordova home. Not only was she baking, but she was also serving at it, and with her past experiences with Grayson, she was more than a little uncomfortable at the prospect.

She was terrified that he would find her at the party and say something about how she had shut him down, not once but twice! She had been pretty cold at the candy shop and Belle was positive that if given the chance, the movie star would somehow make her life miserable.

"Good thing he doesn't know my name," she muttered as she folded over the dough for her croissants. She'd been up since four-thirty that morning making the pastries they needed that night and Belle was already exhausted. But this was what she was here for. These were her special recipe and she was eager to share them with a large crowd. Not to mention, this was the life she was trying to build. Early mornings, early nights, and sharing her flaky goodness with the world. "Except for Grayson Cordova," she grumbled.

"What was that?" Mrs. Stallings asked as she swept through the room with an armful of tablecloths.

"Nothing," Belle said quickly, plastering on a smile. She hesitated, then asked, "Do you really need me to serve tonight? Don't you think I'd be better in the kitchen? I haven't really been trained to handle guests..." She trailed off when Mrs. Stallings gave her a look.

"Do we have a problem, Ms. Kerr?"

Belle kept eye contact, but couldn't seem to hold back the feeling that she was behaving like a naughty school child. It made her feel bad for the kids who had been in Mrs. Stallings' classroom. "No. No problem."

Mrs. Stallings waited a second before nodding and moving onto another task. "We leave in two hours," she called over her shoulder. "Please have the bread packed by then."

Belle clenched her jaw but went back to work. Most of the food would be prepared completely ahead of time, but her breads would be a last-minute thing. Some of the desserts would actually be baked at the house in order to bring them out hot to the guests. *I suppose that means I'll serve less than some of the others,* she reminded herself. The thought was comforting. The less time she was out of the kitchen, the less her chances of running into Grayson.

Firming the idea in her mind, she threw her weight into rolling out the dough before folding it over again. She wouldn't let one man stop her. She hadn't let her ex husband stop her, and she wasn't going to let someone she barely knew stop her either. Belle was on a mission. Start a new life that had nothing to do with men and their fickle ways and build a business that brought only happiness to everyone who came through its doors.

She hated to admit it to herself, but this catering gig was going to be the start of that. She was absolutely positive that if she could get people to eat her baked goods, she could start to build a following that would be the very foundation she needed in order to get her bakery started.

The afternoon rushed by. Soon she was helping load everything into the trucks and they were driving around the back of the Cordova mansion.

Belle's heart was beating rapidly and her stomach was churning, and neither one had anything to do with people trying her pastries for the first time. She put a hand to her stomach and took a deep breath before leaving the confines of the van. She felt like Daniel, heading straight into the lion's den.

He's just a man, she reminded herself. *A jerk of a man who isn't as faithful as he should be, but still...just a man.*

Not for the first time, Belle wondered if she should mention something to Mrs. Cordova. She deserved to know that her husband spent his afternoons flirting with unsuspecting women in grocery stores. But just as she had every time, Belle hesitated. She knew that with her background and divorce, she was more sensitive to things like flirty comments. It may very well be that Mrs. Cordova was fine with her husband's behavior. She might know exactly how he acted around others and it didn't bother her at all. Perhaps it was just part of the movie star husband package.

And the last thing Belle wanted to do was create tension that she didn't need to. Alienating Mrs. Cordova with accusations from a stranger was probably not the best way to start a possible career in Seaside Bay.

"Ms. Kerr!"

Belle snapped into action. She needed to quit worrying about "what if's" and get into work mode. "On it," she responded, hurrying around to the back of the van. She immediately began lifting out trays and loading them on the shelves of the rolling trolley. Together, the team worked to get the food inside and Belle immediately began working to finish her pastries.

Later, she put the first batch of croissants in the oven with a relieved sigh. She was going to be ready on time for the party.

"Get your jacket on and fill a tray," Mrs. Stallings snapped. "The others are already serving."

Shoot. Belle had been so busy with her baking that she had forgotten about serving. Reluctantly, she headed back out to the van to grab her black jacket. Once inside, she moved slower than she should have, filling a tray.

"Take those crostinis to table three," Mrs. Stallings hollered from the other side of the kitchen. "You can refill trays on the tables. I think that'll be more useful at the moment."

Belle nodded and tried not to let her relief show. Filling tables was fine. She could be in and out very quickly and if she kept her head down, hopefully she wouldn't even have to make eye contact with a single party guest.

She balanced the tray over her shoulder, used her back to open the kitchen door, and swung around. Belle stuttered just a moment when she saw the size of the mingling crowd, then quickly decided that the more people there were, the better off she was.

Dodging other servers, she quickly made her way to the right table and switched out the platters of food. Taking a deep breath, she rushed the empty plates to the kitchen, taking a deep breath that she had managed to avoid speaking to a single soul.

She could still hear the strains of soft, orchestral Christmas music coming from the front room and she couldn't help but feel bad about her Scrooge-like attitude at a place that was so obviously meant to be a happy occasion. The ballroom was stunning and looked like a Hallmark movie come to life, but Belle wasn't enjoying any of it. Tonight was all about survival and she was simply grateful she had survived her first run.

Time to check on the bread.

She took care of her work with the pastries, then filled another tray. With a little more confidence than she had the first time, she headed back out, praying for another round of being the silent worker in the middle of the merry chaos.

*****

"You don't even want to meet her?" Brook asked in exasperation.

Carson held back the desire to rub his aching eyes or go grab some medicine for his raging headache. Grayson had promised he would convince Brook to leave him alone, but apparently Brook wasn't willing to listen to the message. "Brook," Carson said in as gentle a tone as possible, "I love you. But please, if you have any feelings for me as a brother...leave my love life alone!"

Brook huffed and folded her arms over her chest. "I just thought you two would get along so well," she argued.

"I get it, but I really want to be able to meet someone on my own terms," he said. "You have to understand that."

Brook made a face, but nodded. "I do. I guess I didn't realize how much it would bug you," she muttered, then gave a heavy sigh. "All right. I'll back off." Her eyes roamed the party. "But still..."

"Don't say it," Carson warned. "If there's anyone here I want to meet, I'm plenty man enough to take care of the introductions." He winked when she gave him a pouty look. "I'm not exactly the shy type," he reminded her.

Brook laughed. "True." Her shoulders fell. "All right. No more interfering." She put a hand in the air. "I promise."

Carson pointed a finger at her. "On your honor."

Brook laughed again. "Yes, sir."

He nodded. "Good." With one last grin, he turned away from his sister-in-law and headed deeper into the crowd. His aim was to fill a plate with food and then become invisible in a corner while he stuffed his face until he couldn't eat anymore. The food was surprisingly delicious, especially the savory pastries.

There were some small rectangles filled with cheese and spinach that just about melted in his mouth, along with something he was sure was some kind of meat pie. Whoever Brook had hired was completely wasted in this tiny town.

He loaded up his food, then worked his way through the laughing guests. There were several people he recognized and Carson tilted his chin at Caro, Jack, Chief Wamsley, his new wife Rose, and their little girl, Lily. The group were standing together, enjoying each other's company.

If he looked around, Carson was sure he would find the rest of Brook's friends. Felix and Hadlee had to be around somewhere, along with Benny, and... Carson scrunched his nose as he tried to remember Benny's wife. *Allison!* he thought triumphantly. *Her name is Ally.*

He finally found the empty space he'd been looking for and Carson put his back to the wall, sighing in relief at being away from the masses. The week-long party wasn't going to be nearly so big, but this big opening night was supposed to be for everyone, which for Brook meant practically the entire town.

Carson let his eyes drift over the crowd. He smiled at the few people he knew, made sure not to make contact with too many women who appeared to be single, and filled his stomach until he wanted to take a nap for the whole week.

"I think you and I have the same idea."

Carson shifted to leave a little more room for Jude in the corner. "Did you lay the law down with Brook?"

Jude gave Carson a look. "No." He sighed. "I don't have the heart to."

Carson chuckled. "It's the only way you're gonna escape the noose."

Jude pushed a hand through his hair, messing up his normally well shaped do. "I like Brook. I don't want to hurt her."

Carson snorted. "I like her too, but that doesn't mean I'm all right letting her pick out a date for me."

"It's not like we're going to be here that long," Jude muttered, looking down into his glass of punch.

Carson frowned. "Jude, man, I'm worried about you. Are you ever gonna tell me why you're so down?"

Jude shrugged and threw back the rest of the glass.

Carson had the feeling his friend wished it contained alcohol, but there was no such luck.

"I guess I'm just getting old," Jude responded, stepping to the side in order to drop off his empty cup on a table corner.

"And what makes you say that?"

Jude folded his arms over his chest. "I'm just getting tired of it all," he admitted. "And at this point, I'm not sure I trust my own judgment any more."

"Hello, gentlemen." Brook's too perky voice drew Carson's attention and immediately let him know she was up to something.

When he turned and saw a lovely young woman standing next to his sister-in-law, he raised an eyebrow. He pinned Brook with a look that he hoped said, *I thought we talked about this?*

Brook gave him a helpless shrug.

She was in for it later.

The woman smiled shyly and tucked a piece of dark blonde hair behind her ear. "You're Grayson's brother?" she asked.

Carson had to physically lock his knees to keep from walking away. Even in Seaside Bay, even with his sister-in-law's approval, he couldn't get away from his brother's shadow. "Yep," he said, popping the last letter a little too hard.

She gave him an odd look, then nodded. "That's, uh, great. I'm Ruth. My grandma owns the motel down on Main." Her eyes went to Jude, who had gone completely silent when Brook walked up. "Are you visiting as well?"

Carson looked at his friend, who appeared oddly sad.

Jude nodded and put out his hand. "Jude Lisbon. Nice to meet you." His eyes went up to Carson's, then back to the women. "If you'll excuse me."

Carson wanted to curse. Jude was supposed to be his wingman, not ditch him at the first sign of trouble!

"What's wrong with Jude?" Brook wondered. She looked at Carson. "Did something happen?"

Carson shrugged. "Not that I know of." That wasn't quite true, but he didn't have a real answer for her.

"Well…" Brook chewed her lip. "I need to mingle." She grabbed Ruth's arm. "Are you okay if I walk around? You're welcome to come. I know you don't know a lot of people."

Ruth glanced at Carson, then turned to Brook. "Actually, I think maybe I'll find my grandma." She looked at Carson. "As long as that's okay?" Her voice sounded unsure, as if she was afraid Carson would be offended she wasn't sticking around.

"That's fine," he assured her. "No worries."

The woman was lovely, but she definitely wasn't the type of person Carson was usually drawn to. She smiled softly, ducked her head, and weaved her way through the crowd.

"You promised," Carson growled as soon as the guest was out of earshot.

"I know," Brook said breathlessly. "But she kept saying she wanted to meet you and I couldn't find the heart to say no."

Carson rolled his eyes. "Well, at least she decided she wasn't interested."

"She didn't hang around very long, did she?" Brook tapped her bottom lip. "Which is odd, considering that she practically dragged me over here." She shrugged. "I'm completely lost."

Carson chuckled. "I'm just grateful to be free." A black-clad worker slid past him and Brook and Carson glanced over, only to do a double take. *It can't be.* His Irish Butter Woman was switching out an empty platter for a full one.

Suddenly, the obsession for Irish butter made sense. She was part of the catering team!

"Do you want to come with me while I walk?" Brook asked. "I hate to see you standing here in the corner."

Carson shook his head. "Nah, but thanks." He forced himself to turn back to his in-law. "I think I'll introduce myself to a few people."

Brook's smile was nothing short of beaming. "Thank you," she gushed. "People have been so excited to meet Grayson and his family and with your sister cancelling at the last minute, I'd be forever grateful if you helped alleviate some of their curiosity." She leaned in closer. "I can barely talk to Grayson with how many ladies are swarming him tonight."

"Yeah...good luck with that," Carson said with a sympathetic smile. "I'm sure you're aware it never seems to stop."

Brook nodded. "I know. But it'll die down after tonight. This was the only chance anyone in the town was going to get to see him."

Carson nodded, but his mind was on the beauty to his left. He could tell she was about to leave and he needed to follow. "Okay, well, good luck and don't be afraid to break a few noses if you have to." He patted Brook's shoulder. "I'll be sure to handle the lawsuits."

Before she could answer, he began heading toward the table just as his elusive butter lady darted out of the room.

Carson grinned. The chase was definitely on.

CHAPTER 8

Belle took in a deep breath as she finally reached the kitchen. She had seen him! Grayson and Brook had been in the corner near the table she was refilling. Belle had made sure to keep her head down and he hadn't said anything, so she was fairly certain she had managed to stay under the radar.

It had been interesting though, that Grayson hadn't been surrounded by a crowd of women. In fact, there had been a large crowd of women on the complete opposite side of the room from where Belle had been working. With Grayson Cordova in the house, she had been sure that that would have been the main attraction of the party, but apparently there was something even more interesting elsewhere.

Of course, with the way Brook had the home decorated, Belle couldn't blame anyone for being caught up in other interests. The greenery swags, poinsettias, golden bells, and soft white lights were so stunning that Belle found herself caught up like a gawking toddler every time she walked through the kitchen door.

"Table two needs a new cheese plate!" Mrs. Stallings hollered as she swept through the door.

"On it," Belle said, doing her best to hide her weariness. She had no idea that trying to be invisible was so hard. But there was nothing for it except to go back out. At least table two was away from where Grayson and his wife had been chatting.

Belle grabbed a platter of cheese, plus another of her pain au chocolates and headed back out. She was extra wary now that she'd spotted the man she was trying to avoid, but she made it to the table without any confrontations and swapped out the empty plates. Breathing out a sigh of relief, she grabbed the tray of empty plates and started back for the kitchen. She was almost home free when she heard a voice that made her want to throw up.

"Hello, Irish Butter."

Belle's feet stumbled, but then she quickly debated the merit of moving on without acknowledging he had spoken. But considering the fact that he was her host at the moment and it was his money paying her paycheck, she forced her feet to slow and she turned toward him. "Mr. Cordova," she said in what she hoped was a polite, but cold tone.

He chuckled and smirked, his hands in the pockets of his suit pants.

Heaven help her if he didn't look absolutely delicious and completely off limits. She had a fleeting thought of her messy hair and the smear of chocolate on the side of her pants that her apron hadn't been able to stop, but she quickly pushed it aside. She shouldn't care what she looked like. This man was *married*! She wanted nothing to do with him!

She shifted the tray on her shoulder. "Can I help you in some way?"

His grin grew and the playfulness behind his eyes was far too enticing. "I'm sure you can." He tilted his head. "So did you manage to get that butter? Or am I eating sub par food tonight?"

Belle's face heated like the inside of a boiling volcano. "I'm sure I don't know, Mr Cordova," she ground out. "Why don't you speak to my supervisor if you feel the food hasn't been to your liking."

He laughed. "You get angry so easily."

"Any woman should when a married man can't take a hint," she snapped. Belle pinched her lips together. She shouldn't let him egg her on like this. She was a full grown woman who had already survived a terrible marriage and divorce. She had come out a survivor and was on her way to true independence. What was it about this man that irked her so much? Why couldn't she just brush him off like she did every other guy who tried to get a word in edgewise?

Grayson stepped a little closer. "What if I told you...again...that I'm not married?"

"Then I would again have to call you a liar," she said, putting her chin in the air to hide how much his nearness affected her. She refused to back down. He was in the wrong here, not her. "The entire country heard about your wedding and I've met your wife." Belle raised an eyebrow. "She's lovely, by the way, and definitely deserves better than you flirting with other women."

Grayson scratched the edge of his jaw. "Brook is lovely and she does deserve better than that kind of behavior." One side of his mouth quirked up as he stepped even closer. "Which means it's a good thing that's how my brother treats her."

Belle felt the blood drain from her head as quickly as a deflated loaf of bread. "Your brother?"

Grayson...or whoever he was...nodded, amusement still prevalent in his gaze.

"You're not Grayson Cordova?"

He shook his head, taking another step forward. They were only a couple feet apart now. If she had wanted to, Belle could have reached out and touched his perfectly tailored suit.

"I don't believe you," she whispered, her voice barely audible.

The man opened his mouth to answer, but another voice cut in. "Car!"

Belle turned and her vision nearly went black. A man who was the spitting image of the stranger in front of her came hurrying in their direction. The new arrival was built bigger and had much bluer eyes than the man Belle had been talking to. In fact, those eyes were almost exactly the same color as all the images she had seen in movies and on billboards.

Grayson Cordova...

She gulped and swayed. He'd been telling the truth. The man she had been treating horribly for the past week wasn't the movie star. He was the movie star's brother.

"'Sup, Gray?" the brother said casually. His gray eyes darted to Belle and all humor drained from his face. "Hey...are you okay?"

He reached out, but Belle stumbled back. "Excuse me," she said hoarsely, nodding her head at both men. "I need to be getting back to the kitchen." She could hear voices behind her, but Belle felt as if her head were under water. She couldn't make out the words and she didn't have the wherewithal to stop and figure it all out.

Once inside the kitchen. she collapsed against a counter and forced her lungs to take in enough air to keep her from passing out. Shame and embarrassment hung over her like a heavy cloak in the summertime, threatening to cut off her air supply and take her to the ground.

"Belle!" Mrs. Stallings' stern voice could be heard behind her. "What's the matter, girl?"

Belle couldn't bring herself to answer. She closed her eyes and let her forehead rest against the cold granite. She hadn't been this ashamed of herself since finding out her husband had been entertaining other women for almost their entire marriage. All the confidence she had worked on building during the last few years fizzled like the ends of a firework. How could she not see what was right in front of her face?

She had been judge, juror, and executioner to a man who had done nothing wrong except look like his family and try to speak to a woman at a grocery store.

Belle groaned.

"Are you sick?" Mrs. Stallings demanded, her voice now right next to Belle.

"You could say that," Belle managed.

"Ms. Kerr!"

Belle shook her head. "I'm sorry, Mrs. Stallings. I had a bit of a shock, but if you'll let me have a five-minute break, I'll be back to my duties."

She wanted to go home and bury her guilt in flour and yeast, but Belle had committed to this job, just like she had committed to coming out of her divorce a better person. And since she had failed horribly at one of those promises, she was determined to succeed at the other.

It was the least she could do.

*****

Carson watched the woman leave, frustrated that he *still* didn't know her name! What the heck kind of timing did his brother have? He turned his full glare on his brother.

Gray put his hands in the air. "Hey, I didn't say anything!"

"You arrived," Carson muttered, dropping his folded arms. "That was enough."

Gray rolled his eyes. "If your brother showing up is enough to scare her off, then she's probably not going to survive this family."

"I wasn't looking to marry her, Gray," Carson argued. "Just get her name."

"She's one of the caterers," Gray said, shaking his head. "Brook'll know her name."

"No!" Carson shouted, then forced himself to bring his voice down. "I don't want Brook to know about this."

Gray stilled. "Just what is going on here?"

"Nothing nefarious." Carson spread his hands to the side. "Why is it so hard to understand that I simply don't want any of my family interfering? I don't want you to set me up on dates, or introduce me to single women, and if I find a woman I want to get to know, I definitely don't want to have to ask you how to get in touch with her."

Gray sighed and rubbed the back of his neck. "I was actually coming over here to apologize for Brook bringing Ruth over, but now I'm starting to think we should have left you in Cali." Gray stepped back. "Is your family really that bad?"

Carson scrubbed at his face. "No," he said in a defeated tone. "You're not that bad." His arms dropped to his sides. "I love all you guys, but..." He growled. "You just won't understand, Gray."

"Try me."

Frustration was building inside of Carson. How could he tell his brother the truth? And yet how could he withhold it and expect them to comply to his wishes?

"You sure you want to hear?" Carson warned.

Gray nodded firmly, set his legs, and folded his arms. "I just survived thirty women ignoring their husbands and keeping me from my wife for the longest hour of my life. I think I can manage it."

Carson rubbed the edge of his jawline. "I want to meet someone who doesn't want you."

Grayson blinked. "Uh, what?"

Carson threw his head back. "See? You don't get it." He waved a hand at his brother. "Do you have any idea how hard it is being in your shadow? Almost every woman who shows an interest in me doesn't actually care about me as much as they find me an easy stepping stone to get to you."

Gray frowned and Carson continued.

"I don't want your hand-me-downs. I don't want a woman who settles for second best," he continued, his argument growing heated. "I don't even want a woman who *sees* me second," he said. "I want to be seen for me. Not because I'm a lawyer, not because I live in California, and definitely not because I'm your brother." His fight wound down and his shoulders sagged. "Is it so wrong to want to be seen as more than your lookalike?"

"And that woman I just scared off?" Gray asked, his eyebrows raising in question.

Carson chuckled. "When I teased her in the grocery store, she thought I was you and she was so mad!"

Grayson scowled. "Why? What did I do?"

Carson smirked. "You flirted with a woman who wasn't your wife."

"No, I...Oh." Grayson nodded slowly as he came to an understanding. "You flirted and she thought it was me and the fact that she blew you off has you intrigued."

Carson tapped the side of his nose. "So can you *please* get Brook off my back, no matter how much her friends beg?" Carson grew serious. "And can you please not tell her about this woman? I don't want anything or anyone interfering."

Grayson shrugged and shook his head. "Brook already feels bad about Ruth, so that'll be no problem, but good luck keeping the rest of this a secret." He made a face. "She just wants you to be happy."

"I know, but I'm going to be happier if I'm left to my own devices."

Grayson chuckled. "I had no idea being related to me was so hard. Sorry."

Carson shrugged. "I'm sure there's worse and I'm sure others wouldn't care, but I'm just not one of them."

"Yeah... you always did like doing your own thing. I don't know why this surprises me." Gray clapped his brother on the shoulder. "Good luck. She didn't exactly look welcoming even before I came up."

Carson scrunched up his face. "I had just told her that I wasn't you."

"And that's the face she made?" Grayson laughed. "I'm not sure if I should be offended or excited for you."

"Grayson!"

Both men turned as the sound of Brook's call. For the first time since she'd left, Carson was grateful his mystery woman had chosen to run off...again.

"Hey, sweetie." Gray wrapped his arm around his wife's waist and kissed her temple.

"You're not mingling," she said with a teasing pout.

"I have to breathe sometime," Gray shot back.

Brook rolled her eyes. "You knew this was coming." She began tugging on his arm. "Come on. After tonight it'll just be close friends and family. You only have to pretend for a few more hours." Her eyes went to Carson. "You doing all right?"

Carson nodded and rocked on his heels. "Yep. Just dandy. Thanks."

Gray pulled against his wife for a second and dropped his voice. "There's mistletoe near the first serving table," he whispered with a wink. "I'll bet that'll shake off some of that cold reticence."

Carson burst out laughing. "Maybe if I want a black eye."

Grayson shrugged as Brook pulled him farther along. "Might be worth it though."

Carson watched them go down the hall and back to the party.

"Excuse me."

He quickly stepped back, making room for another server to walk past with a tray over their shoulder. His eyes went to the kitchen and Carson debated his next move. With Brook being taken care of, Jude off doing who knew what, and Grayson playing interference, that left Carson free to pursue his baking beauty without any setbacks.

But how to go about it?

Grayson's suggestion about the mistletoe flitted through his mind and Carson couldn't help but grin. He'd been serious. Irish Butter would more than likely punch him if he pulled something like that. But...

"Pardon me."

Another server went past and Carson decided it was time to act. He headed back toward the party, planting himself in another corner so he could wait and watch for the right server to come through. And if it just happened to be near table one...well...

CHAPTER 9

Belle hesitated before leaving the kitchen again. She'd taken five minutes to get herself back under control, then had loaded the cart she was going to use to refill the trays on table one, and the only thing left was to reenter the fray...but she was nervous.

She had wrongly accused the brother of her *boss* of being the boss and a wife cheater, and now she was supposed to keep moving as if nothing had happened.

Something is seriously wrong with me.

The thought made her depressed. She used to be a very hopefilled, push forward type of person, but her ex had stolen that part of her, and Belle's belief in the human race, particularly the men, was almost nonexistent.

Logically, she knew not all men were horrible liars, but sometimes it was hard to get the heart to follow the head.

"Get going, Ms. Kerr!"

Belle grit her teeth against the reprimand, knowing her boss was correct. She was an adult. She shouldn't be cowering in the corner because she made a stupid mistake.

Throwing back her shoulders and taking a deep breath for courage, Belle maneuvered her way out of the kitchen with the rolling trolley. The front left wheel squeaked with each inch it moved, and Belle hoped no one would be bothered by it. Hopefully the Christmas music and noise from all the chatting would cover the annoying sound.

She kept her eyes open and her ears tuned in to any smooth, deep voices, but a little holiday luck must have been on her side because she made it to the table without having to grovel at anyone's feet for forgiveness.

The longer Belle went without being spoken to, the more relaxed she became. She kept her eyes and head down as she worked, slipping as seamlessly as she could around the table to replenish the food and not bother the party guests who continued to fill their plates.

A small prick of jealousy ran through Belle, but she ruthlessly pushed the feeling aside. She used to be in the position of the people here. She used to be the type who enjoyed going to parties and spent an hour doing her hair and wearing fancy jewelry. She used to be the type who loved to socialize and share a meal with a friend.

But not anymore.

Belle felt like a shell of the person she used to be. Life had given her a wake up call and everything she had once enjoyed was all part of the past, and more than likely had no place in her future.

She set the last of the croissants on their tray, then grabbed the handle of the trolley and moved away from the table. She paused, however, when her way was blocked by a group of people chatting while slowly filling their plates.

Knowing she wouldn't be able to get around them without garnering more attention than she wanted, Belle settled back on her heels and decided to just wait. Surely they would either notice her and move to the side or their conversation would eventually wrap up and they would walk away from the table.

"Pssst."

Belle stiffened. *Oh, no.*

"Hey. Irish Butter!"

She closed her eyes and fought the temptation to hang her head. This was exactly what she had been hoping to avoid, but there was nothing for it. Belle had seriously wronged the guy and she needed to make amends. Slowly, she turned her head. "Yes?"

The too-handsome movie star lookalike smiled and waved her toward the room entrance he stood in. "You can come through this way." He pointed to the side. "The hall leads back to the kitchen."

Glancing to the group, who still hadn't moved, Belle nodded and pulled the cart around so she could follow his advice. "Thank you," she murmured as she crossed under the room threshold. "I was kind of stuck."

The man smiled, but didn't move to the side, forcing Belle to brush up against him as she walked past.

"Hey," he said softly.

Belle paused and looked up. They were entirely too close. From here she could see the lovely gray of his eyes was swirled with the lightest of blues, made more visible by the colors in his tie. It was the same color his brother, Grayson, sported, but less dominant. The light tone was magnificent against his darker skin and hair, making him every bit as handsome, maybe even more so, than his famous family member. "Can I help you?" she asked, her voice embarrassingly breathy.

"I never got your name," the man said, his eyes roaming her face.

Heat suffused her cheeks and Belle unconsciously tucked a piece of hair behind her ear. "I guess I've been a little...standoffish," she said, scrunching her nose. "I really am sorry about it all."

He put his hands in the air. "Just give me your name and all is forgiven."

Belle tilted her head to the side. "Why is my name so important?"

His look was entirely too smug. "Because I usually get a woman's name before I kiss her."

Belle felt all the blood drain from her head for the second time that night, and this time when she swayed, she only stayed on her feet because the man next to her held her up. "What?" she asked.

He chuckled and she felt the vibration of it as he kept her on her feet. "Look up."

Putting two and two together, Belle knew she'd not only been a fool for a second time that night, but that she had no good way of getting out of the situation. Her eyes went up and found exactly what she had been looking for. Mistletoe.

"I don't usually capture strangers under the greenery," the man said, tilting his head back and forth. "But you're making it awfully hard to keep that standard."

"Why do I get the feeling you did that on purpose?" Belle stiffened her knees and put a few inches of distance between them, though it did little to slow the wild beating of her heart.

"Because you're brilliant," he replied. His now free hands went in the air. "Guilty as charged, your honor."

"But as you said, we *are* strangers, so—"

"You're really going to just walk away?"

Something about the tone of his voice kept Belle's feet planted on the hardwood floor. "You really care if I do?"

He shrugged as if he didn't care, though some of the playfulness in his eyes seemed to have dimmed. "I guess I figured it wasn't much to ask after basically being called a lying cheat."

Belle's shoulders slumped. "You're right," she said. Her eyes went to the party, but since the room entrance was behind the buffet, no one seemed to be paying them much attention. "You do realize that I'm part of the help, right?"

"You do realize that I'm not famous, right?"

Belle smiled, she couldn't quite help it. "If you were, we wouldn't be having this conversation."

His hands rested on her upper arms, warm and strong. "And that's exactly why I have to know your name."

"Isabel," she said automatically. "But my friends call me Belle."

"And which do I get to be?"

Her eyes drifted up, then back to his. "You've seen my penchant for fancy butters, so I suppose Belle is fine."

Slowly he pulled her in, and her heart began to beat against her rib cage. She wasn't sure if he was trying to build anticipation or if he was giving her a chance to pull away, but Belle could barely breathe by the time his mouth hovered over hers.

"Nice to meet you, Belle."

*****

Carson had made a very grave, tactical error.

He had initiated the chase and eventual kiss of Ms. Irish Butter because he was intrigued by the fact that she so obviously was not someone who would fall for his brother. He had apparently played his cards right and now he was kissing her under the mistletoe.

He had never expected, however, to feel as if he never wanted to let her go.

The kiss lasted mere seconds, but it was enough to have him wanting to pull her into his chest and do much more than let his lips linger against her for a moment. He forced himself to pull back, but his male pride took a flying leap when her eyes stayed closed a few seconds after the kiss.

Those dark brown eyes looked slightly glazed when she finally fluttered them open. "I don't know your name."

There was a pause as he processed what she said, and when it finally penetrated, he couldn't help but laugh. "After all that work I went through to get yours, and I never told you mine?"

Belle's cheeks were beautifully flushed as she stepped back from him. "No. Sorry. I was so embarrassed about everything that I totally forgot to ask."

He held out his hand. "Carson Cordova."

Her smile was shy. "Isabelle Kerr." She gave him a firm shake.

"Nice to officially meet you," he said. "Though I had intended for that to happen before I caught you under the mistletoe."

"Ms. Kerr." The snapping voice brought both of them out of the post-kiss haze. An older woman, looking none too pleased, stood only a few feet away from the two of them. Her eyes went to Carson, then back to Belle. "I believe you have a job to do?"

Belle nodded. "You're right. I'm sorry." She ducked her head. "Excuse me."

Carson let her go, but he wasn't about to forget. He was fairly certain the older woman must be the boss because he'd seen her with Brook several times throughout the day. He stuffed his hands in his pockets. "Sorry," he said cheerily, not being truthful in the least. "I couldn't help but take advantage of tradition."

The woman stared him down and Carson began to grow slightly uncomfortable. "I believe Ms. Kerr has enough on her plate," she finally said, her tone brooking no argument.

Carson looked around. "Tonight she does for sure." He smiled, but it fell when the woman didn't smile back. "I'm sorry. I'm being rude." He stepped over and put out his hand. "Carson Cordova."

"I know who you are, Mr. Cordova," the woman said, giving his hand a short shake. "And again, I repeat, she has enough on her plate." One white eyebrow rose high. "And you don't live here."

Both of Carson's eyebrows shot up. "Thank you for the reminder." He was growing irked. Usually he was pretty good at winning grumpy people over, but right now this lady was starting to get on his nerves. He hated being treated like a little kid, and he doubly hated when people assumed they knew him without actually knowing him.

Belle's situation had been funny and intriguing, this lady's was just plain rude.

The woman grunted and turned around, nearly smacking Carson with the tray she held at her waist.

He stepped quickly to the side and watched her go. It was probably time to get back to the party and let the situation with Belle cool down a little bit. He was half afraid that if he caught her again anywhere near the mistletoe, he wouldn't be able to keep himself from sneaking another kiss.

Grabbing a drink, Carson meandered through the crowd.

"Carson!"

He smiled, waved his drink in the air, and headed over to say hello to Ken Wamsley and his wife Rose. "Hey, Ken!" Carson nodded. "Rose." He looked around pointedly. "Where's the squirt?"

Rose groaned. "Aunt Caro has her." Rose shook her head. "I'm pretty sure Lily is going to be so hopped up on sugar that she'll never sleep tonight."

Carson chuckled as he took a drink. "Sounds about right." His back pocket buzzed. "Excuse me a second." Turning away slightly, he grabbed his phone and checked the text.

Looking forward to the holidays with you!

A kissy face followed the words and Carson grimaced. "Why can't she take a hint?" He turned. "Hey, would you hold this for a second?"

Ken nodded and took the drink, leaving Carson to go back to his phone.

Enough, Emme. Stop texting me.

Carson angrily stuffed his phone back in his pocket. Something was seriously wrong with that woman. Other than being neighbors, Carson had never pursued even a casual friendship with her, but he knew her type. She'd never made it a secret that she wanted to get to know him, and Carson was very much aware that in Emme's eyes, he was a gateway to Grayson. Most women who tried that tactic, however, found out quickly that Carson didn't play games and they went away frustrated, but still went away.

Emme didn't seem to want to take no for an answer.

"Everything okay?" Ken's eyebrows were furrowed as he handed Carson his drink.

Carson smiled. "Just peachy." He turned back to Rose. "So...how's marriage to the big guy?" Carson tilted his head toward Ken, who was the biggest of their friends at Seaside Bay. "Please tell me it's good, because I'm not big enough to beat him up."

Rose laughed and her eyes traveled to her husband. "It's wonderful," she said softly.

Carson wanted to groan. That had been a stupid move. His second of the night. First he'd kissed a woman, completely underestimating how it would affect him, and now he'd brought up marriage to a pair of newlyweds who were still in the honeymoon stage of their relationship. If he was concerned about being a third wheel, that had been the wrong move.

Ken winked at his wife and Carson took a long drink of his cider, nearly choking on the carbonation.

"Hey! Look what the jury drug in!"

Carson would know that sassy, Southern twang anywhere. "Caro!" he said, beyond grateful for her interruption. "I heard you were up to no good." His eyes went to her bulging belly. "But it looks like you're growing that little guy just fine, if you ask me."

Caro smirked and rubbed her stomach. "If this little girl doesn't show up soon, I may have to do something drastic." She glanced at Rose, then came back to Carson. "And I was up to no good. I was filling Lily with sugar." Caro leaned in. "Have you tried those chocolate croissants? They're insane!" She frowned. "I wonder who made them."

"I'll bet Brook could ask the caterer," Rose offered. "I heard she was an old teacher of Brook's from middle school or something."

Carson tucked another piece of information away. He would bet good money that was the woman who had warned him away from Belle. He took a more manageable sip of his drink and let himself settle into conversation with his friends. It would help take his mind off the working beauty who was going to make his time in Seaside much more fun than Carson had ever anticipated.

CHAPTER 10

Belle plodded into the kitchen the next morning using more than her use of sight, since her eyes were nearly completely shut. It was late morning, but the bright sun was sending shooting pains through her eye sockets, straight to her brain.

Her hair was a rat's nest, the once contained bun now half in, half out and smashed against her head as if crafted by her darling nephew during a particularly crazy fit of temper.

She was fully aware that her mascara was smeared under her eyes, making the black, half moons even more prominent, but right now...she didn't care.

Sofia was running errands with Cole, and Rich was at work, leaving the house quiet and perfect for lounging around after a *loooong* night keeping a large group of people fed and happy.

And avoiding men who kiss too well for my sanity.

Guilt still riddled Belle's system, but at this point there was little she could do about the situation. She had apologized, he had let it go, and then she had allowed him to kiss her as a way of making amends. The problem was, it wasn't just any kiss.

Even her ex-husband hadn't moved her the way that two-second kiss had last night, which was the exact reason behind Belle's messy and sleep-deprived state. Even getting home late, she could have gotten a decent night's sleep by shutting off her alarm this morning, but what was a girl supposed to do when she couldn't fall asleep *until* the alarm was set to go off because her mind couldn't shake the feeling of Carson Cordova's lips?

Belle rubbed her eye, grimacing at the traces of black left on her palm, and set the tea kettle to boil. A nice, steaming cup of tea would go a long way in helping her wake up right about now.

She leaned her back against the counter and yawned as she waited for the kettle to whistle. When the noise finally sounded, Belle jolted slightly, having almost fallen asleep again.

"Oh my word," she breathed, pouring the water into a mug. "Get yourself together!" The scolding words did little to push Belle's body into compliance, though she did enjoy the lovely smell of mint wafting from her mug as the leaves began to steep.

Dumping a couple pieces of bread in the toaster, Belle grabbed the butter and a plate for her pitiful breakfast.

She had just finished grace and was holding a piece of toast to her mouth when the doorbell rang. She looked toward the door, debating the merits of staying quiet rather than seeing what the person needed, when the knocking came again.

Grumbling under her breath, Belle defiantly took her toast with her, gnawing off a rather large bite just before pulling on the knob. It wasn't like she was trying to impress whoever was there. Odds were it was just a package anyway. Sofia liked to do her holiday shopping online.

When Belle recognized the dark head of hair and light gray eyes, her eyes nearly bugged out of her head and she began to choke on the suddenly dry bread in her mouth.

Carson's initial smile fell and he stepped forward to slap her on the back. "Can you breathe?" he asked.

Belle knew her face had to be Rudolph red as she waved him off and forced herself to swallow the half eaten bite. "I'm fine," she rasped, stepping back to create some distance between them. She put her hands on her knees while she caught her breath, grimacing as she thought about how much she must resemble a homeless person at the moment.

Knowing he was waiting, she finally straightened. Her arms folded over her chest as if that could protect her from the awkward situation and she sent him a tight smile. "Hello. Can I help you?"

Carson wiped a hand over his mouth, but there was no hiding the grin he was sporting as his eyes went from the top of her head to the cold floor beneath her toes. "Nice uniform you're sporting."

Belle tugged at the oversized T-shirt. "Thanks. It's been in the family for generations."

His dark eyebrows shot up. "Wow. That's quite an heirloom. Are you sure you should be sleeping in it?"

Belle's lips twitched. "I'm pretty sure it's fine."

Carson nodded thoughtfully. "Well, if you decide you want to put it in your will or anything...let me know."

Belle frowned. "Uh...I'm lost."

He winked. "I'm a lawyer."

"Oooooh..." Belle responded, drawing out the word. "I'm guessing that explains your tenacity in following me around town, and how you figured out where I lived."

Carson rubbed the back of his neck, as if slightly uncomfortable. "Well, to be honest, running into you in town was completely a work of fate, but last night you gave me your last name, so I'm afraid I can't take as much credit for my being here this morning as I would like." He glanced over his shoulder. "It is kind of cold though. Are you sure you want the door to remain open like this?"

Belle tilted her head to the side. She really should just ask him to leave. She looked and felt horrible, and her handsome visitor was more enticing than he should be. She wasn't looking for another relationship right now...or maybe ever, if she was being honest with herself. She was here because she was out of money and was looking for a way to earn her keep until she could start a business.

"Is that your subtle way of asking to be let in? Because it sure didn't sound like you expected to be left out in the cold."

A slow, completely heartwarming smile spread across Carson's face. "I don't usually leave my friends standing on the stoop of my house," he explained. "So I naturally assumed it would be the same with you."

"Friends?" Belle gave him a disbelieving look.

"You told me I could call you Belle."

Her heart fluttered slightly at his use of her name. Taking a risk, which was completely against everything she stood for since her divorce, Belle waved him in. "I'll grab another mug," she said softly.

*****

Carson watched Belle move around the small kitchen, grabbing a mug, filling it with water, and dropping a tea bag inside. "Thank you," he said as she set it in front of him. He let his hands go around the ceramic, enjoying the warmth as it seeped into his palms.

He couldn't help but grin as he studied Belle's appearance yet again. There was absolutely nothing pretentious in the way she looked at all. Everything was completely natural and real. While he was pretty sure she hadn't been prepared to host company in her ratty pajamas and cockeyed hairdo, she also hadn't rushed out of the room to fix it as soon as he'd arrived, which meant she saw no need to impress him. The idea of a woman not caring was so foreign, he could hardly believe it.

It was perfect.

"Do I offend your sense of style?" Belle quipped, giving him an arch look.

"Not at all," Carson responded. "I've always loved 'Look like a mental patient day.'"

Belle snorted and took a sip of tea. "I'd say thanks, but I'm pretty sure I was insulted in that remark."

"Only in the best of ways."

"You lawyers and your silver tongues." Belle shook her head. "You can make anything sound good."

He chuckled. "You have experience with that?"

Her humor fled. "You could say that."

The words were spoken so softly that Carson wasn't quite sure he had heard them correctly. His natural curious nature demanded he ask questions, but one look at Belle's face told him that wouldn't be the best choice. He cleared his throat. "Thanks for the tea," he said. "It's warming me up."

Belle's smile wasn't quite as bright, but at least it was back to a degree. "You're welcome." She took a bite of her toast. "So what brings you by this morning? I don't recall asking for legal advice."

He smiled. "I wanted to see if you'd go to dinner with me."

Belle began to cough, her face going just as red as it had when she'd choked at the door.

Carson started to rise out of his seat to help, but Belle waved him off yet again, grabbing her mug and chugging what was left of her drink. "Are you asking me on a date?"

"Yes." Carson saw no need to beat around the bush. He was interested in Belle. He wanted to get to know her more. And he wanted to do it in the little time he had while he was in town.

Belle blinked at him. "Really?" she squeaked.

Carson nodded. "Is that so crazy?"

"I..." Belle tucked her hair behind her ear. "I just...I don't know...didn't expect it."

"Does that mean you're turning me down?" He gave her a look. "After everything you put me through?"

Belle leaned back. "Are you *guilting* me into saying yes?"

"Would it work?"

Belle frowned. "I don't know."

He leaned in. "I'll press any advantage I can get," he admitted. "So if telling you that being mistaken for my brother damaged my emotional health for life and the only way to cure it is to be seen for myself in a setting which allows us to speak without being interrupted by any family, friends or bosses, all while eating a delicious dinner, then I'm not too proud to do it."

Belle paused a split second before breaking out in laughter. "That was quite the speech."

"I get a lot of practice."

She nodded. "I think maybe I need to say yes, just to make sure you aren't damaged for life."

He wiped imaginary sweat from his forehead. "My emotional state thanks you."

Belle was still smiling as she shook her head. "I'm not quite sure what to make of you."

"The feeling is mutual," Carson murmured right before taking a sip of his drink. "Have you lived in Seaside Bay long?"

Belle shook her head. "No. I just got here a couple weeks ago."

"And you live with your brother?"

Belle nodded. "Yeah. He's married and running the hardware store on Acorn Street."

"Ah."

"Considering who your brother is, I'm guessing you don't live here full time," Belle hedged.

Carson shook his head. "No. I live in Hollywood. My sister and her family are there, and Grayson used to be there, though he and Brook travel a lot for movie shoots, so it's only a part-time residence for him now."

"Huh." Belle frowned. "That must be kind of a tough life. Moving around all the time."

He shrugged. He really didn't want to get into his brother's life. There was a small skeptical part of Carson that was afraid if they spoke about his movie star brother, Belle would eventually show that she was just like all the other women.

"Do you enjoy it?"

He jerked his head up. "What?"

"Do you enjoy living in Hollywood?" Belle asked. "I've done the big city thing and I know it's not for everybody."

He shrugged again. "I suppose so. I grew up in the area and it made sense to stay close to my siblings."

"Your sister is married? You mentioned she had a family."

Carson hesitated. He didn't like telling too much about his family. The paparazzi seemed to thrive on buying information from people close to them, but Belle's eyes were wide and innocent and he hoped he could trust her. "She has a daughter. She's coming up on her second birthday, just after the new year."

Belle's easy smile relieved his fears. "My nephew, Cole, is a little bit younger. Christmas is going to be a hoot this year with him around." She leaned forward as if imparting a secret. "We already have to block off the Christmas tree. He won't stop grabbing at the ornaments."

Carson laughed. "I'll bet my sister is doing something similar. Little Kaylee is into everything from what I understand."

"Honey! I'm home!" a female voice called into the house.

Carson turned in his seat to see a lovely woman come around the corner with a toddler on her hip. She stuttered to a stop. "Oh. Hello."

Carson stood up and pointed to Belle. "She let me in."

Belle stood up and glared at him. "Way to throw me under the bus."

Carson glanced her way and winked.

Belle rolled her eyes, much to Carson's delight. "Sof, meet Carson Cordova. He's a lawyer from Hollywood. I met him at the party last night."

The smile splitting Carson's face couldn't be helped. She hadn't introduced him as Grayson's brother, or even mentioned movie stars at all. Belle had introduced him as himself and it was the greatest compliment Carson had ever received.

CHAPTER 11

"You're sure about this?" Sofia asked as she bounced Cole on her hip. The child was chewing on a teething toy and leaving a line of drool that would make a bulldog jealous.

Belle made a face. "As sure as I can be." Belle opened her eyes wide to put on her mascara. She wasn't about to meet Carson for dinner looking like she had this morning. The least she could do was not put him off his appetite.

"I mean, I get that he's good looking, but how much do you really know about him?" Sofia switched hips.

Belle paused and blew out a breath, her hair jumping at the movement. "I know that he's Grayson Cordova's brother. I know that means he's related to Brook, who is one of the sweetest women I have ever met. And I know that I misjudged him for a long time and said some things I shouldn't have."

Sofia scrunched her nose. "So you're going out with him because you feel guilty?"

Belle hesitated before shaking her head. "No...at least I don't think so."

"He better keep his hands to himself," Rich grumbled as he walked up to the bathroom door and took Cole from his wife. "Guys who live in that kind of world don't know how to take no for an answer."

Belle did her best to hide the heat in her cheeks. Rich had no idea that she and Carson had already kissed, and she wasn't going to be the one to tell him. "I'm a full grown woman," she said instead. "I think I can handle myself."

"Do you have mace in your purse?"

Belle rolled her eyes. "Of course."

Rich chuckled. "That's my girl."

"I thought that was my job," Sofia said, folding her arms over her chest.

Rich's smile widened and he leaned down to give his wife a kiss that was a little longer than it should have been for the audience. "You're not a girl, you're a woman."

Belle put her hands over her head. "Oh my gosh! For the sake of my sanity, stop!"

Rich's laugh, mixed with his son's squeals, could be heard as they made their way down the hall and stairs.

"Sorry," Sofia said, tucking her hair behind her ear, though she couldn't quite keep the grin off her face.

Belle shook her head. "No. I'm sorry." She smiled. "He's my brother. I'm legally obligated to give him a hard time."

Sofia laughed softly. "Maybe you do need to go out with a lawyer. You certainly know the lingo."

Belle dumped her make-up back in the case and studied herself in the mirror. She wasn't the bright-eyed teenager she had been when she'd met her first husband. Her frame was a little curvier and her skin slightly less dewey. But it was her eyes that had changed the most. Instead of seeing the world through rose-colored glasses, she had a jaded look. *Or maybe it's just experience.*

Belle looked away and shook her head. It didn't matter. It's not like this was going to get serious. Carson seemed fun, now that Belle wasn't trying to bite his head off. But he lived in California and she was basically homeless. They could have a little fun while he was in town and eventually say their goodbyes and there would be absolutely no risk to her emotions or her heart.

The doorbell rang and Belle's pulse jumped up a notch.

"Want me to get it?" Sofia asked.

Belle shook her head. "No. I better do it." She hurried into the hallway, hoping she beat Rich. If he opened the door, she was positive there would be an interrogation.

"Mr. Cordova, I presume?"

Belle stopped mid-stair and bit back a groan. *Dang it.* Grumbling under her breath about interfering family members, she made a little extra noise on her way down in order to let her brother know she was coming. Perhaps it would remind him to behave.

"And you'll have her home when?" Rich asked, still standing in the doorway.

Belle hurried up behind her brother. "Carson! Hi!" Her eyes didn't want to leave the handsome visage in front of her, but she forced them to turn to Rich. "Thanks for getting the door," she said, sidling her way around her brother's bulk and out the door. Carson, very smartly, moved back so he wasn't blocking her. "I'll see you in the morning!" Belle pulled the door shut just as Rich opened his mouth to argue. "Hurry," she whispered, grabbing Carson's arm. "If we don't get out of here, he'll probably come hunt you down for more questions."

"He seemed nice," Carson said with a laugh as they rushed to his car. He lunged in front of Belle in order to open the passenger side for her.

Belle's eyes nearly bugged out of her head. "This is your car?" she choked.

Carson shook his head. "Rental." He shrugged. "Merry Christmas to me, right?"

Belle nodded and swallowed hard as she got in her seat. The last few years of her life had been pretty tough financially, and somehow she felt...unworthy to sit in such a nice car. She didn't dare tell her date that her vehicle was the one held together by duct tape on the corner of the driveway.

Why do you care? her inner voice scolded. *It's not like this is a real date. In a couple of weeks, you'll go your separate ways. That's it. You don't really want a man in your life anyway. Just enjoy the meal and let it be done.*

She took a deep breath, willing the little speech to become a reality.

Carson started the car and pulled them out into the street, but his head kept coming back to her. "Are you okay? Did I say something wrong?"

Belle pushed her heated cheeks to the side and kept a smile in place. "Nope. Everything's fine." Her fingers rubbed the soft leather seat. "Do you always treat yourself to such nice gifts?" She didn't mean for her words to come across as accusatory, but even she could hear the edge in her tone.

Gifts had been her ex's way of hiding his other activities. Distract Belle with a pretty bauble they couldn't afford and he could do whatever he wanted. It was why Belle hadn't fought for much of anything during the divorce. She didn't want a *thing* from him. What she wanted was loyalty and genuine care, but being thrown back into the dating world with her naivete gone, she had quickly seen that those character traits were a dying art.

"It's just a car," Carson said, the confusion in his voice audible. "I thought it would help me make it through the holidays if I had something fun to look forward to."

Belle turned toward him in the dark. "You don't think Christmas is fun?"

He chuckled. "Christmas is great. But being the only single person in a family of matchmakers is terrible." He shrugged. "So I dragged my best buddy along and rented a car that puts a smile on my face and gave me a way to have quick getaways when needed." He turned that smile in her direction and the flash of his white teeth made Belle blink. "Does that bother you?"

Belle shook her head and gave a small smile in return. "No, actually. I think that's a good way to handle it." She frowned. "But I didn't notice anyone playing matchmaker with you at the party the other night."

"You were watching me?"

Belle froze. Crud. Why did she say that? Although, it was unfortunately true. After being made to understand who he was and how wrong she had been, Belle had barely been able to keep her eyes off of him. Apparently, she'd been lucky enough that he hadn't noticed...until now.

*****

The silence in the car let Carson know that Belle was embarrassed by his teasing, but this was too good to pass up. Belle was fairly aloof, although intriguing, and Carson wasn't sure that she actually liked him at all, let alone was interested. But if she'd been watching him at the party...well, that changed things.

"Wait." He made a face. "I need to know whether this was before or after you thought I was Gray."

Belle groaned. "Do you have to keep bringing that up? I said I was sorry."

Carson chuckled. "I know and I accept your apology. But knowing whether or not you watched me before or after really does mean something." He waited with bated breath. So far she had passed all his tests, and it was doing funny things to him. He had been so excited to go on this date tonight that Carson was positive he had driven Jude absolutely crazy.

His physical therapist friend had finally just up and left, walking out right in the middle of a conversation that may or may not have been all about Belle's disdain of Grayson.

Belle huffed. "After," she grumbled, turning to look out the window.

It was too bad she was too embarrassed to look his way, because Carson's grin could have guided ships on a stormy sea. He pressed his turn signal and pulled the car into a small parking lot. "Have you ever been to The Crab Pot?" he asked, turning off the engine. "I've heard it's the best restaurant in town."

Belle leaned forward to look out the windshield. "I haven't," she said softly. "I've only been here a couple of weeks."

"Well, there's no time like the present." Carson stood up and began to walk toward Belle's door, but she beat him to it. He frowned. "And here I was raised a gentleman," he quipped.

Belle gave him a sheepish smile. "Sorry. I'd forgotten those exist."

"Now that's just sad." Carson tsked his tongue and lightly put his hand on her back to guide her inside. "We'll have to fix that." As he held the door open for her, Belle gave him a funny look, but didn't speak, so he let the subject drop. Belle was a beautiful woman, just like her name implied. There was no way she was completely inexperienced with men. If none of them had ever bothered treating her like a lady, then that didn't say much good about Carson's gender.

"Welcome, Mr. Cordova," the hostess said with a wide smile. "Your table is ready and waiting."

"Thank you," Carson said politely, but he kept his focus on Belle. The hostess's smile was a little too eager for his liking and he'd learned over the years there was a reason for it. Maybe he should have taken Belle somewhere out of town, where people didn't know who he was.

"Thanks," Belle said softly as Carson held out her chair for her. She had been very quiet ever since they'd entered the restaurant, and Carson was starting to wonder why.

He waited patiently for the waiter to fill them in on the specials before leaving them with menus and heading off to other tables, before leaning in. "What's wrong?" he whispered.

Belle looked up from her menu. "Nothing. Why?"

"You're quiet."

She made a face. "And that's a bad thing?"

Carson shrugged and tapped his fingers on the table. "No. But it usually means a woman is upset."

Belle gave him an amused look and raised her eyebrows. "And you're a woman expert? I thought that was your brother."

Carson's grin fell and he leaned onto his elbows, folding his hands. "I'm curious. I mean, don't get me wrong...it's not uncommon to see a woman not fawning over Gray, but just what do you have against him? He didn't have any idea who you were the other night." A light bulb went on. "Oh...did you meet him before and he didn't remember you?"

A lead ball landed in Carson's stomach at the realization. All this time he thought Belle just wasn't into fame, but if she held an actual personal grudge against Grayson, that was different. And it meant she was more than likely just like all the other women he knew...only angrier.

Belle's cheeks turned red and she dropped her gaze to her lap. "I'm sorry," she said softly, glancing at him from under her eyelashes. "I shouldn't have said that." She took a deep breath. "I've never met your brother. Judging by how sweet Brook is, I hope he's a wonderful guy." Her lips trembled ever so slightly and she pinched them together. "I, uh..." She clenched her jaw and seemed to come to some kind of decision because her shoulders straightened and her chin went into the air. "I'm divorced."

Carson waited for her to continue, but she didn't. "Okay."

Her brows furrowed. "That doesn't bother you?"

He shrugged. "Why should it? I'm a lawyer. I see it all the time." He leaned back and studied her. "So if you haven't met Gray, then I'm guessing the ex is the one who made you so edgy around men."

In hindsight, that might not have been the best thing to say. Carson knew he tended to be blunt, but normally he was aware enough of his company to keep his words within the bounds of manners he was taught as a child.

Belle looked less than impressed and when she folded her arms over her chest in a defensive manner, Carson knew he'd blown it. "Yes. I guess you could say that." She ground her jaw for a moment. "You know, I think this may have been a mistake." She started to stand and Carson put out his hand.

"Hold on." To his surprise, she actually did pause. "Why don't we call a truce?"

Belle narrowed her eyes. "Why?"

That hadn't exactly been the question he'd been expecting. Then again, most of Belle had been surprising him from day one. He splayed his hands to the side. "Do you mind if we just lay our cards on the table?"

Belle softened just a little. "Okay..."

"When I realized in the grocery store that you thought I was my brother and you still didn't fawn at his feet, I knew I had to meet you."

Belle nodded.

"Not to get too deep here, but I've spent most of my life dodging women who only want one thing."

A single dark eyebrow rose high.

"My brother."

Belle's eyes flared and her demeanor further softened. "So that's why you keep asking me all those questions."

Carson made a face. "Yeah. I hate to admit it, but that's the whole reason I kept trying to get to know you." He shrugged. "Running into you was a coincidence because I never actually managed to find out your name before you beelined it away from me, and none of my friends in town knew who you were."

"Because I'm new." Belle huffed a laugh. "So it wasn't my bubbly personality that drew you in, huh?"

Carson chuckled, grateful she wasn't upset. "Not at first...but I can't say I haven't been intrigued by what I've seen so far."

"A sharp-tongued woman who carries a grudge the size of Manhattan?"

His smile widened. "A beautiful woman with a quick wit who isn't using me for a stepping stone."

Belle sighed and gave him an understanding look. "I guess we accomplished the first date purpose."

"What's that?"

"Getting to know each other."

Carson laughed. "Maybe too well."

"Are you sure you want to stick around for dinner?" Belle leaned forward. "I can't promise I won't be sarcastic once in a while, but I can promise that I'm not here because of your last name."

"Are we ready to order?"

Carson glanced up at the waiter, then back at Belle. "Yes," he said, replying to them both. "I think we're ready."

CHAPTER 12

"Thank you," Belle murmured as Carson pulled back her chair to make it easier to stand up. "That was delicious," she told him, walking toward the restaurant door.

"Not bad for a podunk town like this." He pushed the front door open for her.

"It's not podunk," Belle defended, though she hadn't spent too much time in Seaside Bay. "It's just...small. Small and charming."

Carson laughed, then ducked his head against the cold wind. "Brr...I was going to see if you wanted to go for a walk, but..." He made a face.

Belle grimaced. "Not exactly a pleasant evening, is it?" She pulled her coat tighter around her. It would be nice to get home to her brother's warm house, though she understood Carson's sentiment. After they had basically laid out their weird pasts, it had ended up being a very enjoyable night. The food was good and fresh, and the company had left her laughing more than once.

Belle couldn't remember the last time she had felt so carefree. A heavy weight had been sitting on her shoulders ever since her divorce, but tonight it had been lightened, and as cold as it was, she wasn't sure she was ready to pick the mantle back up.

Carson pulled open her door. "Mother Nature seems to be having a bad night," he agreed, closing it as soon as her legs were inside. He rushed around and jumped into his seat, before pausing. "I hope this doesn't come off as too forward, but since we can't take a walk, would you like to go...for lack of a better word...park at the beach with me?"

Belle snorted. "I think maybe I should ask what all would be included in this parking session." Carson's bright white smile was pure mischief, but somehow, Belle found she wasn't worried. After finally figuring out who he was, Carson had been flirty, fun, and ultimately...a gentleman. He could have pushed things when she agreed to a small mistletoe kiss. He could have made suggestive comments during dinner. He could have made comments about taking her back to his place. But he hadn't done any of those things.

He was blunt and it was easy to see he was a lawyer when he asked direct questions, but Belle found herself relaxing more and more knowing that Carson was not the type of man who would push her boundaries.

"A good view of the ocean and some more get to know you, talking," Carson said with an understanding grin. He put his hands in the air. "I'll keep these babies to myself."

A small part of Belle huffed in disappointment, but she shoved it to the side. She wasn't here in Seaside to find a man, but to find herself. Carson was fun, but he could never be anything more than a sweet distraction. She had a bank account to fill and a business to start. He was only here for the next week and then she'd never see him again. Which meant that tiny voice that wanted another chance to experience his kiss in a less public and hurried circumstance needed to be quiet and pull itself together.

"Then I think that sounds just fine," Belle said with a smile. "You're sure you want to keep chatting?" she asked as he pulled out. "This is your chance to get rid of me."

Carson chuckled. "Get rid of the first woman who didn't fall at my brother's feet? Are you kidding?" He glanced her way before going back to the road. "I might have to pack you in my luggage when I go home just so I can show you off to my friends."

Belle shook her head, but couldn't help her smile. "There's no way that *every* woman you meet is after Grayson." Yet, as she watched his face fall, Belle realized that maybe she just had never experienced what the life of a celebrity was really like. Besides, her husband was more than popular with other women, so she had a sliver of first hand experience in how crazy fangirls could be.

"You'd be surprised," he muttered.

"Sorry," Belle said sincerely. "I shouldn't have said that. But my point was, you seem like a really nice guy and you're every bit as attractive as your brother, so I guess I don't understand why everyone would be that way. "

Carson shrugged. "The crowds we mingle with probably don't help. Grayson is famous enough that we're friends with all the bigwigs and followed by all the crazies." He looked her way again. "Take your pick."

"You're right, that probably doesn't help," Belle conceded.

Carson parked the car, the front facing the boardwalk, which was empty at the moment, considering the time and weather. Just beyond the walkway was wild grass, followed by sand and ocean. It wasn't as easy to see as normal, since the moon was only half full, but with the car off, Belle could hear the crashing waves and she could imagine what the water looked like. It really was quite peaceful, despite the temperature.

"So..." he hedged. "Tell me about this ex."

Belle's eyebrows furrowed together. "And here I thought our chat was going to be fun."

Carson tapped his fingers on the steering wheel, looking through the windshield. "I didn't push too much earlier, but we already discussed that he played a large part in how you view the world at the moment." His head turned her way. "I want to get to know you more, and I think that knowing where you're coming from is one of the keys."

Belle forced herself to relax in her seat, though her stomach was still in knots. "There goes that silver tongue again," she whispered. He must be deadly in the courtroom. She *hated* talking about Dale, and yet Carson made it sound like it was not only okay, but something flattering.

He gave her a sad grin. "You intrigue me," he said, just as softly. "Can you blame me for wanting to understand as much as possible?" He shrugged one shoulder. "Maybe the lawyer in me is a little stronger than I thought."

Belle sighed and laid her head back against the seat. "It's not a pretty story."

"The fact that you're sitting here next to me means it ends up okay," he responded.

Belle's low laugh was anything but amused. "Okay, but remember, you asked for it." She sighed. "Dale and I were high school sweethearts."

"Really?" Carson whistled low under his breath. "That's impressive. I didn't think most of those worked out."

"Mine only lasted five years, so…"

"The average marriage in the U.S. only lasts eight years," Carson supplied. "If you count your high school years, you were probably together close to that."

Belle huffed a laugh. "Being a normal statistic doesn't make me feel better."

"Sorry." Carson waved a hand in her direction. "On with the story."

Belle took a deep breath. "Dale was one of the most popular boys in school," she began. "He was a definite jock and I was the epitome of a high school cheer bunny."

Carson snorted, but didn't speak.

"We were the ultimate couple, I suppose." Belle felt the normal pain in her chest as she spoke. Even after all this time, she still hated how it had all turned out. She hated how stupid she had been, how blind, how young and naive. Her promising start had ended with her penniless, living at her brother's home, and with a chip the size of Texas on her shoulder. Despite Carson's assurance that her being here tonight was a good thing, Belle wasn't quite so sure she was grateful for the journey.

*****

He had touched on a nerve. The very air in the car felt slightly sour and Carson braced himself for what she was going to say. He had seen hurt women before and Belle definitely fell into that category. What he was enjoying, however, was the fact that instead of sulking and feeling sorry for herself, Belle was up, doing and working. Many of the women he worked with who were left behind in a harsh divorce went through a terrible depression that was hard to come out of. He was grateful Belle didn't appear to be doing the same.

"Dale's specialty was baseball and he'd been recruited early in our high school career," Belle continued. "So we worked hard and I got into school with him and after graduation, we headed to college together and eloped before Christmas."

Carson's eyes nearly bugged out of his head. "You eloped? Really?"

Belle laughed. "Yeah. I was a little more...reckless back then, I guess."

"Wow. You guys must have really been serious."

"Too serious." Belle groaned. "We could only see two things. Us and Dale's baseball career." She rubbed her forehead and Carson had the urge to push her hand away and soothe her himself.

He quickly shoved the feelings aside. Yes, he wanted to get to know Belle, but he didn't know her well enough to be that familiar with her...even if he had kissed her already.

"At first, we both went to school, since Dale was on scholarship, but eventually, I dropped out to support him." Belle looked pained as she spoke. "That was mistake number one. The second was not recognizing that Dale's long hours *practicing* were much more than practicing."

She shrugged and picked at her dress as if it didn't matter, but it did. Carson could tell it mattered to her, and it definitely mattered to him. He saw the exact story she was describing all the time in his office. Men and women who didn't have any regard for the treasure they held in their hands, and spent their lives making choices only for themselves. It rarely resulted in anything good and the fact that the victim this time had been Belle made him extra frustrated.

"Of course, I didn't realize that until several years down the road. I just continued working, paying the bills and feeding his ego until he made it into the big leagues." She took in a long breath and turned back to the ocean, as if it held all the answers she sought. "By that time, I was worn down, grumpier than I should have been at that age, and ready for a break." She laughed, but it was bitter. "And that's when he served me the divorce papers."

Carson scrubbed his face. "Wow, Belle. I'm...so sorry."

She shook her head. "I don't want pity," she said fiercely. Her eyes were hard as they turned toward him in the semi-dark. "In fact, I should probably thank Dale. I walked away from the divorce a free woman. I didn't want anything from him. I got just enough of our savings account to help me get through culinary school, and I'm going to open a bakery and spend the rest of my life elbow deep in dough and relying on no one but myself."

Carson hadn't actually felt any pity for Belle until that very moment. What a sad existence she described. Standing on her own two feet was fine—he could understand the need to do so—but never letting others in? Never wanting another relationship? An actual prick of pain hit his chest at the thought and he knew that he was deeper in like with her than he should have been. He'd finally found a woman who wasn't obsessed with his brother, only to find out she refused to be obsessed by anyone. Including him.

Belle relaxed a little and tilted her head. "Not what you expected?"

Carson shook his head. "No. Again, I'm sorry."

She pursed her lips and looked away. "I'm fine, but thank you."

"So...those chocolate croissant things at the party the other night. They were yours?"

Belle nodded and a smile finally graced her lips. The air in the car changed dramatically from hurt and anger to pride. "Yes. Pain au chocolat is one of my specialties."

Carson grinned. "One of your specialties? What else do you like to bake?"

Belle laughed softly. "I love baking bread. I paid special attention to French style breads, but when I said I wanted to open a bakery, I didn't mean cookies and cakes. I want to build a bread store."

"Is that why you came to Seaside Bay? And can I have the recipe?"

Belle shook her head. "Sorry, but no. Those are my own design and they're top secret." She smiled when Carson groaned. "Though I think a storefront might do well here, I came because of my brother." She grimaced and dropped her gaze to her lap again. "He settled here a couple of years ago. Bought the hardware store. Since I used all my money on school, I'm living with him until I can earn enough to get my own place."

"That's really nice of him," Carson said, making a note to meet the brother again. He had been very protective tonight, but Carson wasn't ready to be done with Belle yet. Despite her aversion to relationships or anything that hinted of reliance, he still found her fascinating. She was beautiful, stubborn, determined, and had a quick mind, which was one of the things he enjoyed the most. A meek, quiet woman would never do it for Carson. He enjoyed banter and a good healthy argument once in a while, and he wanted a woman who could keep up with that.

"It is," Belle agreed softly. "Rich is a life saver and his wife Sofia is a saint." A grin tugged at her lips. "My nephew Cole is already pretty fun. He keeps things lively for sure."

"I've got a niece myself," Carson offered. "She's great."

Belle nodded. "I'll bet."

Carson glanced at the clock and disappointment hit him. He really should get her back. He had Christmas activities with the group tomorrow and Belle probably had work, but Carson wanted to spend more time with her. "Well, Miss Belle," he said in a teasing tone. "If we don't get you home soon, I'm afraid your brother's going to strangle me when I show up with a pumpkin instead of his beautiful sister."

Belle laughed. "Wrong fairy tale," she corrected.

Carson gave her a wink while he started the car and got them back out on the street. "So...what are your plans tomorrow?"

Belle's mouth opened and closed a few times. "You want to get together again?"

Carson nodded. "Of course." He glanced her way before going back to the road. "Don't you?"

She was silent for a moment, which sent a fissure of worry down Carson's spine. He knew his question was bold, but Belle was strong enough to handle it. Had he misinterpreted their evening together? She seemed attracted to him and even if she wasn't interested in a relationship now, it didn't mean her mind couldn't be changed for the future.

"I don't know," she admitted.

"Well..." Carson's mind churned for answers. "Let's think about this logically. Did you have a good time tonight?"

"Yes," Belle answered easily, making him feel slightly better.

"Do you have other commitments to fill your time?"

"Not really, unless I'm working."

"Then why not say yes?" Carson pressed. "If nothing else, it gives you something fun to do for the next couple of weeks leading up to Christmas and then, if you want me gone, it won't matter, because I live in California anyway." He smiled at her as he parked the car in her brother's driveway. "Easy come, easy go."

Belle studied him for a few minutes in the dark and Carson did his best to hold still. He really, really hoped she said yes. There was just something about this strong, but strangely vulnerable woman that made Carson want to step up and show her the world. And while that couldn't happen in the next couple of weeks he was in Seaside Bay, it would at least give him a foundation to work from.

"Okay," she said softly, and when her eyes rounded, Carson knew she had been surprised at her own response.

His smile just about split his face. Try as she might to hide it, apparently, Belle, was just as intrigued as he was. "Great! Hold tight and I'll come get your door."

CHAPTER 13

The next day, Belle couldn't seem to keep her date off her mind. Carson had been blunt but sweet and a complete gentleman the whole time. If she was being honest with herself, other than the fact that she spilled her whole stupid, pathetic backstory, she thoroughly enjoyed their evening together.

Carson was fun and sarcastic and fiercely intelligent, which was almost more attractive than his movie star looks. Belle's ex-husband had been smart, but a jock all the way, and as a teenager, it had been his confident and suave ego that had drawn her in. In the end, that had also driven her away. They had both changed during their time together, but it had been in opposite directions.

While Belle had been forced to grow up and realize the importance of work and bills and the tedious part of being an adult, Dale had been able to enjoy glory, fame, and fun without ever understanding all Belle did to support him. Their balance as a married couple had been so lopsided, it was a wonder it lasted five years.

"Are you done?"

Belle spun to look over her shoulder at Mrs. Stallings. "Not quite," she said sheepishly. She hadn't been working quite as fast as she should have been today, since her mind was so preoccupied. "I wanted to get these muffins in the freezer for the office party tomorrow."

Mrs. Stallings nodded. "It would be good to have them done." She made a face. "The other prep is finished. Are you okay to do this on your own?"

Belle nodded enthusiastically. She loved working alone in the kitchen. Being pulled away by other coworkers or being asked to do other work drove her crazy, though she didn't complain about it. Belle was just grateful to have a job at the moment. She could save the quiet, do her own schedule thing, for when she had her own bakery. "Sure. I can take care of it, and then I'll clock out and head home. No biggie."

Mrs. Stallings' lips firmed, but then she nodded. "I do think it will make tomorrow easier. Thank you." Without further ado, the older woman left the kitchen.

Belle couldn't help but smile as soon as it grew quiet. She closed her eyes and let her head fall back. Sweet smells, peace, and a warm oven. This was the ultimate picture for Belle's life.

A fleeting picture of Carson's handsome face floated through her mind and she gently pushed it aside. He was fun, he was intelligent, and his kisses were sweeter than creme brulee, but he was not in her long term plans.

She had shocked herself last night when she'd agreed to see him again. Why bother to spend time getting to know each other if it would, and could, never go anywhere?

A knock on the back door brought Belle out of her thoughts and she frowned as she walked to let in whoever had been locked out. She peeked around the large metal door. "Carson?" Her eyes widened. "What in the world are you doing here?"

He grinned at her as he stood shaking in the cold. The peacoat he wore was tailored and emphasized his wonderful build, but apparently it wasn't very warm. *Which makes sense since he's from California. He probably doesn't have much use for coats in Hollywood.*

"Can I come in?" he teased. "I think my knees are actually knocking together out here."

"Oh my gosh," Belle gushed, stepping back and opening the door wider. "Hurry. It's plenty warm inside."

Carson blew out a breath as he stepped in and shook himself hard. "Ahh...you guys have been baking." He grinned. "Lucky me."

"Are you stopping by because you're hoping for free handouts?" Belle asked with a laugh as she shut the door. "In that case, I hate to disappoint you, but all the food in here is bought and paid for."

Carson shook his head. "Nope. No free handouts. But it's extra warm because your ovens have been on." He pointed to the door. "Mother Nature definitely hasn't been baking."

Belle grinned. "Well, grab a stool if you want to warm up. I need to finish making some muffins for tomorrow."

"What kind of muffins?"

"Blueberry lemon," Belle said, walking back to her station.

"It's a good thing we don't live close to each other," Carson quipped. "I think I'd gain twenty pounds just being neighbors."

Belle laughed, but inside, his words hurt ever so slightly. She would actually probably enjoy living near Carson...maybe. While he seemed really nice, there was a part of her that whispered that he couldn't be as sweet as he appeared. She'd fallen for sweet words before and they'd turned out to be a lie. Over and over again.

Why did she think Carson would be any different?

You can't. The words were harsh, but true. Belle barely knew the man. There was no way she could assume he was anything different from every other man in her life other than her brother. While his attention might be nice for a couple weeks, she wouldn't let herself mourn or wonder when it was over.

Carson sat across the stainless steel counter, watching her every move.

"Haven't you ever seen someone bake muffins before?" Belle teased, mixing her batter vigorously.

"Sure, but none as pretty as you."

Belle rolled her eyes. "I'm not dealing with cheese today, Mr. Cordova."

He chuckled and folded his arms over his chest. "Truth isn't cheesy."

She shook her head, but a small smile remained despite her scolding. "You never did say what brought you by?"

Caron raised his dark eyebrows. "You didn't answer your phone."

Belle wanted to smack herself. "Sorry," she said. "I don't always keep it on me while I'm working."

He shrugged. "No big deal. I figured if I couldn't get you to go out, I'd come in to where you were."

"How did you know where I was?" Belle asked, narrowing her eyes. "Twice now you've shown up without me telling you where to go."

"This is Seaside Bay," Carson said slowly, as if that should explain everything. "Do you really think anyone sneezes in this town without everyone else knowing about it?"

"Really?" Belle gave him a disbelieving look. "I didn't think anyone knew who I was."

"A few obviously do," Carson said with a smirk. "And I have to tell you that I'm pretty darn good at getting information out of people."

"I would hope so," Belle said, wiping her spatula against the edge of the bowl. "Otherwise your career as a lawyer wouldn't last very long."

Carson tapped his nose. "So!" His exuberant voice said he was changing the subject. "What did you get your brother for Christmas?"

Belle leaned back a little. "What kind of question is that? I thought you said you were good at this."

"That, my dear, is the kind of question you ask a person when you have no idea what to get your own brother, so you're hoping someone else has a better idea and you can copy it."

It took Belle just a split second to comprehend everything he'd just said before she burst out laughing. "You really think your brother would be happy with the same things as mine?"

"I don't know," Carson mused, his eyes twinkling with humor. "You never know when Gray might need a chainsaw or something."

*****

Carson wanted to close his eyes and simply soak in the laughter coming from Belle. It took ten years off of her face when she laughed and he was enjoying every second of it. It made him feel like a teenager again, where he was trying to impress the prettiest girl in his class.

"So tell me about your day," Belle said. She began to pull out paper cups and put them into muffin tins.

"As you probably know, my sister-in-law, Brook, has set aside the next week for a Christmas party with all her friends."

Belle nodded. "Yeah. That night I catered at the house was the first part, right?"

"Right," Carson agreed. "That was the kick off and that was for everyone." He grimaced. "She knows that the whole town goes crazy with Gray here, so she figured why not just invite them all over for one night and then she wouldn't feel bad about locking the doors for the rest of the week."

Belle paused. "I thought you said you were here for two more weeks."

"I am." He grinned. "I'm family."

She nodded. "Got it. But...that means you still won't be here for Christmas." She raised her eyebrows. "Planning to spend it down in warmer weather?"

Carson shrugged. Truth was, the more he thought about how short his time was with Belle, the more he thought about simply staying on through the new year, but whether or not he did that would depend on Belle's response. She hadn't blown him off yet, but she hadn't welcomed him in either. The next few days might be a little tricky...and telling. "We'll see," he said. "My niece and sister and brother in law are down there, so I wouldn't be completely alone, but I like it up here too."

"Not too cold?"

Carson scowled. "Are you saying I'm not manly enough to handle the weather?"

Belle made an innocent face and shook her head. "I would never."

Carson hopped off his stool and marched around the table, crowding into Belle's space. The smell of cinnamon and spices lingered in the air and he wanted to soak it in, but right now he had a reputation to defend. "Say that again to my face," he whispered, lowering his head until they were nose to nose.

The pulse in Belle's neck began to flutter and her breathing changed, exciting Carson all the more. There was no sound for just a few moments before she responded. "You're a wimp in cold weather."

Carson paused, then snorted. He hadn't thought she would actually do it. Especially after he got right in her face. Without thinking, he leaned in and kissed her forehead. "Belle, you're a jewel."

Her face was flushed as she turned back to her muffins. "You're not as intimidating as you think you are," she said breathlessly.

Carson stayed right by her side, her shoulder rubbing against his chest as she worked. He was enjoying her reaction far too much. "You're absolutely right," he admitted. "Now...what can I do to help?"

Belle gave him an incredulous look. "What?"

"How can I help? I hate sitting there while you do all the work."

Belle shook her head. "This is my job," she said. "I'm supposed to be working."

"And I'm your friend. Let me help."

"I get paid for this," she argued.

"I do too."

Belle stopped and gave him a look. "How? I'm pretty sure Mrs. Stallings doesn't have you on her payroll."

"I get paid in time," Carson explained. "Time with you."

Belle smiled. "You never give up, do you?"

"Not when I find something I want." The words were out of Carson's mouth before he could think better of it. They were true, but it was probably too soon to admit something like that, especially after hearing Belle's story last night.

Her cheeks turned pink again and she went back to the muffins. "I suppose you could get me a couple more pans," she said, her voice slightly tense.

Carson looked around. "And where would those be?"

Belle thrust her chin to the side. "Right over there. I can use two more."

"On it." Carson took his time, knowing she needed a minute to breathe. He did as well. The desire to taste another one of those sweet kisses was a little too strong at the moment. "Now what?"

Belle handed him the stack of paper cups. "Put one of these in each one." They worked quietly side by side before Belle spoke again. "You never did say what activities Brook had you all do today."

"Let's see," Carson murmured. "We made ornaments."

"What?" Belle laughed.

Carson grimaced. "I know. It was like kindergarten crafts all over again."

"What exactly were they?"

"We all had these clear glass balls," Carson explained. "And we poured paints in them, then swirled it all around until it was completely coated on the inside."

"Huh." Belle poked out her bottom lip and nodded. "That actually sounds kind of cool."

He shrugged. "It wasn't horrible, I suppose, but man...women take their crafting way too seriously."

"Uh-oh." Belle gave him a look. "What did you do?"

Carson jerked back. "What's that supposed to mean? Do you really think I would do something to ruin it?"

Belle just gave him a look until Carson chuckled.

"Okay, so maybe I wasn't as cooperative as I should have been."

She continued to wait, a perfectly shaped eyebrow shifting straight up her forehead.

"Fine." Carson groaned. "I might have taken the opportunity, when presented, to throw weird colors in other people's glass bulbs." He shrugged. "It's not like these were masterpieces or something! And it was Benny's idea to begin with!"

Belle frowned. "Who's Benny?"

"Oh, yeah. Sorry." Carson gave her a sheepish grin. "I forget you don't know everyone here. Benny, or Bennett Frasier, is Brook's friend and the town mailman. His wife teaches music at the school."

"Okay, so why did you make it sound like him being the mastermind made it all okay?" Belle pressed.

Carson shrugged again. "Benny may or may not be the group prankster."

"And you just followed right along," Belle said, tsking her tongue and shaking her head. "Why is it that men turn into boys when they get together?"

"Ah-ha!" Carson shouted. "You just admitted I'm a man."

Belle rolled her eyes. "I never said you weren't."

"You said I was a wimp," Carson argued.

"Yes, but wimp and man are two different words with two different meanings." Her lips twitched with amusement. "Perhaps you should get your brother a dictionary for Christmas and then borrow it."

Carson laughed. "I'll take that under consideration." He went back to his job, both of them still lightly laughing several seconds later. This was exactly the type of interaction that Carson dreamed of. Why did it have to happen with a woman who didn't want anything to do with a relationship?

He could feel his resolve building as the minutes ticked on. It didn't matter that she wasn't completely convinced that this was the start of something great. Carson determined then and there that he would do whatever it took, even work from Seaside Bay for the whole month of December if necessary, in order to convince her.

He'd spent his life winning cases in court. This, however, might be the most important one he'd ever taken on.

CHAPTER 14

"I can't believe I let you talk me into this," Belle said through chattering teeth as she boarded the large boat. It was winter for crying out loud! Why in the world was she currently getting onto a boat that was going to leave the harbor and all good sources of heat behind, in order to be out on freezing cold water, when they could easily buy any fish they wanted in the grocery store, rather than have to catch one?

Carson chuckled and held out a hand for her.

Belle grasped the offering and finished walking across the gangplank. "Remind me why we're doing this again?"

Carson's smile never wavered. "I spent time where you have fun. Now you get to join me where I like to have fun."

"And that's in the middle of the ocean in freezing cold weather?" She blew on her hands and rubbed them together. "The other morning you looked like you didn't enjoy lower temperatures."

Carson laughed and wrapped his arms around Belle, pulling her into his chest. "I know it's cold, but Felix has heat inside and there's nothing quite like the peace of being out on the water."

Belle rolled her eyes, but the complaining was mostly a joke. She knew exactly why she was out here. Because she was an idiot. She was dangerously close to letting down her guard when it came to this charming man and so she allowed him to pull her along between his Christmas activities with his family, as they continued to get to know each other.

She kept telling herself the situation was temporary, that Carson was going to go back to Hollywood and they'd never speak again, but deep inside, the thought terrified Belle. Their friendship had started out rough, but was quickly emerging into the highlight of Belle's life. She loved her family and especially enjoyed spending time with her nephew, but there was just something about Carson's bright outlook on life and his quick sense of humor that drew Belle in like a bee to honey.

And just as one voice said she wanted more, another screamed that she was going to be hurt.

The biggest problem came with not knowing which voice was right. Belle *wanted* to believe Carson was good. He'd shown her nothing but respect and friendship. But life had taught her that men could hide their true intentions and that sometimes it took years to figure them out.

"Hello, Ms. Kerr." A deep, slightly gravelly voice brought Belle out of her Carson-induced stupor and she reluctantly pulled herself away from the cocoon he'd created.

She turned to the man, who was thickly built with dark hair and a serious, but kind expression. "Hello." She turned to Carson, not knowing who she was talking to.

"Belle, this is Captain Felix Mendez," Carson explained, holding out his hand and shaking Felix's. "He's the captain of this fine vessel and has promised that you and I will be bringing in a haul to keep us fed until next Christmas."

Felix grunted, but his smile widened slightly. "Every time I meet you, I'm reminded how acting runs in the family."

Belle stiffened slightly, the words giving evidence to her dark thoughts of Carson not being everything he said. But when the men laughed with each other, she forced herself to relax. Captain Mendez's words were those of a teasing friend. Belle knew she needed to lighten up a bit. Along with her sense of self worth, she was aware that her sense of humor had seriously been lacking the last few years.

"If you're cold, Ms. Kerr, you're welcome to join me in the wheelhouse, or downstairs you'll find coffee, tea, and hot chocolate, plus a few hand-held snacks."

"That sounds wonderful, thank you," Belle responded with a smile. Right then and there, she decided that she was going to command herself to enjoy the day. She might not be interested in fishing and she was probably going to come home a human Popsicle, but maybe...this was exactly the type of thing she needed to break herself loose from the grumpy, old woman persona she had been sporting ever since her divorce.

Carson more than likely wouldn't be in her life for long, no matter how much Belle was beginning to hope otherwise. But that didn't mean it was a bad thing to enjoy it while he was here. They could be friends. They could have fun together. In fact, Belle could use this opportunity as one to practice getting back into the real world. If she was going to run a bread shop, she couldn't stand behind the counter with a dour expression on her face, scaring away all the customers. Carson could be the perfect way for her to soften the person she had become lately.

Carson bumped knuckles with Felix and then put a hand on Belle's back and led her toward the stairs. "Careful," he murmured, going first. "They're kind of steep and narrow."

"Got it," Belle responded, putting a hand toward the ceiling as she went down. She knew she wasn't tall enough to hit her head, but it certainly felt that way. When she finally landed at the bottom, she let out a relieved breath. The large room was cozy with couches and a small kitchenette.

"Can I get you that hot chocolate you so desperately wanted?" Carson asked with a smile.

Belle couldn't help but respond in kind. "Thank you," she said, "but I've got it." She went to the counter and tore open a packet, dumping it in the Styrofoam cup. "Would you like something?"

Carson shook his head. "Nah. I'm good." He plopped onto the couch, laying his head back against the cushions.

"Tired?" Belle asked as she walked toward him while stirring her drink.

"Mm-hm."

"Late night?"

Carson cracked an eye open. "Trying to get a peek into the famous Cordova household schedule?"

Belle gave him an exasperated look. "Hardly. You just always seem like the Energizer Bunny, so I was wondering why you're so tired."

Carson closed his eyes again, but a small smile hung on his lips. "We stayed up late playing games," he said. "I should have called you to come over. You would've had a ton of fun."

"Well, that depends on the games," Belle said, blowing on the chocolate. "Not all of them are created equal."

"True, but these were fun. They were the dumb ones, like having to dig a quarter out of flour without using hands, and shaking a ping pong ball out of a box of tissues that's been strapped to your waist."

Belle laughed softly as she took a tiny drink. The warmth traveled to her stomach and then spread to the rest of her body. "I might have paid good money to see you all acting like idiots."

Carson picked his head up, his smile never wavering. "Whatever. If you'd been there, you'd have jumped right in."

She ticked her head back and forth. "Okay. Probably." With a smirk, she elbowed him in the upper arm. "But I wouldn't have just played, I'd have won."

"Oh, ho! A competitive streak, huh?"

Belle shrugged.

Suddenly, Carson stood up and walked over to the snacks. "Then I think maybe we need to have a little showdown." He ripped open a package of sandwich cookies.

"Right now?" Belle asked in shock.

"Right now." Carson held out the cookie. "Come on. I'll tell you what to do."

*****

Carson held back his laughter at the skeptical look on Belle's face. He could understand the emotion. What he was doing was a bit silly, but there was a purpose behind it. He wanted Belle to loosen up. He wanted her to laugh and play. He enjoyed the banter they had with each other, but there was still a bitter, hard edge that was always lurking just behind the corner and would often be audible when she gave a sarcastic response to something.

The best cure Carson knew for being over the top serious was being over the top silly.

"Okay," he began after she finally took the cookie. "We start by putting it on our foreheads." He leaned his head back to give her an example and laid the treat right in the middle. "Like this."

"Why do I feel like at any time, someone is going to jump out with a camera," Belle muttered. Still, despite her protesting, she followed suit.

"No prank, I promise," Carson said. "But now we have to put it into our mouths without actually touching it."

"Are you serious?"

"Deadly," Carson said in a low tone. "Want to make a bet on the outcome?"

"Do I look like I was born yesterday to you?"

He laughed and the cookie fell. "Hang on." He grabbed another one and got resituated. "If I win, I want a kiss." The desire to see Belle's face when he threw that out there was overwhelming, but Carson kept himself focused. She needed to know he wasn't going to beat around the bush or hide his intentions. He had told her he wanted to spend time with her and get to know her, and now he was announcing that he wanted more than just their friendly banter.

It was quiet for several moments before she answered. "If I win, you have to clean up next time I bake."

"Done." Carson grinned. "On your mark, get set, go!" He immediately began scrunching his face in weird ways to make the cookie move. What he hadn't shared with Belle was that he had won last night, so he had an advantage up his sleeve. He would use it for all it was worth.

"Oh my gosh," she breathed through a laugh. "This is ridiculous."

"That sounds like a person who's going to owe me a kiss in a minute," Carson said, bending his body in a weird way to keep the cookie from falling to the ground.

"What happens if it falls off your face?" Belle asked.

"You lose."

"What?" she squeaked.

"Hey! I don't make the rules. I just follow them." He smiled at her grumbling. "Aaaannnddd..." He shifted one more time, feeling the cookie at the edge of his mouth.

"No way!" Belle shouted. "You can't be that close already! I'm stuck on my eye!"

"Almost..." Carson maneuvered his face just right and...*yes!* "Got it," he said through his chomping.

Belle straightened and her cookie fell from her face. "Already?" She huffed and wiped all the dark crumbs from her skin. "I think this thing is rigged," she muttered as she looked on the ground for the cookie she dropped.

"Uh, uh, uh," Carson teased, gently taking her arms and pulling her closer. "I didn't cheat and it definitely wasn't rigged." His arms were fully around her now and he was enjoying the red flush to her cheeks. When her hands landed on his chest, he almost sucked in a gasp. The heat that traveled through him was a new sensation, but wasn't unpleasant. In fact, he wanted more of it.

"You already had a kiss from me," Belle said, her voice slightly shaky. "Why in the world would you want another?"

Carson studied her dark brown eyes and traced the lines of her face. She really was quite beautiful. He enjoyed how she felt tucked into his chest and knew he would continue to touch her at every opportunity as long as she didn't pull away from him. "I think the real question is...why wouldn't I?" he argued. He dropped his head and brought them nose to nose. "Didn't you feel it last time?"

"What?" she breathed, her eyes fluttering closed.

"The intensity, the electricity..." Carson rubbed his nose along her cheek, inhaling the smell of sweet cinnamon. "Didn't it make you curious?"

The only answer was a shaky sigh as he kissed her temple.

"I've always been the type of guy to find the answers," Carson continued, coming back to the front of her face. "And since I won the bet, I intend to find out." Without allowing her any more time to think about it, he brought their lips together.

If a comet had crash landed in the sea at that exact moment, Carson was positive he wouldn't have noticed. Their first kiss has been short and sweet, though full of sparks. This one...he intended to savor, and it was everything he could have hoped for.

Her lips were soft and after the first few seconds, became just as hungry as his own. Tilting his head, Carson cupped her cheek in order to better control their exchange. When Belle's arms slid up and around his neck, he closed the few inches between them and allowed himself to kiss her exactly how he had been dreaming about since the mistletoe incident.

If he thought he'd been warm before, it was nothing compared to what Carson was feeling now. Right here, in this moment, he'd found heaven...and he wasn't about to let it go.

Mother Nature, on the other hand, wasn't quite as enthusiastic about the situation. The boat rocked hard, as if it had been hit by a rogue wave.

Belle pulled back, gasping and breathing heavily. Her hand went to her red lips and her eyes were wide with a mixture of wonder and shock. "I think I fulfilled the debt," she croaked.

Carson couldn't find it within himself to laugh at how affected she was, as he was also struggling to pull himself under control. The boat shifted again and he widened his stance to balance. "Maybe so," he stated. "But after that, there's no way I'm going to let that be our last kiss."

Belle's eyes widened even farther and her cheeks flared. She turned away from him and squeaked as she came to a stop.

Felix stood on the stairs, leaning against one side with his hands folded over his thick chest. An amused look was on his face.

"Is there a problem, Captain?" Carson said, unsure how long his friend had been watching them.

Felix pursed his lips and shook his head slowly. "Not for me..." His eyes drifted to Belle and he raised his eyebrows. "Everything okay down here?"

Belle pinched her lips between her teeth and tucked a piece of hair behind her ear. "Yep. Hunky dory."

Felix's smirk widened. "Good to hear." The boat rocked and he put a hand against the wall. "The wind is picking up and I wanted to see how set you were on fishing. We can throw down the lines where we're at, though it's not exactly my favorite spot. But according to the radar, the wind is worse where I want to go and it's not exactly going to be pleasant there."

Carson looked to Belle. "Brave it? Or go home?" he asked.

Belle glanced his way, holding his eyes and slowly straightening. Once she looked a little less vulnerable, she turned to the captain. "Is the situation dangerous?"

Felix shook his head. "No. I don't think so. Just some heavy rocking."

Belle's eyes came back to Carson and there was a challenge in them. "Did you bring me out here to fish or what?"

A slow smile crept across Carson's face as Felix choked on his laughter. "I did."

"Then I expect you to be a man of your word," Belle threw back at him.

Considering what he had said right before they were interrupted by Felix, Carson couldn't have been more proud of his date in that moment. "Consider it done." Holding out his hand, Carson waited for Belle to take it and then guided her up the steps and into the cold sea air.

They followed Felix and got their poles set up properly, listening to the instructions. All the while, Carson watched Belle shiver until he was sure she was going to shatter. He waited politely for Felix to finish his demonstration, then made his move.

Setting his pole in the holder, Carson stepped up behind Belle and brought her chest to his front.

"What are you doing?" she asked, looking over her shoulder.

Carson tucked her in close. "Warming you up and blocking the wind."

Belle paused as if checking to see that he was being truthful, then melted against him, much to Carson's enjoyment. "Thank you," she whispered.

He kissed the top of her head. "Anytime." The outcome of this little trip wasn't exactly what he had expected, it had been even better. But Carson knew he couldn't let his guard down now. He needed to settle things at work so they knew he wouldn't be back in the office until after the holidays, and he needed to convince Belle that this relationship blossoming between them was worth fighting for.

He'd made progress today, but he'd seen too many other women with chips on their shoulders to believe everything would be smooth from here on out. When Belle snuggled back into his hold a little tighter, Carson had a burst of hope that perhaps he wasn't exactly on the wrong track.

CHAPTER 15

"You want me to what?" Belle screeched over the phone. She was currently sitting next to the fireplace at her brother's house trying to thaw out from her trip on the ocean. By the time they'd gotten back to shore, Belle had been an absolute ice cube. She could barely walk and her teeth had chattered so hard, she was sure one of them was going to break before she got warmed up.

Carson had done his best to shield her from the wind and use their combined body heat to help, but even that hadn't been enough.

"I want you to come over and help decorate the tree with us tomorrow," Carson said over the line.

He'd dropped her off after their little excursion, but only a half-hour later, they were already talking on the phone. Belle wasn't complaining though. She enjoyed talking to Carson and after that earth shattering kiss earlier today, she knew it was going to be harder and harder to get him out of her thoughts.

He had been completely upfront with the fact that he was interested in more than friendship with her and Belle appreciated the bluntness, but she was still struggling with the logistics of it all. They lived in two different places and Belle was not about to move for a man she barely knew. That would only put her right back where she began. In a vulnerable position to be hurt again.

And even though Carson had been honest and kind, that tiny voice in the back of her head wasn't completely convinced he was genuine. No one could be that perfect, could they? If Belle had created her perfect man, Carson would have been a doppelganger. He was intelligent and sarcastic. He enjoyed a little fun, but didn't let it interfere with getting his work done. He treated her like a princess, but let her stand on her own two feet.

It all felt like a fairy tale and the rightness of it made Belle even more hesitant. She had been head over heels in love with her first husband and that had ended in a complete disaster with Belle getting the short end of the stick.

"I can't come over to a party I wasn't invited to and decorate a tree," Belle argued, snuggling deeper into her blanket. "This is a family thing."

"Not everyone here is family," Carson retorted.

"Maybe not, but they're *like* family," Belle said. "I'm not."

"You're my plus one."

"And did they say you could have a plus one?"

Carson groaned. "Belle, do you really think I would invite you to come if it wasn't okay?"

Belle slumped. She really enjoyed spending time with Carson, but this all just seemed so fast. Her head was in the clouds instead of in reality where it belonged, and doing an activity with his family, which included a movie star brother, just seemed...like too much. "I don't know," she admitted softly. "Because if I'm being honest, I just don't know you that well yet."

"Belle." His voice was low and patient. "We might not be besties yet, but I have been very upfront with you the whole week that we've known each other."

Belle laughed softly. It all sounded so outrageous. "Well, can I at least bring something? It just feels really awkward to show up and expect them to entertain someone they don't know."

"Actually..."

"Oh, man." Belle threw her head back against the cushions. "Here it comes..."

Carson's chuckle was delicious. "See...just like everything during this party, the whole thing is a competition. We each have our own tree and we're going to have a judge pick the best one at the end."

"You each have your own tree?" Belle shook her head. That kind of excess was crazy and she wasn't sure she would ever get used to it.

"Yeah, but it's not a big deal. Every couple provided their own tree. We're just going to decorate them together."

"Ah, gotcha." That seemed a little less crazy. "Are you sharing a tree with Brook? Or do you get your own?"

"I have my own. So does Jude."

"Jude?"

"Guess I never mentioned him, huh? He's a buddy who came up from California with me for the party."

Belle nodded. "Okay, but are you really sure you want me there? You did just spend the morning with me."

"Isabelle," he growled, making Belle smile. "Do we really have to keep going over this?"

"Okay, okay." She bit her lip. "I might have an idea."

"Sweet. Let's hear it."

"What if we made the ornaments?"

"Please tell me we aren't gluing toothpicks onto wooden soldiers," Carson drawled.

Belle laughed. "Nothing like that. But we might still use toothpicks."

"As long as it means I can spend time with you, then I'm all for it."

"You really never give up, do you?" Belle was in awe of how forward he was. Carson didn't seem to hide anything and it was as refreshing as it was frightening. That was exactly how she needed a guy to be, but was she really ready to accept that he might be someone worth keeping around?

"I think I've already said this, but one more time for the peanut gallery...not when it's something I want."

Belle took a breath for courage. "Then meet me at the commercial kitchen in an hour."

"Done. Should I bring anything?" Carson asked.

"Actually, meet me at the grocery store. We might need to pick out a few things first." Belle's mind immediately began to flood with ideas and thoughts. She wasn't sure exactly how original they were, but they would certainly be fun.

"They still won't have Irish butter."

"How do you know? Maybe the manager ordered some in for me?" Belle challenged.

"Really? You met the manager?"

"No, but it's possible." Belle's smile was wide as she listened to him laugh. Carson's humor was always so carefree and contagious.

"Men have done much worse for a beautiful woman's smile," he quipped. "Grocery store it is. Don't be late."

Without another word, the line went dead and Belle was left fighting both elation and regret. What was she doing, agreeing to continue this...whatever it was? She was setting herself up for failure.

But what if you don't fail?

That thought landed in Belle's stomach like unleavened bread. It could mean that happiness was on the horizon, but at what cost? Was she willing to give up her sense of identity yet again in order to join with someone else?

She liked Carson...a lot...but Belle just couldn't quite bring herself to give in completely to the feelings floating through her system. Hopefully, a little more time would help her see things more clearly. And there was no place better for getting to know someone than knee deep in dough and dishes.

*****

After hanging up his phone, Carson ran straight for the shower. He smelled like fish guts and he wasn't going to meet Belle that way. After a quick, but thorough wash, he was shaving and running a little gel through his hair when Jude showed up at the bathroom door.

"Got a hot date?" he asked with a grin.

"Heading to the grocery store," Carson said honestly.

"You just went a couple days ago." Jude crossed his arms over his chest. "Why would you need to go again?"

"Maybe Brook's sending me." Carson turned and mimicked his friend's pose.

"Eh." Jude made the sound of a buzzer. "Try again."

Carson rolled his eyes. "Maybe I don't want to tell you."

Jude's narrowed his gaze. "It must be a woman."

Carson's eyebrows slowly rose. "What makes you say that?"

"Because you're one of the most talkative people I know," Jude said wryly. "You only clam up when it comes to women, and even that you don't do very much of, because most of the time you complain about how all they want is Gray."

"I've seen you with female company yourself, lately," Carson shot back.

Jude rubbed the back of his neck. "Yeah. So?"

"So, nothing," Carson said easily. "You do your thing. I'll do mine."

Jude sighed. "I suppose." He stopped Carson as he tried to walk through the door. "It isn't…" He swallowed. "It's not the lady from the opening party, is it?"

Carson frowned as he tried to figure out who Jude was talking about. "She was there. She was refilling the dishes."

Now it was Jude's turn to frown. "Refilling? Like, she was working? With the caterers?"

Carson nodded. "Who else would it be?"

"No one," Jude said quickly, stepping back and leaving room for Carson to leave. "It's no big deal."

Carson knew the words were a complete lie, but right now he didn't care. He was headed to meet Belle and Jude could take care of whatever woman he was talking about. "See ya!" He hurried downstairs and out the front door before someone else could stop him.

He knew tomorrow the cat would totally be out of the bag, but until then, he was going to continue to woo Belle and keep his family in the dark.

The engine of his sports car roared as he pressed a little too hard on the gas pedal and Carson forced himself to pull back. This town was too small for him to go zooming down the street, and it wasn't like the grocery store was very far into town.

Easing off the power, he cruised gently down the street and turned into the grocery store parking lot. A rustbucket sedan was parking just ahead of him and Carson realized with a start that it was Belle. He barked out a laugh, realizing she hadn't been kidding when she told him it was held together with duct tape.

He put the car into park and quickly got out, eager to see Belle again, despite the fact that he'd spent the whole morning with her. "Belle!"

Her dark hair swung as she turned his way. "I should have recognized that eyesore," she teased, giving his car a look. "Your engine is loud enough to wake the whole town."

Carson grinned. "At least I wasn't worried about losing my bumper on the speed bump."

Belle groaned, her head dropping back. She looked back up and shrugged. "At least it runs, right? I mean, it could be worse."

Carson reached her side and narrowed his eyes as if studying the car. "I'm not sure how... Ow!" He laughed and held his ribs where she elbowed him.

"Don't make her feel bad," she whispered, putting a finger to her lips. "I need her to think she's wonderful until I can replace her."

"When will that be?" Carson asked, joining the joke and dropping his voice.

"When my business is up and running."

He made a face. "I'm not sure she'll last that long." He glanced over their shoulders. "But weirder things have happened."

"True." Belle held up her crossed fingers. "So for now, we're wishing."

"Speaking of wishes," Carson started. "What are we wishing for in the store today?" They were hit in the face with a blast of warm air as they walked inside and Carson noticed a shudder run through Belle. Without pausing to think of the consequences, he put his arm around her and tucked her under his shoulder.

Belle was stiff for a moment, then relaxed under his hold and Carson gave himself a mental high five. "We're shopping for cookie accessories."

"Cookie accessories? Is that a thing?"

"Yeah. Like sprinkles, frosting tips, edible glitter...you know, the stuff you decorate with?" Belle looked up at him.

"Ah. Gotcha." Carson let go of her to push the cart. "Where to?"

"The baking aisle."

"Lead the way, captain," he said. Carson couldn't seem to wipe the smile off his face as he pushed the squeaky wheeled cart down the aisle.

They reached the right aisle and Belle stopped in front of a display of food colorings, birthday candles, and sprinkles. "What kind of cookies do you want to make?" she asked, her eyes on the shelves.

"Ones that taste good."

Belle rolled her eyes good-naturedly at him. "These aren't for eating, Car. They're for making ornaments."

The thrill that went through him when she called him Car was an unexpected sensation. He'd been called Car by his friends and family since he was a little kid, but none of them made him feel as warm as when Belle did it. Did she even realize what she had said? He wasn't sure, but he wasn't going to point it out either. The more comfortable she grew with him, the better off his case was.

"Why can't they be both?" he asked, leaning his forearms onto the cart.

"I suppose they can, but usually ornament cookies are crisper with less sugar, so they aren't as tasty."

"Yeah, but if we're going to win the competition, then we need to go above and beyond."

Belle sighed and gave him an indulgent smile. "All right. We can use a different recipe, but we'll need to pick up butter."

"Ah, butter." Carson tried to look thoughtful. "I have fond memories of looking for butter in this place."

"Stop," Belle said with a laugh, giving the cart a small push.

Carson straightened and laughed with her. "What would *you* like to do with the cookies?"

"Hmm..." Belle tapped her bottom lip. "Well, we could go with a color theme, or a shape theme."

"Or we could just do everything."

"You don't like to create boundaries, do you?"

He shook his head. "Not when I don't have to. I spend my whole career staying between the lines. When it comes to my personal life, I don't want the line to be straight. I want it all."

Belle considered him for a moment, though she didn't look like she disapproved of his words. "I can see that, I suppose, but doesn't it mean you never really accomplish anything? Because you're always jumping from one place to another?"

"Or maybe I accomplish lots of things, just not the way society says I have to. Can you imagine how many things you learn when you don't stick with only one subject?"

She gave a soft laugh and looked back at the display. "Okay, so lots of shapes and lots of colors." She began pulling sprinkles off the shelves and a couple different boxes of colors. "Let's go get that butter and some powdered sugar, and then we can hit the kitchen."

Carson took a couple of quick steps, catching up to her side, and darted in for a quick peck. "Sounds like a plan to me."

She glanced sideways at him, but didn't scold him for his boldness. "I thought you didn't like plans."

"Oh, now don't put words in my mouth," he retorted. "It's not plans I don't like, it's sticking with them to the point that they stop us from doing anything else."

Belle rubbed her forehead. "I'm not sure I'm ever going to understand all your life rules." She huffed a laugh. "Or lack thereof."

"Don't worry," Carson offered. "Stick around and I'd be happy to show you everything I know."

CHAPTER 16

"No, no, no!" Belle called out, lunging across the kitchen to pull Carson's hand back. "If you shove it like that, you're going to mess up the shape."

Carson raised a wry eyebrow at her. "It's just a cookie."

Belle huffed and put her hands on her hips. "I thought you wanted to win."

"I do, but is a little glitch in the star going to keep me from doing that?" He gave her a look. "Won't the sprinkles and frosting make up for it?"

"With the way you make cookies, I doubt it," Belle teased.

"Oh, ho!" Carson crowed. "It looks like the smack talk has officially begun!"

Belle laughed, feeling like a giddy young girl. Carson was a working professional, in a career that had a very high stress load. How was he always so happy and fun? It brought Belle no small amount of consternation as she wondered how he did it.

He held up his messy hands and wiggled them in her face. "Is this where we start the frosting wars?" He smirked. "I wouldn't mind helping with any that got stuck on your lips."

Belle's cheeks flared a tomato red and she gulped...hard. He was so forward about how he felt about her. Belle had not a single iota of doubt that he was attracted to her. And if he was so upfront with his feelings, she wanted to believe that he was just as open in the rest of his life. Surely he couldn't be hiding some deep dark secret, like a secret girlfriend back in California or something. Could he just be that good of an actor?

Captain Felix had been right when he'd joked that acting ran in the Cordova family. But was Carson acting? It didn't seem like it.

But how do I know for sure?

That was the million dollar question. Yet every time they spent more time together, Belle found her skepticism fading a little bit more. Carson never seemed to change. She never caught him hiding something, or appearing guilty or trying to avoid talking about certain parts of his life, other than being the brother of a movie star.

"Is that a yes?" Carson prodded, pulling Belle from her very vivid imagination.

"No!" she croaked out, before clearing her throat. She stepped back just a little and laughed nervously. "We don't even have any frosting."

Carson turned back to the cookies. "I'm sure we could fix that."

Belle let her breath out in a whoosh. *This guy is going to be the death of me. I can see it now. Dead by heart attack before the age of thirty, all because a guy flirted with me.*

"So how do you get them out of the cutters if you can't push?" Carson asked, flinging a cookie cutter through the air in an attempt to dislodge the dough.

Belle's anxiety melted and she laughed, stepping up to his side. "Best way is to do it before you lift," she explained. "Or dip the cutter in flour. Let me show you." Belle took the star-shaped cutter and reached across Carson's body to dip the metal edges of the cutter in a pile of flour. As she pulled back, heat raced up the top of her arm where she was brushing against Carson's chest. Doing her best to act nonchalant, Belle straightened and pressed her cutter into the dough, gently removing it without the dough getting stuck. "See?" Her voice squeaked and she closed her eyes, completely humiliated that he could hear exactly how he affected her.

Carson leaned in close to her ear. "Don't worry," he said, his tone lower than normal. "I feel the same way." He nuzzled her neck. "Are you sure we have to make cookies? I can think of other things that might be more fun."

When his lips brushed just under her ear, Belle pulled in an embarrassingly loud gasp. "I think we should stick with the cookies," she said in a shaky tone.

"Pity." Carson pulled back and studied the dough. "Looks like you're an expert." He pulled up the cut out and set it on the pan.

"Lots and lots of practice," Belle said, brushing away the compliment. She was equal parts grateful he had listened and disappointed his attention was elsewhere. What in the world was going on with her? She didn't want a man in her life. Even one as fun as Carson. She was supposed to be focused on setting herself up to be as independent as humanly possible. Giving into the pull between her and Carson would be a step backwards...wouldn't it? The answer to the question was more difficult with each touch and caress.

"Okay, so let's get this first batch in the oven and then we'll cut out some more." Belle hefted the pan and walked over to the commercial stove, opening the oven door and plopping the jelly roll pan inside. The heat from the oven hit her face and Belle blinked a few times. Maybe it would now look like her flushed face came from the appliances, rather than from her reactions to a handsome man. This situation was getting absolutely ridiculous. She needed to get control of herself!

"What should we cut out next?" Carson asked.

Belle turned back and scowled. "No eating the dough!"

Carson rolled his eyes. "Belle," he drawled. "Why are you always so stuck on the rules?" He threw another piece of dough in his mouth. "Lighten up a bit." He broke off one more piece, then walked her way, holding the bite in the air. "Open up."

"What?" Belle ducked backward, dodging his attempts to feed her.

"Come on," Carson cajoled. "Just take a bite!"

"You're not feeding me," Belle argued, though her laughter ruined any authority she might have had. "Carson!"

Carson wrapped an arm around her and tugged her into his chest as he moved the dough around, trying to catch her mouth. "Come on! You know you want to! Just eat it!"

"You're ridiculous," Belle said with a laugh.

"I think you need to turn that back to yourself, Ms. Priss. It's only a piece of cookie dough!"

Belle groaned and stopped moving away from him. "Will you stop if I take the bite?" Carson's smirk was so triumphant that Belle kind of wanted to wipe it off his face.

"For now," he promised.

"That's not good enough," Belle stated, pressing against his chest. "I'm here trying to help you, and all you want to do is eat cookies!"

"No, I want to have fun with a beautiful woman," Carson corrected. "What's the point of company if you don't find a way to enjoy it?"

Belle slumped a little. "You really think I'm good company?" She hated how vulnerable she sounded. More and more Belle had been recognizing how stiff and grumpy she had become. Where was the bright, bubbly young woman who had tried to take on the world to support her brand new husband? Who was determined to give selflessly until they succeeded together?

There were parts of her old self that Belle was glad were gone, but as a whole...Belle missed who she had been. She missed not looking at everyone with suspicion and trying to figure out what their ulterior motive is. She missed smiling and laughing without feeling like she was breaking some hidden rule. She missed being spontaneous and taking life by the horns in a way that brought triumph rather than grudging acceptance.

She searched Carson's laughing gray eyes. If ever she was going to take a chance on letting a little of that woman back in her life, this was surely it. Carson had been nothing but wonderful, and perhaps their temporary situation was the right way to test the waters.

Like an obedient bird, Belle opened her mouth and accepted the treat. Sugar, butter, and vanilla danced on her tongue, and she was reminded of why she loved baking so much. Bread was her soulmate, but baking in general was her creative outlet. "Thanks," she said softly.

Carson leaned in. "Anytime."

*****

If he didn't kiss her soon, Carson was positive he was going to implode. For the last hour they'd danced around each other in the grocery store, and now the kitchen, and he couldn't take much more.

He worked hard to be a disciplined man in his professional career, but in his personal life, he didn't want the same restraints. He wanted fun, spontaneity, and adoration. He wanted a woman to tease and laugh with, one who understood the need to break free of life's rules once in a while.

He had been starting to despair whether or not Belle could ever be that woman...until right this moment.

She had held him at bay for a long time, but something had shifted. He had seen it in her eyes. When she took the dough, she made a decision and judging from her actions, it was going to be in his favor.

He kissed the edge of her mouth. "Belle," he said sweetly.

"Hmm?"

"I know something sweeter than that dough."

Her lips spread with a smile. "You do, huh?'

"Yep. Want some?"

She pushed a hand through his hair, eventually teasing the skin on the back of his neck. "I think I do."

That was all the encouragement Carson needed and he wrapped both arms around her, closing every inch between them. For several minutes he allowed himself to indulge in the sweetest dessert he'd ever had. When the desire to hold on almost overpowered his self control, he knew it was time to stop.

Slowly, he brought their kisses to a halt and rested his forehead against hers. Both of them were breathing heavily and Carson wanted to groan with the sweet scent of vanilla and sugar he could smell in her hair. "Belle," he said hoarsely, kissing her cheek and working his way around her face. He just couldn't seem to stop touching her.

"What?" she asked just as breathlessly.

"I like you a lot."

She laughed softly and continued playing with the hair on the back of his head. "I like you too."

"Do you think you might be willing to really give this a chance?" He moved down to her jawline. "Not just the weeks I'm here in Seaside, but even after?" Belle stilled and Carson pulled back so he could look at her. He knew it was too soon for a question like that, but he didn't want to wait. He wanted to know where this was going, and he wanted to know now.

"Do you really think we can make a long-distance relationship work?" she asked.

Carson nodded. "If we want it to." Her eyebrows were pulled together and he reached up to smooth the wrinkles.

"And you really feel that strongly about me...about us, to commit to that now? We've only known each other for a little over a week, and the first couple of times, I thought you were someone else."

Carson considered his words carefully. He wasn't in love with Belle...yet. He wasn't ready to say their relationship would last forever. But he did think it could last longer than the next three weeks until Christmas. "I'm curious why you think I'm so fickle that I wouldn't want to continue dating you after only three weeks."

Belle scrunched her face, then jumped when the cookie timer went off. "Oh my gosh, we totally forgot to make another batch!"

Carson chuckled. "I think what we did was better." He opened his arms so she could rush to grab the pan out of the oven. The cookies smelled delicious, and he knew they'd probably have to make more dough if they were going to have enough for a tree.

Belle carried the hot pan over and settled it on the stainless steel counter. "Okay, we need to fill another pan because these won't be enough."

"Not after I get done with them," Carson quipped.

Belle pointed her finger at him. "You will *not* eat these."

He grinned. "I make no promises." His grin grew. "I have a definite sweet tooth."

Belle shook her head, her cheeks bright red again. "You're incorrigible."

"Thank you."

Belle laughed softly and tucked a piece of hair behind her ear. "Let's roll out some more dough."

Carson went along with her plan for a little longer, behaving himself quite well, but as they started to break out the frosting and sprinkles, he knew being a Boy Scout couldn't continue much longer. There just were too many resources to work with.

"You never answered my question, you know."

Belle looked up from the mixer. "What question?"

He gave her a look. "About whether or not you're willing to give this a try for longer than while I'm in town."

Belle sighed and looked back at the mixer. She waited to answer him until she had turned off the appliance. "If I'm being honest, I'm kind of torn."

"About what?" Carson tried not to take her hesitation personally. He knew where she was coming from. He'd seen it before. He wasn't going to sit back and not push her, but he also knew this wasn't going to be an overnight transformation.

"About whether or not it's the right thing," she admitted. Belle folded her arms over her chest and rested a hip against the counter. "I went back to school so I didn't have to depend on anyone ever again."

"And what does that have to do with us?"

"Getting in a relationship means relying on someone," Belle said. "I lost myself in my marriage and ended up burned for it. I don't ever want to do that again."

"Any man worth his salt would never ask you to." Carson shook his head. "I'm not asking you to be a damsel in distress. I'm asking you to explore a mutual relationship." He quirked an eyebrow. "You can't deny that we have insane chemistry."

Belle snorted and dropped her eyes to the floor.

"But I also think you're just an amazing woman, Belle."

She looked up from under her eyelashes.

"You're smart, you're resourceful." He chuckled. "You give me back snark for snark and aren't afraid when I argue just for the fun of it."

Belle rolled her eyes and shook her head at him.

"You're right, you were burned, but I'd dare say that the woman who emerged from those ashes is even more wonderful than the one she was before." Slowly he began walking her way. "And that new woman is one I'm not ready to say goodbye to." He stopped just in front of her. "I've already talked to my firm and worked out being able to stay in Seaside until after the holidays."

Belle gasped and her eyes widened. "Really?"

He nodded. "Yes. And I'm asking that you meet me in the middle. I've done what I can to give us more time... Are you willing to do the same?"

Her eyes were slightly misty as she studied him. "And after Christmas?"

"Let's see where we are and we'll go from there." He waited a beat. "So...are you in?"

The room was deadly quiet. The only sound was the ticking of the oven timer as the last batch of cookies baked.

Belle took in a shaky breath, then another one. Her face was pale and her fingers trembled as she pushed that same chunk of hair behind her ear again.

Carson thought he would die from anticipation. He'd thrown his cards on the table and his heart felt as if it would break through his ribcage any second.

"Okay." The word was so quiet, Carson almost missed it.

"Okay?" he clarified, unable to keep the hope from his voice.

She gave him a small smile. "Okay. Let's see where this goes."

With a whoop, Carson wrapped his arms around her and lifted Belle into the air before dropping her back down. "You know what this means, don't you?"

She wiped her eyes as she laughed. "What?"

Carson reached into the mixing bowl and took a little bit of frosting, then turned and smeared it across Belle's cheek.

"Hey!"

He pulled her into his chest. "Now I get to do exactly what I said I would do earlier." He grinned. "Better prepare yourself, Ms. Kerr. The can of worms has officially been opened."

CHAPTER 17

Belle's heart was nearly in her throat as she walked up the grand entrance to Grayson and Brook Cordova's home. The temperature might have been chilly, but Belle was nearly sweating through her sweater as she raised a shaky fist to knock on the door.

She shifted her weight from side to side as she waited for someone to open it, then jumped almost out of her skin when Brook pulled it back.

"Hey!" Brook said cheerily. "I'm horrified to say that Carson had to remind me of your name." Brook leaned in a little. "In my mind, I kept referring to you as Croissant Girl."

Belle laughed stiffly. "I don't think I mind that."

Brook smiled wide. "Still, I think it's best if I call you your *real* name, Belle. And Carson told me I shouldn't even ask for the recipe."

Belle ducked her head. "Sorry. They're...special to me."

Brook nodded her understanding and opened the door wider. "Come on in. Carson is in the family room."

"BELLE!"

"Or not," Brook muttered under her breath, followed by a snicker.

Belle tried to hide her blush at Brook's obvious amusement concerning Carson's enthusiastic greeting, but when Carson wrapped his arms around her and lifted her into the air, all sense of being shy was gone in a hot wave of embarrassment.

"Carson," she scolded, holding onto his shoulder automatically. "Put me down!"

He shook his head. "Not yet." His light eyes looked around and Belle realized Brook had left. Without another word, he gave her a short, but fierce kiss. "Hey," he whispered afterward.

"Hey," Belle managed back. Her breathing was now heavy for a far different reason than being nervous about meeting Carson's friends and family.

Smirking, as usual, Carson gently set her feet on the floor. "I missed you."

"I can see that," Belle teased. She tucked a piece of hair behind her ear. "I think everyone could see it."

Carson shrugged and took her hand, leading her farther into the house. "That's fine. I had kind of kept everything a secret from them, until yesterday where you finally agreed to officially date me." He winked. "Now all bets are off."

"Are you sure this is a good idea?" she whispered as they continued down the hallway. Belle could see the grand ballroom in front of them, the one the party had been held in, and she could feel herself panicking.

Carson squeezed her hand a couple of times. "Absolutely. I want everyone to know how amazing you are."

"It's just still so new," Belle argued weakly.

"I know," he agreed. "But we don't have tons of time before we'll be doing this long-distance, so I'm going to utilize it to the best of my ability." He paused in the room opening.

Belle gulped as a large amount of eyes turned her way.

"Just like pulling off a Band-Aid," Carson whispered just before turning to the crowd.

With growing horror, Belle realized he was just going to shout his introduction of her to everyone at once. She tugged on his arm. "Could we maybe walk around to meet people?" she asked under her breath. "I'm not really into the idea of a shouting match."

Carson chuckled. "It's quicker this way."

"It's also more embarrassing this way." She narrowed her eyes. "I thought you were some hot shot lawyer. Aren't they supposed to be all suave and stuff?"

"And weren't you listening when I said I saved the rules for work?" He raised his eyebrows and tilted his head.

Belle rolled her eyes. "Fine. But I still would rather walk around."

Before they could begin to move around the group, the group came to them.

"Belle?" Brook asked.

Belle turned from her staredown with Carson and her eyes felt like they would bug out of their heads. So many people! And every single one of them was staring. "Hey," she squeaked, tightening her grip on Carson's arm.

Brook smiled understandingly. "Don't worry," she said in a fake whisper. "There's a lot of us, but I promise we don't bite."

"Speak for yourself!" came a voice from the back, followed by a smack then, "Ow!"

Brook hung her head and shook it from side to side. When she finally looked back at Belle, she was smiling sheepishly. "Please excuse Benny. He's a dork."

"Hey!" Another smack followed the outburst.

Grayson stepped up beside his wife and Belle had to wonder how she ever mixed the two up. While it was easy to see that they were related, now that she'd gotten to know Carson, the differences were stark. The least of which was the difference in eye color.

Grayson put one arm around his wife's waist and the other was held out to Belle. "Nice to officially meet you, Belle. I'm Grayson, or Gray for friends and family." He grinned. "And I promise I'm not as bad as you thought I was. And I'd never stray from my wife." He shrugged. "No offense. You're quite lovely, but I'm happy where I'm at."

Did people spontaneously combust? Belle was absolutely positive that she was close to doing so. Her cheeks were so hot she was afraid to touch them as she realized that Carson had told his brother all about her reaction to Carson when she thought he was Grayson.

"Would you stop it?" Brook hissed, smacking her husband's chest. "You're going to scare her off."

Carson tucked Belle into his side. "Don't listen to him," he said, glaring at his brother. "He doesn't know when to keep his mouth shut."

"Sounds to me like it runs in the family," Belle grumbled, much to the amusement of everyone who could hear her.

"I like her," Grayson said as he chuckled. "Maybe we've finally found someone to keep you in line."

"Oh, for the love!" a very loud, very Southern voice called out. The crowd shifted as the tiny, but very pregnant blonde from the cookie and chocolate shop worked her way forward. She glared at the gawking crowd, then turned and immediately smiled sweetly at Belle. "Hey," she said. "I know we sorta met before, but I'm Caro." She searched over her shoulder. "The handsome one in the back is my husband, Jack."

A man with dark blonde, sort of longish hair, waved. "That's me."

"Actually, I think she had that wrong," the same voice from earlier said. "She said handsome." Another blond peeked his head over the crowd and smiled. "She must have meant me."

Jack socked the guy's shoulder, while Caro groaned. "Okay, let me just tell you all the names and maybe as the day goes on, you can get to know us a bit." She scrunched her petite nose. "But right now, I'm afraid if we keep this up, not only will you run from the building before anyone can stop you, but you'll be so overwhelmed you might go into a catatonic shock."

A burst of laughter broke free from Belle and she tried to cover it with her fist. "Sorry," she said. "But you're right, this is kind of crazy."

Caro pursed her red lips and nodded. "We hear you." She turned around and stepped back so she was beside Belle. "Right. You've met Brook and Gray. And Jack." Her manicured finger moved around. "The loud one in the back is Benny. His wife Ally is next to him and most of the time, she's good at keeping him under control, but he must have had too much sugar at breakfast."

"Sorry!" Ally called out, and shrugged.

Belle smiled at the lovely woman, who appeared to have some kind of scarring on the side of her face. She would have to ask Carson about it eventually. This was all so much, but despite her anxiety, the feel of the group was warm and welcoming and Belle forced her feet to stay still as she listened to Caro.

*****

Carson could practically feel Belle's desire to bolt. For a woman who had kept to herself for the last several years, this had to be the ultimate nightmare. He hadn't really planned for this to be such a big event, but now that it was happening, he didn't know how to say no.

"Genni and Coop." Caro leaned toward Belle. "They have a cute mini me at home, but she's just the right age for pulling the tree over."

"Gotcha," Belle said.

Caro rubbed her own large belly. "There are three of us who are about to add to the bunch, and by next Christmas, we might not be able to get together without something burning down."

Belle's smile was completely at ease and amused, and Carson found himself able to relax a little.

"Speak for yourself," a Hispanic female said from the side. Her stomach was almost as large as Caro's. "My child is going to be perfect."

Caro rolled her eyes. "Perfectly cute, sure," Caro said. "But if you think yours isn't going to be as much of a troublemaker as her mama, you need your head examined."

"Sounds like you started the party without us," a deep voice came from behind Carson and Belle.

"Well, if it isn't Captain Ken," Carson said, turning and holding out his hand to the police captain. Carson looked around. "Where's the lovely Lily?" he asked, referring to Rose's daughter.

"We left her with her sitter," Rose explained. She smiled shyly at Ken, then turned her attention back to Carson. "We wanted to speak to you, actually."

Carson raised his eyebrows. "Legal advice?"

"Sort of." Rose laid her head against Ken's shoulder. "We'd like you to help us work out the adoption papers for Ken to adopt Lily for Christmas."

The crowd broke into shouts of joy and Carson stepped back with Belle to allow the friends to swarm Ken and Rose. "Lily is Rose's daughter," Carson explained. "Ken and Rose got married a few months ago and Lily is from her first marriage."

"How sweet," Belle said, her eyes slightly misty. "I'm so happy for them."

"Yeah...it'll be great." He grinned. "Ken's a great guy. But don't tell him I said that."

Belle laughed softly.

"Come on." Carson took her hand and led her toward a bare fir tree. "Let's get started."

"Shouldn't we wait for everyone else?"

He shook his head. "Nope. You snooze, you lose." He opened the storage containers they had placed the cookies in. "Besides, who knows how long they'll stay there. We might as well get ahead while we can."

"If you say so," Belle said, though she was smiling.

"So..." Carson hung a cookie and turned to look at his lovely date. "What do you think of the massive crew?"

Belle blew out a breath and looked back at the crowd. "I'm not gonna lie, it's a lot." Her dark eyes met his. "But I think it's pretty great you all are such good friends."

Carson nodded. "I can't really claim to be on the inner circle of things, especially as I live down in California, but this group seems to take in strays faster than they're created."

"Were you a stray?" Belle asked. She wasn't looking at him as she stretched for a branch.

Carson came up behind her and helped lift the tasty ornament to where she wanted it. "I didn't know it until I met these guys," he said in a soft tone.

Belle looked over her shoulder with a frown. "I don't understand."

Carson shrugged. "I have a great family, though my parents are nuts. But my siblings and I have always had each other's backs. However, once I met Brook's friends and they took me under their wing, I came to realize just how…" He grimaced. "Lonely I was." He dropped his voice. "But don't tell anyone I said that."

Belle turned and put a hand on his cheek. "I'm sorry," she said softly.

Carson trapped her hand against his cheek. "Don't be. I wasn't unhappy, just…missing something." He huffed a laugh. "Now I have more friends than I can keep track of every time I come up for a visit, and I've met a beautiful woman who lets me eat ornaments whenever I feel like it." He started to reach for one, but Belle turned and slapped his hand.

"Don't even think about it," she scolded.

"Too late!" Carson went back to the storage containers. "And the challenge has been accepted."

"Why do I get the feeling that decorating this tree is going to be like dealing with a toddler?"

He grinned and kissed her cheek as he passed her. "Because you're brilliant."

Belle rolled her eyes, but smiled. "Come on, man who acts like a five-year-old. Let's get this taken care of."

Carson couldn't stop smiling as he went back to putting their cookies on the tree. It was easy to see who had decorated each one. His fit the talent of that five-year-old Belle had just mentioned, while hers were simple but lovely.

Time passed companionably with people calling out insults and teasings at each other from around the room. There was lots of laughter and treats and enough hot chocolate to fill a swimming pool and Carson found himself enjoying every minute of it.

Now that he didn't have to face any matchmaking endeavors or feel like a third wheel, he could easily find happiness in the holiday's celebrations. It was amazing how the company of one person...the right person...could change everything.

"Car?"

He turned and smiled at Brook, who was standing in the room entrance. His smile fell when he realized Brook didn't look very happy. Frowning, Carson walked over. "What's wrong?"

Brook's eyes moved over his shoulder, then back. "There's a woman at the door for you."

His frown deepened. "What?"

"She says she came to join you for Christmas."

Carson quickly glanced at Belle, who was watching him, but trying to look like she wasn't. It was clear she was curious. His mind spun. Who in the world could he even know in town that would think...no. It couldn't be. He jerked back to Brook. "Please tell me she's not a too-skinny bleach blonde with a fake tan."

Brook's raised eyebrow was all the confirmation he needed.

Carson hung his head and groaned.

"Who is she?" Brook hissed.

"A woman who can't take a hint," Carson whispered back. "Look, just keep Belle busy for a second and I'll get rid of her."

"You better," Brook threatened. "I like Belle a lot."

Carson gave her a stern look. "So do I, and I would never compromise that with someone like Emme."

Brook nodded and moved around him, leaving him to his business. Taking a fortifying breath, Carson prepared himself to enter the lion's den. He had no idea where she got the idea that following him to Oregon was okay, but she had just moved from overly friendly neighbor to creepy stalker, and he wasn't going to let her get away with it.

CHAPTER 18

Carson looked anything but happy as he stormed from the room.

Belle frowned and set down the cookie she had been about to hang up. Brook was headed in her direction, but she also looked upset. "What's going on?" Belle asked. "Was there an emergency or something?"

Brook tucked her hair behind her ear and shook her head. "No, nothing like that." A fake smile spread across her face. "He just had something he needed to take care of." Brook's hazel eyes moved to the tree Belle and Carson had been working on. "Oh my goodness," she gushed. "Did you two make all those cookies?"

Belle shrugged, her attention still down the hall with Carson. "Yeah. We worked on it yesterday."

Brook pushed one of the star cookies covered in edible glitter. "They're stunning." She paused at one with a mass of red and green frosting all over it, then turned and grinned at Belle. "I'm guessing that the ones *you* decorated are amazing. Carson might be all thumbs when it comes to cookie decorating."

Belle laughed softly. "He had fun. That's the important thing, right?"

Brook laughed a little louder. "I'm sure he did."

Belle felt her face heat up. Every single person in here was part of a couple and probably knew all too well how her and Carson's cooking session had gone yesterday.

At the thought of Carson, she turned back to the hallway. What was he doing? Why would he walk off without saying anything to her?

"Would you like to come help me in the kitchen for a few minutes?" Brook asked, her eyes wide and innocent.

Belle wasn't fooled by the performance. She knew that Brook was doing her best to keep Belle from following Carson. That ugly voice in the back of Belle's head began to sneer.

You knew he had something to hide.

They always do.

This is how it starts.

Her bottom lip started to shake and Belle bit it hard between her teeth. It was just yesterday that she had agreed to trust him and work on a relationship. Thinking about how he was keeping a secret was a betrayal of that trust. But on the other hand, why was Brook so obviously trying to keep her away from following? Why didn't he want Belle to know what was going on?

"Belle?"

Belle blinked and came out of her argumentative thoughts. She sucked in a deep breath. "Sorry. What was that?"

"Would you like to come help me in the kitchen?"

The inner fight was deafening. What was she supposed to do?

Enough!

Belle shoved aside the cynical voice that had been gaining strength in the last five minutes.

"I'd love to," Belle said. Her smile was tight, but she kept it in place as she followed Brook farther into the house. It took every ounce of self control she had to keep her bitter, distrustful side from rising to the forefront.

This was exactly what Belle had been afraid of. She was becoming a jaded woman who couldn't see the good in anything. She didn't want to be the crazy cat lady, who screamed at kids to get off her lawn. She wanted to be happy and full of love.

Carson had pursued *her*. He had initiated their relationship and had just now introduced her to most of his friends and family. Surely he wouldn't do that, then turn around and break her trust. It simply didn't fit with the man Belle had been coming to know in the last few days.

"What can I do?" Belle asked.

"Why don't you grab that tray and we'll fill it with more toppings for the hot chocolate," Brook directed. She smiled, a smile that was much more sincere than before. "I'm pretty sure Benny and Cooper have eaten so much sugar this afternoon, they'll never sleep again."

Belle laughed. "Sounds about right."

"So...you're a baker?"

Belle glanced up from her work. "Uh-huh."

"And you want to do catering?"

Belle shook her head. "No. That's just the first job I found after coming here."

"And what brought you to Seaside Bay?" Brook asked. "I've been here a long time, and I don't remember you as a local."

Belle smiled. "I'm not. My brother moved in a few years ago. Richard Kerr? He owns the hardware store."

"Ah, gotcha." Brook nodded and filled the tiny pitcher with more cream. "So you're living with him?"

"He was nice enough to let me get my feet under me before I get into something more permanent."

"It's really nice to have family around, isn't it?" Brook responded.

Belle shrugged. "Yeah. I mean, I love him and his wife and my nephew, but sometimes my brother is still a pain, ya know?"

Brook shook her head. "Nope. Only child." She leaned over a little. "But I've now got experience with Carson as a brother and I can imagine."

Belle laughed as intended. "I think brothers are worse than sisters, but I don't have a sister, so I don't know for sure."

"Sounds right to me," Brook quipped.

Belle and Brook both laughed and Belle went back to filling the container with mini marshmallows and pulling some mint stirrers from the jar. A loud gust of wind blew past the window and drew her attention up, where Belle promptly froze.

From her place in the kitchen, Belle had the perfect view of the driveway, where Carson was standing with a stunningly beautiful blonde. She was thin and poised and looked completely put together in her designer coat and boots. In other words, she was everything Belle wasn't.

Belle wasn't usually the type of person to feel inadequate, but right now she couldn't help comparing the side braid she had thought so cute this morning to the woman's flowy locks. Belle had picked her sweater to show off her brown eyes, but now she wished she'd pulled something a little more elegant from the closet. Not that Belle had *anything* that could compare to this woman, but still...

"It's not what it looks like."

Belle was pulled from her comparisonitis, back to the fact she was standing in the kitchen staring. "What?"

Brook's face was solemn as she nodded toward the window. "Carson...and that...woman. It's not what it looks like."

Belle quickly nodded. "I'm sure it's fine." She refused to look back out, instead going back to the tray. "He's a grown man. He can certainly have other friends." Belle kept her eyes down and eventually Brook moved away, but the sting in Belle's heart refused to budge.

There had to be an explanation, but as she struggled to stay calm, Belle wondered if she would be able to hear it without letting her suspicions take over.

*****

"You need to just go home," Carson stated bluntly. "I've never given you any reason to think there's anything between us."

Emme pushed out her overly glossed bottom lip. "But Car..." she whined, making Carson want to scratch his eyes out. "We've been neighbors for so long." A slow smile crept across her face. "You can't tell me that you're not attracted to me." She began to step forward and Carson scurried back.

"I'm not, Emme."

Emme paused and frowned. "What?"

"I'm not attracted to you." Carson put his hands in the air. "Look. You've been a good neighbor, but I'm not interested. I've never been interested. I don't know why you decided you should follow me to Oregon—in fact, I'm not even sure *how* you knew I was in Oregon—but it doesn't matter." He tried to give her the most serious look he could. "I'm with someone else. Someone I have very strong feelings for. Please go home and don't contact me again or I'll be forced to take out a restraining order."

Emme's lips pinched into a thin white line and Carson prayed his message was finally hitting home. She flung her hair over her shoulder. "I understand," she said tightly. "Though I hope you understand that if I walk away now, I won't be coming back. You'll be losing your chance."

Carson nodded. "Thank you for the warning. Please go."

Emme's lip curled, but she spun on her heel and yanked open her car door, plopping herself inelegantly in the driver's seat before peeling out of the driveway.

Carson blew out a breath and pushed his hand through his hair. The wind was blowing it everywhere, but he was less affected by that than he was the situation with Emme. The woman was crazy! How did she even know he was here?

Carson shook his head. All he wanted was to get inside and warm up. If he was lucky, Belle would be part of the warming up process. He hurried inside, shutting and locking the door behind him. He wasn't taking any chances that Emme would change her mind and come back, this time making her way into the house.

He could still hear the chatting and laughter coming from the ballroom and he hurried in that direction. At first glance, he couldn't see Belle and it caused him to pause. But after a moment, she walked through an opening on the opposite side of the room with a tray in hand. She and Brook seemed to have come from the kitchen, since they were both carrying trays full of drinks and food.

He smiled at her and rushed over. "Let me help with that," he said, winking. He nearly stumbled when her brown eyes met his. There was a very clear conflict going on and Carson had no idea what it was.

He looked to Brook, who gave him a sympathetic look. "The kitchen overlooks the driveway," she said with a shrug.

Crap.

Carson nodded and finished lifting the tray from Belle's death grip. "Come on," he said, taking her hand and leading her across the room. Once they were semi-alone, he pulled her up closer until she was facing him. "Go ahead. Ask me."

Belle played with the end of her braid. "I don't know that there's anything to ask. I know you have other friends."

"Friends, yes. Girlfriends, not a chance," Carson clarified.

Belle's dark brown eyes looked up from under her lashes. "She was very beautiful."

Carson shrugged. "I suppose if you're into fake tans and plastic."

A smile tugged on Belle's lips, but it never fully emerged. "Is she someone you...knew before?"

"She's not an ex, if that's what you're really asking," Carson stated. He reached out and rubbed his hands on her upper arms. Emme was the absolute last thing he wanted to talk about right now. He just needed Belle to trust him that nothing was going on. "She's someone I know from back in California, but there's nothing between us. There never has been, and there never will be."

Belle hesitated, but nodded. "Okay. If you say so."

Trying to portray the confidence she needed, Carson nodded as well. "Let's just forget about her, okay? I'd much rather spend my time thinking about you and those delicious cookies we made than nosy neighbors."

Belle's smile wasn't quite as bright as before, but it did appear and Carson decided to take that as a win. "Okay."

"Great." He took her hand and they walked casually back to the tree. "I think we're a little behind," he whispered loudly enough to be heard by several people.

"It isn't a race," Brook called out.

"No, but how can everyone see the tree that's going to win if we never finish it?" Carson hollered back.

"You wish!" Caro argued. "All we'd have to do is let Scottie in here and your tree would be toast!" she said, referring to Genni and Cooper's dog.

"Already looking for a way to cheat." Benny tsked his tongue. "One of these days you're just going to have to admit that someone is better than you."

Caro put her hands on her hips, looking like she was seriously debating whether or not she could take Benny in a fight.

"Don't even think about it," Charli called out. She rubbed her stomach. "There's no going into labor until after the holidays."

"Yeah, well, if I get much bigger, my stomach will pop whether the baby is ready or not," Caro muttered.

"Won't it be wonderful?" Melody sighed, leaning into her husband's side. "All our kids growing up together?"

"All I'm saying is that in three years, we are *not* coming over to my house for Thanksgiving dinner. I'd like it to still be standing at the end of the day."

Carson snickered along with everyone else as they continued to banter back and forth. He looked to Belle, who was smiling softly, but not participating in the chatter. "Doing okay?" he asked softly, this time making sure his voice didn't carry. "I know they can be a lot."

She looked up at him. "They're fun, but yeah...a little overwhelming." She tilted her head to the side. "I'm kind of surprised it's who your brother hangs out with though. I would have expected him to be attracted to a...more elite group."

"Well, first off...these were Brook's friends, and family. I'll have to tell you Brook and Grayson's story someday, because he used to only hang out with those elite. But Brook has been good for him, helping him step out of his rich and famous bubble. She also helped him overcome a severe injury to his back that could have left him paralyzed."

Belle's eyes widened. "I heard about that. It's why he went into directing, right?"

Carson nodded. "Yep."

"So her friends became his friends."

Carson nodded again, though it had been a statement, not a question. "And truthfully, they've become our extended family. I mean, I have family and they're great, but this group just never lets you go."

"I can see that." The words were said in a thoughtful tone and after a moment, Belle shook herself, then smiled. "If you're wanting to win, I suppose we better get this tree done, huh?"

"Sounds good to me." Carson left a quick kiss on her soft cheek, then headed for the container of cookies. "Come on, Ms. Irish Butter. Your canvas awaits."

"I'm never going to live that down, am I?"

Carson knew his grin was answer enough.

CHAPTER 19

Belle hummed as she kneaded her dough the next morning. Christmas tunes were stuck in her head on repeat and there didn't seem to be anything she could do to stop them. Every time the name Carson or a picture of him flitted through her head, songs from the tree decorating party would come back, causing her to smile and stare off into the distance like an idiot.

The worst part was, she didn't exactly hate it.

It had been a long time since Belle had felt so light and carefree, and she knew...she *knew*...exactly what this feeling was.

She was falling in love.

The whole idea of falling in love with someone in only a couple of weeks was insane. It was what she would have done back in high school. But not now. Not as an experienced, battered, grown woman who ran her own life.

"What has you so cheery today?" Corey asked as he walked by with a pan of cookies in his hands.

Corey was quite a few years younger than Belle, but had been very friendly ever since she joined the team. Corey was saving up to go to college and very quickly, Belle found herself cheering him on. He was a good kid and deserved the chance to get the education he wanted.

"Nothing," Belle said quickly.

Corey paused, then slowly spun and gave her a look. "Your answer was a little too quick."

Belle rolled her eyes. "It's nothing, Corey."

He grinned. "And I believe that even less than I believed you the first time." His eyes widened. "It's a guy. Isn't it?"

Belle threw her sticky hands to the side. "How did we go from nothing to guy? The line doesn't even make sense."

"But it's right!"

"Would you two stop talking and get back to work?" April snapped. She was hugging a canister of flour to her hip. "It's like working with toddlers."

Corey stuck his tongue out at April's back and Belle huffed a soft laugh. "She's crankier than the Grinch," he complained.

"She's right though," Belle said. "We have a job to do."

"Fine, fine, but don't think I'm not on to that secret of yours." Corey pointed a finger in her direction, then quickly righted the shifting pan and walked back to his station. They were catering an office party tonight and everyone was busy with a list of foods they were supposed to have ready.

It was nice to be so busy during the holidays, giving Belle a nice paycheck in order to get started on her own life, but every night she was at work was one less night she could spend with Carson. And with the knowledge that her time with him was limited, she found herself wanting to bask in every moment.

Last night, after they had gotten over the awkward moment of the woman in the driveway, Carson had been perfectly sweet, attentive, and mischievous. He certainly loved to stir up a little trouble and then sit back and watch it all play out. Belle was sure that was part of what made him good at being a lawyer. He wasn't afraid to push the boundaries, though he had always done so in a way that was annoying, but respectful.

Watching him interact with Brook's friends had been enlightening and enjoyable. The group was obviously very close and came from completely different walks of life. Jack was a cookie-making surfer, while Ken was captain of the local police precinct. Jensen taught high school English whereas Hadlee had a doctorate in marine biology.

And then there was Grayson, who seemed to be in a league of his own, but no one seemed to care. Carson had been right. Brook kept him grounded. The movie star obviously had more money than he knew what to do with, but with Brook's pushing, it was being used to help others just as much as it was used for fun.

After finishing the trees last night, they had all spent time chatting while building gift bags of necessities to donate to Bronson and Charli's nonprofit called Father and Sons.

The camaraderie was as warming as it was intimidating, and by the end of the evening, Belle knew she wanted to be a part of it. Her cynical voice had slowly grown more and more quiet the longer their gathering went and Belle found her worries slipping further and further away.

While she couldn't be sure, not yet anyway, she had a feeling that she just might have found exactly what Sofia and Rich had been telling her about for years. A relationship that was fun, exciting, and passionate. The type of relationship that made her a better person rather than sucking out all her energy.

Carson knew her situation in life. She was bumming off her brother while waiting to build a savings account. Her car was one bump away from the dump and she would barely be able to afford to buy her nephew a gift for Christmas.

But not once had he ever brought up the differences in their social status. He treated her to cookies, treats, and dinners without ever saying anything about the strain on his wallet or how it was her turn or even joking that he was quickly becoming her own personal piggy bank.

"Would you stop that infernal humming?" April shouted.

Belle's breath caught. Once again, she had gotten lost in her thoughts and completely forgotten what she was doing. "Sorry," she offered quietly.

"I think a little music sounds good," Corey called out. "It's almost Christmas, after all."

"There'll be enough of that at the party tonight," April grumbled.

Belle bit her lip to keep from smiling. She couldn't help it. Even April's grumpy attitude wasn't enough to keep her from feeling the residual joy at what was going on in her life.

"You're adults," Mrs. Stallings said calmly from her office door. "I expect you to act like it."

Belle felt her cheeks heat and she kept her eyes on her dough. It was ready to be shaped into rolls and left to rise for a bit. Suddenly, with their boss glaring at everyone, those rolls were the most important thing in the world.

Belle was almost positive that she could feel Mrs. Stallings' eyes boring into her back, but eventually the sensation left. She glanced over her shoulder and let out a breath of relief that the office door was empty.

"Ignore them," Corey said in passing. "Maybe they just need a good pass under the mistletoe. That'd help them lighten up."

Belle snorted, then covered the sound by coughing. Corey had no idea how her own moment under the mistletoe had changed everything. "I'm sure you're right," she whispered back with a secretive grin.

Keeping her humming low enough not to be heard, Belle went back to her work. She really didn't mind the catering, even if it wasn't what she wanted to do permanently. The problem was, it just wasn't as important as the fact that she had once again given her heart to a man.

She just hoped that this time turned out better than the last.

*****

Carson blew on his hands and rubbed them together. It was freezing tonight. But the cold wasn't enough to deter him from wanting to see Belle. He had texted her earlier in the day and discovered she was helping cater an office party tonight.

After a little bit of sleuthing, Carson had figured out which office and how long the party was supposed to last. Now he was waiting outside for a very particular woman, in order to surprise her with a late night dinner, since she more than likely hadn't eaten yet.

He perked up when someone in black walked out the back of the building, but slumped again when it wasn't Belle.

Carson glanced at his watch. The party was supposed to end in five minutes. How much longer could she be?

"Stop partying, people, and let the staff out," he grumbled, knowing he was being unreasonable. He'd attended plenty of work parties himself and knew they rarely ended on time. The spark of reality only made him grumble all the more.

He considered starting his car to get the heater running, but he didn't want to give away the fact that a man, not a part of the staff or the office, was sitting around in the shadows waiting for someone. Said out loud, it sounded creepy and Carson refused to acknowledge that he might have gone a little overboard tonight.

Finally, more than one of the catering staff was seen coming and going. Large trays and full, silver carts were being moved to the two vans backed up to the door.

Carson smiled as he watched Belle come and go several times. He knew he would have to wait until she was fully done to surprise her. He didn't need another scolding from the overprotective boss.

Another half-hour passed with Carson barely feeling the cold as he watched Belle. It seemed to take forever before the van doors closed and the staff started saying goodbye.

Carson had a momentary panic when he realized that a few of the employees would need to go back to the catering kitchen to help unload and he had no idea if Belle was one of them. His question was answered, however, when a few got into the vans and the rest got into cars.

To his relief, Belle was headed to her hunk of junk and Carson quickly opened his door and got out of his own. He didn't want to shout, so he decided to get a little closer before calling her name.

Before he could speak, however, Belle spun and held her hands in the air in front of her. "Stay back!" she shouted in a shaky voice.

Carson stopped and put his hands in the air, but apparently it wasn't quick enough. A puff of peppery gas hit his eyes. "Ah!" He quickly backed up and forced himself to keep his hands to his side. Rubbing this was only going to be worse and at the moment, he wasn't sure he could handle that without crying like a baby.

He leaned over, hands on his knees, and tried to breathe, but the searing pain in his eyes made it difficult.

"Carson!"

He heard pounding footsteps and Belle's body nearly slammed into him. She wrapped her arms around his back. "Inside. Quick. We need to rinse your eyes."

"I'm a little blind at the moment," he said through gritted teeth. "You're going to have to guide me."

"Oh my gosh. I can't believe this," Belle breathed, slowly pushing him forward. "Everybody kept saying there was some guy in a car watching everything. We were worried you were a thief or something, but when I heard you walking up behind me, I was scared for another reason."

"I was going to surprise you." Carson grunted, stumbling on a threshold step. "Wanted to take you to a late night dinner."

"I am *such* an idiot," Belle stammered, her voice breaking on a sob.

"Actually, I think that award goes to me," Carson said, trying to make a joke. It definitely fell flat.

"Right here," she said hurriedly. "Bend your head down and I'll spray the water toward your eyes."

"No drowning," Carson said.

"Stop cracking jokes," she scolded. "It only makes me feel worse."

"I'm not feeling so hot myself," he said, then paused. "That might be a bad choice of words. I'm overly hot, if anything."

"Oh my word," Belle ground out. "Seriously. Be quiet and let me fix this." She didn't give him any more chances to kid around before shoving his head down and hitting him square in the face with a blast of cold water.

Carson sputtered and opened his mouth wide to try and keep breathing through the dousing.

"We need to sit like this for several minutes," Belle said loudly. "I'm so sorry."

"It's fine," Carson sputtered through the water. He tried holding his breath, but breathing like a weird fish creature seemed to work better, and he eventually gave up any semblance of trying to look un-affected. The water ran down his head and neck, soaking his shirt and coat. He had a feeling that going back outside was going to be much worse than before.

"Okay..." Belle shut off the water and began to pat down his face with something soft. "That should be enough."

Carson slowly straightened and took the towel from her, wiping at his face and neck. "Wow. I had no idea what it was like to go face first up a waterfall, but I think I've got it figured out now." He stopped when he saw Belle's stricken face. Her eyes were probably as red as his were and tears were streaming down her chin and onto her shirt. "Ah, sweetheart." He dropped the towel and pulled her into his chest. "Don't cry. You know men can't stand tears."

"I'm so sorry," she blubbered against his coat. Her arms wound around him, squeezing tightly. "I'm so sorry."

"Don't be." Carson framed her face and pushed her back slightly. His eyes still felt gritty, but they no longer stung like he'd been dipped in acid. "You were protecting yourself from someone who certainly should have known better." He made a wry face. "I've worked with people in court who ended up *not* spraying their attacker. I probably should have thought of that when I sat there watching you like a stalker."

Belle shook her head. "If I'd waited just a second, I would have seen—"

"Nope. We're done here." Carson kissed her forehead. "I don't think I'm up to a restaurant tonight. What do you say to takeout?" He took her hand and guided her out of the utility area they were in. Christmas music could still be heard farther inside the building. The party must have been good.

"You can't be serious!" she cried.

Carson stopped and looked at her. "Why wouldn't I be?"

"You need to go home...and, and...I don't know! Rest or something! Maybe we should do an emergency visit with an eye doctor!"

Carson chuckled. "I think my nurse already took care of that. I'm not opposed to stopping and grabbing some eye drops for the next couple days, but otherwise, I'm hungry, not sick." He blinked a few times, noting that his eyes still burned, but it was far less than it was before. Belle didn't need to know that though. "Let's just grab something and we can sneak in the back of Gray's mansion and cuddle on one of the couches that he doesn't even know exists because they have too much space for two people."

"Carson, I'm serious!" Belle cried, looking truly distressed.

"Me too! I'm hungry! So let's get this show on the road!" Carson started pulling her along again and Belle came, but he could tell she was still upset. Carson wasn't though. If she thought for one second he wouldn't milk this thing until the cows came home...she didn't know him very well yet. Carson had plenty of ideas of how Belle could make this up to him and he planned to use every single one.

CHAPTER 20

What if I run into Carson again?

The thought made Belle laugh under her breath as she walked into the local grocery store. This is where she had first met him, despite the fact that Belle had mistaken Carson for his brother.

Maybe if she pretended to look for Irish butter again, Carson would come waltzing around the corner, teasing her and calling her funny nicknames. This time Belle would be sure not to hit him in the face with pepper spray.

She almost groaned as she remembered that disaster. Carson had been so sweet about it, but Belle still felt guilty. In fact, that was why she was at the store right now. She was purchasing the ingredients to make him a treat in order to say *I'm sorry*...again.

The front door pushed apart and Belle marched inside, grabbing a basket along the way. She had picked a recipe this time that had ingredients she was sure even a small town grocery store would carry.

The weather was cold, the wind bit through their clothes, and Belle knew it was time for sweet, cinnamony, apple pie. And since she had noticed Carson ate more apples than anything else off the fruit tray the other night, she figured it was bound to be a hit.

Once the apples were acquired, Belle wandered to the butter section. They might not have Irish style here, but Tillamook was carried in abundance, and that would work wonderfully.

After dumping a couple of pounds in her basket, she turned to head toward the baking aisle, but skidded quickly to a stop.

Perfectly styled blonde hair, smooth tan skin, red lips, and a white smile that most orthodontists would love to advertise with stood between Belle and her destination. "Hello."

Belle blinked, then looked around before frowning at the woman. "Hello." While Belle certainly recognized the beach bunny from the Cordova house, she couldn't figure out why the woman was speaking to her. Carson had assured Belle that she wasn't anyone important and Belle had believed him. Though, with the woman standing right here, Belle's conviction was wavering a bit.

"How rude of me," the woman said. "I'm Emme Spencer." She held out her small, feminine hand.

Belle's frown remained, even as she shook Emme's hand. She had said the name as if it should mean something to Belle. *Maybe she's some kind of actress? Like, with Grayson?* "I'm sorry," Belle said apologetically. "Should I know you?"

Emme's bright blue eyes widened. "Carson hasn't told you about me?"

Belle hesitated. "He said you were a friend from California."

Emme's laugh was pure joy. If she wasn't on the stage, she really should be. Every viewer would be entranced. Especially the men. "He's such a sweetheart. And so humble."

"Humble?" Belle tilted her head. "I don't understand."

Emme waved her hand carelessly through the air. "Well, we certainly haven't made it official, but Carson and I are engaged."

"Engaged." Belle's tone was flat. Her heart began to beat in an uneven rhythm. This couldn't be happening again. Could it? Carson *knew* about her past. He wouldn't do this... He couldn't have!

Emme nodded sweetly, swinging her own basket from side to side. "Oh, yes. It's all been very hush hush. My daddy wanted to make Carson's promotion in the firm official before announcing our marriage." She leaned in. "That way people didn't think he was promoted just because he was part of the family."

"I see." Belle forced a small smile onto her face, even though she felt like she was dying inside. She had no idea whom to believe. Carson had helped pull Belle out of her jaded and cynical mentality and shown her what it was like to laugh and smile again, all while stealing bits of her heart until it was completely gone. And yet, the one thing he had never truly explained between them was the woman standing in front of Belle, spouting words that were enough to crush her.

"I was supposed to wait until Christmas when he got back from Oregon to see him again, but I just couldn't wait," Emme said as if it were a secret. "His brother's wife and I don't always get along, so Carson thought it best if he came up here without me and we'd get together when he came home."

Belle nodded, her stomach in knots and threatening to ruin Emme's designer shoes. Belle glanced at her watch. "Oh, I'm sorry. I'm afraid I have to get to work." Her smile was brittle, but at least her lips moved. "Congrats to you and Carson, but if you'll excuse me, I need to run."

"Oh, of course. I'm so sorry." Emme giggled. "I get carried away when I talk about him."

"Totally understandable." Belle forced her lips to move one more time, then spun on her heel and made her way to the baking aisle. The idea of baking a pie now sounded like the worst idea she'd ever had.

Unless it had a laxative in it...

Belle shook her head, throwing the idea away. She still didn't know whom to believe in this situation. While Emme's words made sense, there were several questions left unanswered.

One of the main ones being about Brook. She was one of the kindest people Belle had ever met. And Emme certainly knew how to put on a happy face. Why in the world would the two of them not get along?

And Carson himself. He seemed so sincere. He had admitted to his feelings about his brother and how it had led him to seeking Belle out. She struggled to see the man she was in love with as the type of person who would double cross her this way.

You thought the same thing about Dale.

Belle paused and had to lean over, breathing slowly through her nose. Her mind whirled and any thoughts of an apple pie went out the window. She needed answers and she needed them now.

Dropping her basket to the floor, Belle rushed out the door. Hopefully a worker would find it and put the food back soon, but Belle's panic was keeping her from caring as much as she should.

She slammed the door to her car, then forced herself to pause. "You can't go in with guns blazing," she told herself with a hoarse voice. "You know Carson, you don't know Emme. He needs to be given a chance to refute what she said."

Her vehicle almost didn't turn over and Belle found that the slight amount of anxiety that it caused put her over the edge. She was breathing heavily and her stomach continued to churn. She knew, logically, that she needed to speak calmly to Carson, but the only thing she could think of was the fact that she had known her ex-husband as well. She had given him years of her life and he had still turned out to be a stranger. Could she really believe that this time would be different?

*****

Carson found himself wandering aimlessly around the mansion. He was bored out of his mind, and it wasn't because he hadn't been entertained for the last two days.

After he'd come back from the mace dousing, he had showered, fallen asleep for much longer than normal, and then endured the ribbing that came from his family after spilling the story of what had happened with Belle.

That had been followed by a cookie decorating party, and then the drawing of Secret Santas, all of which had been without Belle because she had been working at various events.

Today, she said she would come over this afternoon after dealing with some things in the morning, and the clock simply wouldn't move fast enough.

Carson had learned his lesson about surprising her at work, but that didn't make the wait any more endurable. Two days was too long to wait to see the woman he was falling for.

He paused in his pacing, but quickly got going again. He *was* falling for her. There was no way to deny it and he didn't really want to anyway. That beautiful woman with her kind but snarky attitude and wide, chocolatey eyes had stolen his attention, and then his heart.

A slow smile crept across Carson's face. She wouldn't be ready to hear his feelings. Belle needed to move slower than that, especially considering her past. But the idea of a future, a real future with her, excited him in a way he'd never felt before.

He didn't just want to spend time with her now, he wanted to spend time with her five years from now. He wanted to take her to his favorite restaurant down in Hollywood. He wanted to introduce her to his colleagues and feel that smug sensation that she was his and only his. He wanted to—

"Car?"

He turned and nearly lost his balance, much to Grayson's amusement. Carson cleared his throat. "Yeah?"

"You have a visitor."

Carson glanced at his watch. "She's early," he murmured, then grinned. Who cared if she was early. That was great news! "On it!" he rushed past his brother, ignoring Grayson's chuckles, and made for the front entryway. "Belle!" he shouted, the sound echoing off all the fancy tiles in the home. Without waiting for her response, he wrapped his arms around her and spun her around before kissing her soundly. "I missed you," he whispered against her lips. There was something so freeing about admitting his feelings, even if it was only to himself. He was good at keeping secrets, but that didn't mean he wouldn't revel in the feeling of what he would eventually share with the world.

When Belle didn't return his sentiment, Carson finally looked at her and realized her eyes were red rimmed and her mouth was down-turned. "What's wrong?" he demanded, letting her feet fall to the floor. "Did Cole get sick? Did something happen to Rich?"

Belle shook her head and slowly backed out of his arms. "We, uh, need to have a talk."

They were simple words, but there was something about the way she said it that made the request sound ominous. "Okay," Carson said carefully. He watched her body movements. He'd spent his entire career learning to read people, and the edginess in Belle's movements didn't bode well for Carson.

"Is there somewhere we can speak privately?" she whispered.

Caron considered, then nodded. "Let's head to my room. It's big enough for us to talk without being interrupted."

Belle hesitated, then nodded.

Carson reached for her hand and was grateful she didn't pull away. Something was seriously wrong and if he wasn't way off base, it had to do with them as a couple. It took a minute to get to where he wanted to go. "In here." He pushed open his door, grateful he hadn't been exceptionally messy this morning.

His shoes were next to the bed and a jacket was hanging on the back of a chair, but otherwise things weren't in too bad of shape. Two chairs and a coffee table were on one side of the room and Carson led Belle in that direction.

"Thank you," she said in a low tone as she took one of the chairs.

Carson sat in the other. Gently, he leaned forward and took her hand, pressing her cold one between his own. "Okay. Now what's this all about?" Belle wouldn't meet his eyes and Carson moved his head around until he forced her to look at him. "Is this still about the mace?" he teased. "Because I think it only adds to our already fun story."

Belle's lips twitched, but she shook her head and turned away. "Do we have a story?" she asked.

Carson stiffened. "Don't we?"

Her face came back and her eyes were a little snappier than they were before. "Carson. Who's Emme Spencer?"

He jerked upright. "What did she do?" he asked.

"I asked you a question," Belle said more firmly than before. She was starting to gain some of her backbone and Carson wasn't sure if it was a good thing or not.

The wounded bird look wasn't good on her, but he also didn't want to be on the receiving end of her anger. He'd done it before and it had been funny because it was misplaced. This time, she knew exactly who he was and was still treating him this way.

"She's my neighbor." Belle blinked and waited, but Carson had nothing more to say.

"And?" she pressed.

"And nothing," Carson said, his tone a little snippier than it should be. Why were they even talking about her? He'd sent her packing days ago and Carson thought they'd gotten this whole thing out in the open when they were decorating the tree. Why bring it up now?

"Do you work for her father?"

Carson shrugged. "Yeah."

"Are they planning to promote you?"

Carson frowned. "It's been talked about, but nothing is certain yet." He leaned in. "How do you know that?"

Belle shook her head and fell back in the seat. "I saw Emme at the grocery store today."

Carson raised his eyebrows. "She left town."

"Did she?"

"I told her to," Carson stated. "You saw it. The day she showed up unannounced at the tree decorating party. She's been trying to get me to ask her on a date for ages and I've been politely putting her off, but lately she's gotten more forceful."

"You're telling me that a woman, who happens to be your neighbor and whose father you work for, came all the way from California just because she wanted you to take her on a date?"

Carson scowled. "What is this?" he demanded. "I told you what happened. Why the inquisition? I get the feeling I'm on trial."

Belle jerked to her feet and began to pace the room not much differently than Carson had been only a few minutes before. "Emme cornered me in the store," she began, then turned to look at Carson. "She told me that you two were engaged, but were keeping it secret because of the promotion. That the firm didn't want people to think you had gotten the job only because your boss was your father-in-law."

"What?" Carson shouted, jumping to his feet.

Belle stepped back, but then seemed to catch herself and planted her feet before throwing back her shoulders. "I came to find out the truth," she said.

"I don't think so," Carson retorted, his anger simmering. It burned at Emme, at her gall, at himself for not taking care of it earlier, and at Belle for listening to the lies. "You've already decided the truth. Otherwise you wouldn't be here accusing me of being like Dale. You've already pronounced me guilty."

CHAPTER 21

Carson's accusation hit Belle straight in the gut and the bile churned once more, but she did her best to hold her ground. "I came to give you a chance to be open with me," she refuted.

"No, you came to find a reason to get rid of me."

Belle turned and headed toward the door. "Goodbye, Carson." His hand landed on her arm.

"Wait," he said, then dropped his head and took a breath. "Please."

Belle stepped back so he wasn't touching her, but she did wait. She felt like such an idiot. Did she simply have *GULLIBLE* tattooed across her forehead? Why did she always fall for the good liars? It seemed so unfair. She'd spent the last several years with her guard up and all it took was a good looking, charismatic man to bring her protection crashing down. And look where that had gotten her. The only consolation she could think of was the fact that this time she hadn't married him before finding out it was all a lie.

Carson put his hands in the air. "Can we...talk like adults? Rather than growling at each other like a couple of feral cats?"

This wasn't a time for amusement, yet Belle wanted to laugh. Carson's sense of humor was one of the things she loved about him most. The reminder of that misplaced love, however, was enough to keep her from giving into the sensation.

She folded her arms across her chest, giving herself a slight form of protection, and nodded. "I'm not sure what there is to talk about, but sure." She wanted this over with, but he was right. It wouldn't be good to leave things like this. They needed to clear the air so they could both get the closure they wanted. Or at least so she could get closure. He still hadn't confessed to anything, but the way he'd danced around the subject told her all she needed to know.

Belle perched herself on the very edge of the seat, every muscle tight and ready to run if it went south again.

"Thank you," Carson said with forced calmness. He sat in the other chair. "I'm sorry for snapping. I shouldn't have spoken to you like that, but..." He shook his head. "I just don't understand how you could believe that woman over me."

His blue eyes implored her and Belle had a hard time holding herself back. He looked so sincere, but she'd fallen for sincere before.

"You know me, Belle," Carson argued. "You know I'm not a liar. You know more about me than anyone."

"I didn't know about the promotion," Belle said bluntly.

His shoulders slumped. "No. I didn't tell you that." He raised his eyebrows. "I don't usually date a woman by telling her how much I make and that it might become more by the end of the year." He paused a beat. "Not to mention, I don't think those are the kind of things that would impress you." His tone was soft, but the words stung nonetheless. They were a rebuke, plain and simple. This was all her fault.

Well, Belle had heard that before too. She hadn't given Dale everything he needed and that was why he strayed. She didn't look the part and that was why he went to the aftergame parties without her. She didn't know how to let loose and have fun, so he found fun elsewhere...

"You're right," she said, sticking her chin in the air. "Money doesn't impress me. But honesty does. And I'm having a hard time believing that a woman would follow you from California just because she wanted a date."

He threw his hands in the air. "And I'm having a hard time believing that the woman I gave my heart to is so stuck on her past hurts that she can't see what's right in front of her face!"

Belle almost bit her tongue in half to keep from responding to those words. If he had wanted to hurt her, he'd done a marvelous job.

"Then I suppose it's a good thing you don't have to deal with me and my past anymore." Belle rose. "Goodbye, Mr Cordova. All the best to you and Emme."

"Belle...I didn't mean it that way!"

She kept walking. She had lost her heart, her future, and apparently her mind, but right now, Belle refused to let go of her dignity.

"Belle!"

She had no idea how to get out of this house, but Belle pressed forward. Carson hadn't followed her, thank goodness, but she didn't know where the front door was and with her nerves already completely shredded, Belle knew she was only moments away from a complete breakdown.

"Belle?"

She turned at Brook's sweet voice.

"Are you all right?" Brook looked so concerned that Belle actually took a moment to do an inventory.

She reached up and realized her cheeks were wet. She had been so focused on getting away from Carson that she hadn't realized she was crying. "I'm fine," she whispered. "Could you please help me find the front door?"

The words rankled. It made her feel even more stupid than she already did, but Belle had to get out of this house before she couldn't hold herself together anymore. That moment was growing too close for comfort.

"Maybe you'd like to come into the kitchen and talk?" Brook offered, stepping closer with her hand out.

Belle shook her head, breaking more tears loose. "No, thank you. The door, please."

Brook dropped her hand and sighed. "All right." Silently, she led the way through several rooms until they reached the familiar front entryway. Belle moved to the door, walking past Brook on her way.

"He's a good guy, Belle."

Belle paused with her hand on the door.

"I don't know what happened between the two of you, but please give him another chance."

Belle took in a shuddering breath, but couldn't bring herself to respond. If she ever decided to give a relationship a try again, it wouldn't be with Carson. She needed someone she could trust. Someone who would be one hundred percent honest with her at all times. It didn't matter how small or insignificant the matter, she wanted to know about it.

With Brook still behind her, Belle walked out the door, pulling until the latch clicked. The sound was the closing of another chapter in Belle's life. One that she knew would haunt her for a long time to come. But despite the heartache and desire to go to bed and eat her weight in carbs, Belle was proud of herself.

When Dale had admitted his infidelity, Belle had cried, begged, and pleaded for understanding. This time she had done none of that. She had walked away with her head high, even if her heart was dragging on the ground.

She had kept herself under control just long enough to show Carson that she wasn't going to continue to play his game and that she was strong enough to handle anything life threw at her.

This time her grieving would be kept to herself. And Carson would never know how much he had broken her.

*****

She had walked away... She. Had. Walked. Away.

Carson growled and stormed across the floor, pushing both hands through his hair. "How could she think that I would lie to her about something like that?" he ground out. "After all we've been through together? I was *completely* honest with her the other day, and yet she believes someone she doesn't even know over me."

His door flew open. "What did you do?" Brook snapped.

"Me?" Carson put a hand to his chest. "Are you kidding?" He waved toward the door. "She came accusing me of cheating behind her back with Emme. *Emme!* Of all the stupid..."

"Wait, wait, wait... Who's Emme?" Brook asked.

"My neighbor," Carson said. "The one who showed up the other day out of the blue."

"You mean the beautiful blonde who seems to think she has some kind of claim to you?"

"Yeah. That one." Carson plopped in the seat again and put his head in his hands.

"The one you specifically told me to keep Belle away from?" Brook pressed.

"Yep. That one." Carson was getting tired of this line of questioning.

"The one that you *didn't want Belle to know about*?"

"Yes, Brook!" Carson shouted. "That one!"

Brook folded her arms over her chest and leaned her shoulder into the doorframe. "Are you hearing yourself, Car? You tried to *hide* Emme. Can you blame Belle for being upset about that?"

"What's going on?" Grayson asked, coming up to join his wife. "Why all the shouting?"

"Your wife is poking her nose into my business," Carson sneered. He was done. He had never felt such emotional whiplash. One moment he couldn't wait to see Belle because he knew for certain he was ready to give everything to her, and the next she was walking away after calling him a cheat and a liar.

"Watch it," Grayson said with a scowl.

"Your brother broke Belle's heart and refuses to admit it was his fault," Brook said over the top of the men's argument.

"How is it my fault?" Carson demanded, jumping to his feet. "She should trust me!"

"You tried to lie to her," Brook retorted. "It's hard to trust the person who's keeping things from you."

"I didn't lie to her."

"A beautiful woman showed up at the house, wanting to see you, and you brushed it under the rug," Brook said, throwing her arms to the side. "How is that not lying?"

"Not true." Carson walked toward his sister-in-law. "I told Belle to ask me anything about the situation."

"*After* she caught you speaking to Emme."

"Emme. Who's Emme?" Grayson inserted.

"His neighbor," Brook explained.

"Your neighbor." Grayson turned to Carson. "Your neighbor from California? What's she doing in Oregon?"

Carson threw his head back and groaned. "Why is my life such a mess?"

"Because you hurt the person you love." Brook's words were soft, but poignant.

Slowly, Carson brought his head back to rights and looked at her. "How do you know I love her?"

Brook shrugged. "It's written all over your face every time you see her." She smiled softly. "I've never seen you get so excited to spend time with a woman before."

"You ought to know." Carson snorted. "You've tried to set me up with enough of them."

Brook huffed a sarcastic laugh. "It was only because I wanted you to experience what you're feeling."

"Anger and heartache?"

She pursed her lips and gave him an unimpressed look. "The elation of knowing there's someone out there meant just for you."

Carson turned sideways and collapsed on his bed. "But I don't have that anymore, do I?"

"So do something about it," Brook said.

"Do what?" Carson raised his head. "She walked away from me. She's the one who said goodbye." He pounded his chest. "She's the one who didn't trust me."

"How well do you know her?" Grayson asked, reminding Carson he had a bigger audience than he wanted.

"What do you mean?" Carson propped himself up on his elbows.

Grayson shrugged. "If she so easily distrusted you, the thing to do would be to figure out why."

Carson narrowed his eyes. "Since when did you become a psychologist?"

"Since I had a brother who asks questions for a living," Grayson retorted. "If you were representing someone like her in court, what would you say led to her behavior?"

Carson paused and swallowed hard. He had to give Grayson credit. He had certainly gotten to the heart of the matter rather quickly.

It hurt that Belle hadn't believed him, true. But despite Carson's deep feelings, they hadn't known each other all that long, and with a background of trust issues and lying husbands, Belle might have a good reason for her struggles.

It had been foolish of Carson to think that a couple of euphoric dates and mind-blowing kisses would be enough to erase years of hurt and emotional abuse. He had known from the beginning that winning Belle's heart would take time, but when she'd been so favorable to his advances, Carson had forgotten his vow to move at her pace.

Now he'd scared her off by demanding she give something he hadn't yet earned. Brook was right. The situation with Emme had been handled badly. In his efforts to get rid of Emme, he'd made it seem like he was hiding something, rather than allowing Belle to understand the whole situation.

Now Emme had apparently taken advantage of that, and was using Carson's idiocy to her advantage. He knew her kind. She had probably told a completely believable story, one that apparently included details of Carson's life that Belle hadn't known.

He groaned and let his head flop back. "She might have been cheated on in the past and now has trust issues," he said softly.

"Oh, Car," Brook said softly. "No wonder she's so skittish."

"So what are you going to do about it?" Grayson asked.

"Honestly? I'm not sure," Carson responded.

"So you're going to let her go?"

Carson shook his head. "No. I can't do that. At least, not until she knows the truth and still walks away. But I'm not sure how to handle it yet." He sat up. "The first thing is probably to find Emme and get her out of town. If she's hanging around, anything I tell Belle is going to continue to seem bogus."

Grayson nodded. "All right. Why don't we call Ken and go from there."

Carson nodded. "It's a start."

CHAPTER 22

Belle wove the plastic spoon through the air and eventually landed it in her nephew's mouth, only to have him clamp his teeth and refuse to let go. "Come on, buddy," she whined. "I can't get you any more until you open."

She wiggled it back and forth until finally pulling the utensil free.

"Sorry," Sofia called from her place at the stove. "It's been his favorite thing lately."

Belle shrugged, her eyes on the bowl of chunky applesauce. "It's fine." A few moments went by with Belle managing to get another bite in Cole's mouth without him snapping the spoon in half.

"When are you going to tell me what's going on?" Sofia asked, slipping into the seat next to Belle.

Belle made sure she never looked away from Cole. After all, who knew what a kid like him would do if left unsupervised. "I don't know what you mean."

"Belle...I'm a mother, not an idiot."

Belle jerked her head toward Sofia. "I never said you were an idiot, or that mothers were."

Sofia smirked and tilted her head to the side. "I know. But I also knew that would get your attention. You've been working a little too hard to stay away from me."

Belle went back to feeding the now protesting Cole. She sighed. "I'm not sure what to say."

"How about you start at the beginning."

Belle stretched her neck. She really did want to talk to someone, but Sofia was her sister-in-law. What if she told Rich? Rich would be so ticked and would probably ream Belle for falling for a movie star's brother in the first place.

"I won't tell him."

Belle jerked her head up. "What?"

Sofia's smirk was still firmly in place. "I don't have to tell Rich. I don't keep much from him, but this is your life, and that means you choose who gets to hear about it. I should have done that from the beginning." Sofia raised a single eyebrow. "Unless I feel like you're in danger."

Belle shook her head. "I'm not in any danger."

"Okay. Then tell me why you've been looking on the verge of tears since yesterday."

Another sigh escaped Belle's lips. She was starting to understand those women in romance novels who went about acting all dramatic and stupid when they got their hearts broken. Dale had done a number on Belle, but falling in love as a mature, adult woman was breaking her in different ways. This one hadn't been based on overeager, teenage love. Carson had captured her in a different way. He had used wit and humor, not hormones. "Carson has a fiance."

There, she said it. Belle managed a glance at Sofia and cringed. Her sister-in-law's mouth had dropped and her eyes were wide enough to rival a Disney princess.

"You can't be serious."

Belle nodded. "Deadly."

"What did he say?" Sofia demanded.

"He says it's not true."

Sofia twitched, then held up her hand. "Wait... What?"

"I ran into a woman named Emme at the grocery store," Belle explained. "She introduced herself as Carson's fiance."

"And you believed her?"

Belle made a face. "I had seen her before! She showed up at Brook and Grayson's house when we were having the tree decorating competition. She and Carson talked out in the driveway, but I saw them through the kitchen window, and after it was over, Carson didn't want me to know about it."

"So he lied about her being there? His own fiance? And she was okay with that?" Sofia put a hand to her chest. "What kind of soap opera did you walk into?"

Despite the situation, Belle's lips twitched. "He told me she was someone he knew from back home and then promised I had nothing to worry about."

Sofia paused, then leaned on the table, her hands folded together. "What exactly did you see in the driveway?"

"Them talking."

"Did they kiss? Hug? Did they look affectionate with each other at all?"

Belle let her mind go back to the scene. She hadn't wanted to watch it, but at the time it had been like a car wreck and she had been unable to look away. "No," she admitted, a little sheepishly. "They were talking from several feet apart and they never touched."

Sofia frowned. "And she told you they were engaged?"

Belle nodded.

"Did you meet her when she showed up at the house?"

"No."

"Then how did this woman know who you were?"

Belle opened her mouth, then paused. "I...don't know." Her eyebrows pulled together. "Come to think of it, she didn't say my name. She simply introduced herself and then announced she was Carson's fiance."

"Then tell me why...out of all the people in the grocery store, would this woman come to *you*?"

Belle had no answer. It was a legitimate question, one which hadn't bothered to cross that mature, logical mind that Belle had been so proud of yesterday.

"Belle, sweetie." Sofia reached out and put a hand on Belle's arm. "Do you think she could have been lying?"

"But why would she do that?" Belle asked.

Cole squawked, apparently finished, and Sofia jumped to her feet. "Hold that thought." She grabbed a graham cracker out of the cupboard and handed it to her son, who was now content once again, before sitting down. "I don't know, especially since you hadn't met her before." Sofia tapped the table with her finger. "I'm assuming you confronted Carson, since you said he denied it."

Belle nodded as she bit her bottom lip. She was starting to think she had made a terrible mistake. Things had been so heated between her and Carson yesterday... Could she have jumped to conclusions? Did she miss something important that would prove his innocence? Would he ever consider letting her apologize if that was the case? "I did," Belle said in a small voice.

"And his explanation was?"

"He said she was his neighbor and had followed him up here because she wouldn't take no for an answer."

Sofia made a face. "That's pretty weak."

"That's what I thought, as well," Belle said.

"But her story doesn't make sense either."

Belle dropped her chin to her chest. "What's wrong with me?" she mumbled. "Why am I always falling for the wrong thing?" Tears which Belle had hoped had been stopped forever, broke free and she covered her face with her hands.

"Oh, hon." Sofia stood and wrapped her arms around her sister-in-law. "We'll get this figured out. Don't worry. And there's nothing wrong with you. You've just been the victim of some cruel and horrible people. But that's their problem, not yours."

Belle sniffed. "I feel like that's the kind of talk you give a kid in middle school."

Sofia pulled back and smiled down at Belle. "And yet it still holds true. There's a reason we learn our life lessons in kindergarten."

Belle shook her head. "If he was telling the truth, he'll never forgive me."

"If he loves you, he will," Sofia assured her.

Belle, however, wasn't convinced.

"Don't make decisions for him," Sofia scolded. "He deserves the chance to clean this up and to decide what he wants to do moving forward, same as you."

Belle nodded. "You're right."

"Darn tootin'," Sofia said with a wink. "And that is why being a mother means I'm anything but dumb."

*****

"Has she threatened you in any way?" Ken asked.

Carson rolled his eyes. "I can see where this is going, you know."

Ken leaned back in his seat. "Then why are you here?"

Carson huffed and folded his arms over his chest. "Because I had hoped that there was some law in Oregon I wasn't aware of that would give me some rights."

Ken made a face. "I'm sorry I'm not more help."

"I know." Carson scrubbed his face. "But how in the world do I deal with her?"

"The great lawyer doesn't know what to do?" Ken chuckled. "I didn't think I'd ever see the day where you were out of words, Carson."

Carson gave Ken a stern look. "Believe me, they disappear just when it matters most."

"Uh-oh." Ken shook his head. "That sounds like woman trouble." He put his hands in the air. "And I am definitely not the right person to talk to about that."

"Wasn't planning on it."

Ken wiped imaginary sweat from his forehead, then leaned forward on his desk. "But seriously. What are you going to do?"

Carson scratched his jawline. "I'm not sure. Emme is going around telling lies, but they aren't the kind I can hit her with slander for. Saying we're engaged doesn't hurt my reputation in a way that I can use in court." He shrugged. "It makes her sound delusional, but no one is going to charge her with anything for saying that."

"Agreed." Ken tapped his desk. "But if her lies are keeping you from the woman you *do* want, there has to be a way to get her to stop." He made a face. "You could try a cease and desist."

"That's usually geared toward illegal business practices."

Ken shrugged. "I'm sure you could come up with some fancy legalese that'll make it sound legit."

"Her father is a lawyer," Carson pointed out. "I doubt she'll be fooled that easily."

"Really?" Ken rubbed the back of his neck. "Well, shoot. That does make it harder."

"In fact, I would bet she knows exactly what she's doing." The more Carson thought about it, the more sure he was. She had to know exactly where the line between legal and illegal was and she was skirting it in a way that gave Carson no logical course of making her stop. He slapped his knees. "Thanks for your time, Ken. I think I'll head out and see what I can figure out."

Ken stood and offered his hand. "Sorry I can't do more. But if I happen to see someone matching her description, I'll be sure to keep an eye out."

"Appreciate it. Thanks." Carson left the police station feeling dejected, but not ready to give up. He was a lawyer for crying out loud! There had to be something he could do, even if it meant being a little...creative.

"Hello, Carson."

He stopped, closed his eyes to keep from strangling the woman behind him, then slowly spun. "Emme."

Her smile was annoyingly smug. "Been having fun with your family stuff?"

Carson glowered. "How did you know who Belle was?"

Her eyebrows went up. "Belle? Who's that?" She frowned and tapped her bottom lip. "I thought your sister-in-law was Brook."

"This isn't funny, Emme," Carson said curtly. "You need to stay away from her."

"I don't even know who she is." Emme's eyes were wide. "How can I stay away from someone I don't know?"

"Should we head to her house?" Carson snapped. "Should I ask Belle if she's ever seen you before?"

"Sure." Emme smiled. "Why don't we ride together?"

He threw up his hands. "What do you want?" he shouted, drawing some attention from the people on the street. Carson dropped his voice, but his tone stayed angry. "Why are you here? I already told you I'm not interested in you, so why are you hanging around?"

Emme's sweet facade slowly faded. "I don't think you understand," she said, her voice barely above a whisper. "I intend to be part of the Cordova family and with Grayson married, the only way in is..." She grinned. "You." Her smile faded. "Now...I haven't bothered to involve my father as of yet. I had hoped you would simply choose to be cooperative." She leaned in conspiratorially. "However, you should know that he never denies me anything..."

Carson's jaw clenched and he felt a muscle in his neck begin to pulse. "I'm not interested." He turned and began to walk away.

"Not interested enough to lose your job?"

He paused, then turned. "Are you threatening me, Emme?" He smirked. "Because there's a good reason your father hired me." He walked toward Emme, trying to be strong without making anyone worry he was going to hurt her. The last thing he needed was some eye witness saying he was making threatening stances in public. "I'm a good lawyer," he said in a quiet tone. "I know the law forward and back, and if your father tries to fire me because you were finally told 'no' for once in your life, I'll slap the firm so hard with a wrongful termination suit, it'll put them out of business."

Emme's confidence never wavered. "You would have...in the past. But now your heart is involved." She tilted her head. "Isn't it?"

Carson frowned. "What do you mean?"

"I saw the way you looked at that pathetic, little tramp," Emme said tightly, showing the first signs of anything other than cool smugness. "I'm willing to bet that if Belle's future was involved, you'd definitely be willing to see things my way."

"Explain." Carson was lost as to how Emme had any control of Belle's future. The woman wanted to open a bakery, and had no plans of moving to California. What could Emme do?

Emme studied her nails. "I heard she had a nasty divorce a few years back. It would be a shame if her ex-husband went public with information that might hurt her credibility...especially if she's looking for a loan any time soon." Her blue eyes flickered up to Carson's from under thick, black lashes. "I heard he's got quite a following online... How embarrassing for her if any dirty laundry was aired."

"Leave her out of this," Carson ground out.

"Not until you're a good little boy and do as you're told," Emme said with a smile that was in complete defiance of the disgusting threat she was giving.

"I won't play your game," Carson said, backing up. "I also won't let you hurt Belle. You go after her, and you're finished. Do you hear me? I won't stop until I've ruined you, your father, and every person who associates with you. Your plush little life will be gone to the point that you won't even be able to afford a manicure."

He must have finally been getting through to her because Emme's face was tight and her cheeks were bright red, despite the flawless tan. "That's the way you want to play this?" she asked.

Carson nodded. "That's the way I want to play it," he lied as he walked away. In truth, he wanted to take Belle and run. The idea of her reputation and dreams being in jeopardy made him sick to his stomach. She didn't deserve any of this, but Carson also wasn't going to back down. Emme had already done a heck of a job playing on Belle's mistrust of men, leaving Carson a long row to hoe if he was going to fix it, but he'd seen this scenario before. He wasn't going to let Emme win, holding this cloud over his head for the rest of their lives.

Belle would never be out of danger, as long as Emme thought the threat would work. So...Carson wasn't going to let it work. He'd be watching the news outlets for her next move, and if Belle's name came up at all, he'd end this once and for all.

CHAPTER 23

Belle thought she had been heartbroken before, but it was nothing compared to now. Two more days had passed. Two more days of not seeing Carson and not knowing if she had been wrong to walk away. At first she had been filled with righteous indignation, but as that had ebbed, followed by Sofia's questions...Belle had sunken lower than a deflated souffle.

Her mind was stuck in a whirlpool so deep she had burned her muffins yesterday while preparing for yet another holiday party and Mrs. Stallings had sent her home.

"You're pale and look ready to collapse," the older woman had said with a concerned look on her face. "Perhaps a day off would do you good. Come back tomorrow in time to serve at the party."

Despite needing every hour she could get, Belle had nodded and trudged home without a single ounce of complaint. She spent more time in her bed than she had when she had finally managed to divorce Dale. This situation, with a man she had only known for a few weeks, had set her back far more than a man she had been married to for five years.

With a groan, Belle shook her head and went back to work. They were heading out to a gig in an hour and despite the music playing on the speaker and the red and green decorations on all the cookies, she was anything but merry and jolly.

Grabbing the jar of sprinkles, Belle began dripping a few of them over the wet icing, wishing fixing her life was as easy as fixing the cookies.

"You feeling better?" Corey asked as he walked past.

Belle forced a nod and a smile. "Sure."

He frowned and brought the tray from his shoulder so he was holding it in front of his body. "What's wrong, Belle? Like, really. What's wrong?"

"We don't care," April sang out. "Leave your home life at home."

Belle rolled her eyes and shook her head at Corey. "Don't worry about it. I just did something dumb."

"Then fix it," he said, hoisting the tray again and starting to walk away.

"If only," Belle grumbled.

"You never know until you try," Corey shouted across the room.

"Seriously!" April snapped. "I don't want to hear it!"

"Don't worry," Belle said as she started to frost the next batch of cookies. "I don't really want to share."

"Poor Belle," April said. "Pining over a movie star she can't have."

Belle paused, then slowly looked up. "Excuse me?"

April curled her lip. "The entire town knows that you've been dating Grayson Cordova's brother."

Belle put her hands on her hips. "So what's that to you? I don't recall it bursting your balloon in any way."

April huffed. "Like I would want anything to do with a man who dates one woman while he's engaged to another."

"Where did you hear that?" Belle asked, stepping around the work table.

"Whoa!" Corey said. "That's quite an accusation."

April held her chin up as Belle approached, but she looked slightly nervous and Belle calmed her body language. "Where did you hear that?" Belle asked more softly.

"I was there," April said tightly. "At the grocery store when that woman told you she was engaged to your *boyfriend*."

"And?"

"And what?" April asked, making a face.

"And how do you know she was telling the truth?"

That caused April to hesitate. "I...I don't," she said carefully. "But why would she lie about it?"

Corey came up beside them. "I'm so lost." He looked at Belle. "Did he lie to you? Do I need to pull out the pythons and defend your honor?"

Belle held up a hand. "I'm not even going to ask what the pythons are—"

Corey held up his arm and flexed it. "I have two of them."

"Oh my word." April groaned, slapping her forehead.

Belle's lips twitched a little, but she kept moving forward. "No one needs to defend anyone, but I think it's possible the woman was lying."

April shook her head. "But why? You still haven't told me why someone would do that."

Because sometimes other people get jealous and just want to ruin anyone else's chance at happiness. The words were on the tip of Belle's tongue, but she bit them back. April was difficult to work with and definitely wasn't someone Belle wanted as a bestie, but for her to be as snarky as she was, Belle was starting to understand that some-times people were prickly because life had forced them to put up their dukes just to survive. Belle should know... She had been exactly like that until Carson had helped her start to soften again. "I'm not sure," Belle said. "Carson told me she followed him from California. That she's not very good at taking no for an answer."

"How do you know Carson isn't the one lying?" April looked a little too smug.

Belle shook her head. "I don't. But I don't know Emme. I *do* know Carson." As soon as she said the words, she felt the truth ring inside of her. How could she have been so blind? Why had she need-ed her sister-in-law to point out that Carson was a good person?

"Then why have you been walking around like a zombie for the past few days?" Corey inserted.

Belle tucked a piece of hair back into her hairnet. "Remember how I said I had done something stupid?"

April laughed and shook her head. "You really have been pining! After that whole speech about knowing him, you didn't believe him, did you?"

Belle nodded. "I made a mistake."

"And I told you to fix it," Corey repeated. He folded his arms over his chest. "Why is this so hard?"

"Would you want to take back a woman who walked away, thinking you were a cheater?"

Corey tilted his head back and forth. "Well...I can't say I wouldn't be hurt, but if I loved her, then I would be willing to work it out."

Belle shook her head. "He doesn't love me."

"What makes you say that?" he asked.

"He's never said it."

Corey rolled his eyes and patted Belle's head. "We've got to get to work. But that answer is *way* dumber than you walking away because you had a moment of panic."

"Is there something you all want to share?" Mrs. Stallings called from her office door. "Or is gossip a new ingredient I should know about?"

"Sorry!" Belle called out as she rushed back to her station.

The others also called out their apologies and everyone went back to work, but Belle's mind definitely didn't settle down at all. *I know him...* The words wouldn't leave her head. She did know him. She didn't know Emme.

Slowly, Belle's confusion drained from her and determination settled in its place. She had to make this right. She wasn't convinced that Corey's vague response was right and that Carson was in love with her, but Belle knew she wanted to find out.

It would have to wait until after her gig tonight, but tomorrow, first thing, she was going to approach Carson and beg for forgiveness. The more she thought about it, the more she realized that risking her pride was more than worth the possibility of a future with Carson. *I know him.* She did. And he was worth the risk.

*****

Brook wiped her mouth with a napkin and set it on the table. "Okay, Carson. It's time to fill us all in."

Carson froze with the fork halfway to his mouth. "Uh…"

She gave him a look. "What's going on with Belle? And that other girl… What was her name?"

Carson set down the bite of rice he was about to eat and huffed. "Emme."

"Wait? Who?" Caro called out from the other side of the table. "I thought Belle was your date the other day."

"She was."

"But there are two women?"

Carson shook his head as chatter broke out around the table. They'd ended the day by having a large family dinner, which the women had all worked on together, leaving the men to watch a basketball game while their wives cooked up a storm. It had been very pleasant, until this very moment. "No. It's just Belle."

Caro pointed her fork at Brook. "Then what were you saying about another one?"

"Maybe if you'd stop asking questions, Carson would be able to answer that," Charli said wryly. She winced and rubbed her stomach. "I think we have a soccer player on our hands," she grumbled.

"Or maybe he's telling you to hush and not interrupt," Caro said with a saccharine sweet smile.

"Ladies, the hormones are getting a little intense," Benny called out. He ducked and grabbed his wife's hand when she tried to smack him. With a grin, he kissed her palm.

Ally rolled her eyes, but smiled and didn't try to hit him again.

"Risking getting smacked myself," Gray said, leaning back from the table, "I'd also like to hear what's going on." His eyes darted to Ken, who sat across from Benny. "I haven't heard what happened since you spoke to Ken."

Carson let out a long breath. "So...there's not much we can do, legally speaking," he began. "But..." He scratched the edge of his chin. He hadn't told anyone about his run-in with Emme. After their confrontation, he hadn't seen her around and had hoped it was all going away, though he still had his eye on the streaming media.

"But what?" Caro demanded. "Don't keep a pregnant woman waiting like that."

"Sweetheart, what does being pregnant have to do with anything?" Jack asked with a chuckle.

"Shh!" Caro held up her hand. "I'm milking this for all it's worth. Don't rain on my parade."

Carson shook his head, amused but frustrated. "I ran into Emme after leaving the station."

"You didn't tell me that!" Brook gasped.

Ken straightened. "What happened?" he asked in his official tone.

Rose put a hand on his arm. "Let him speak," she said firmly.

Carson nodded his thanks at Rose. It was so weird having so many people invested in his life. Usually it was just his brother and his sister. Carson wasn't quite sure if he enjoyed having such a big group of people watching his every move. "I don't think I need to go over everything we spoke about, but it ended with her threatening Belle and me telling her that if she endangered Belle in any way, I would sue her until even her grandchildren were poverty stricken."

The table erupted and Carson sat back. Normally he enjoyed causing a little ruckus, but this time he wasn't as keen on creating mischief. This was his and Belle's lives, and Carson wasn't enjoying the yo-yo motions of their relationship at the moment.

Jude had been completely silent up until now, but he leaned in and whispered. "Remind me not to cross threats with you."

Carson smirked and huffed a small laugh. "I'll warn you next time I'm feeling ornery."

"But seriously," Jude continued. "What's even going on with you and Belle? I thought you broke up?"

Carson rubbed the back of his neck as the table continued to argue and shout over each other. He'd seen this group respond this way before and knew they'd calm down in a minute and then some serious brainstorming would occur. They were nothing if not predictable. "We did...sort of. She believed something Emme told her, but I've decided I'm not willing to let it go at that. I'm working on a way to get her back, but dealing with Emme has slowed me down."

Jude nodded thoughtfully. "What did she threaten to do?"

"I think we'd all like to know that." Ken's voice was loud enough to cut through the fighting and the table slowly calmed down. Ken had stood up and walked over to their side of the table, standing directly behind Gray and Brook. "What kind of threat was it?" he asked. "Is it something we can use to build a restraining order?"

Carson shook his head. "No. It wasn't concrete enough. Plus, it wasn't directed at me." Carson leaned back. "She hinted at getting a hold of Belle's ex and having him 'leak' some juicy tidbits from their married life. Stuff that would ruin her chances of ever getting a loan in order to start her own business."

"She wants to start a business?" Hadlee said with a smile. "What does she do?"

Leave it to Felix's wife to focus on good. She was one of the kindest people Carson had ever met, though he wasn't as close with Felix as he had become with Ken and a few of the others. "She wants to open a bakery." He looked at Caro. "One that sells bread. French breads, like croissants, are her specialty."

Caro slapped the tabletop. "Please tell me those pain a chocolats were hers at the opening party."

Carson nodded proudly. "They were."

"Will she sell me the recipe?"

Carson shook his head. "Nope. They're top secret. Guards them tighter than Fort Knox."

Caro grumbled, then shouted, "She's hired," like an auction engineer.

"She wants her own place," Charli argued.

"Maybe so, but she has to start somewhere," Caro said. "She can start in our shop and maybe eventually she can work out being next door and we can share customers." Caro leaned in. "I heard the bookstore is headed out of business."

"Oh, how sad," Rose said with a frown.

Caro nodded. "Yeah, but Mrs. Gordon is, like, ninety years old. I'm surprised it's lasted as long as it has, especially since she hasn't brought in a new book since *A Hitchhiker's Guide to the Galaxy* was released."

The table broke out in chuckles, but Carson shrugged. "I have no idea how she'd feel about that, but you can ask her."

"You don't want to?" Caro pressed.

Carson could feel his cheeks getting hot. "I'm still working on getting her to speak to me."

"Been there."

Carson had no idea who said the words, since they echoed around the room from multiple sources. He grinned, realizing that no one else in the room had had a smooth path to love either. Perhaps he wasn't quite as alone as he thought. He turned to Jude. "Are you still leaving tomorrow?"

Jude pinched his lips together and shrugged. "I'm not sure. You?"

Carson shook his head. "No. I'm here until the new year for sure. I'm just hoping it ends up being worth it."

Jude slapped him on the back. "I'm sure you'll work it out. Belle seemed really nice." He hesitated. "You're sure she's the one? You haven't known her long."

Carson nodded. "I'm sure. Now I just need to convince her of that."

"Good luck, man."

Carson nodded. "Thanks. I'm gonna need it."

CHAPTER 24

"Oh my gosh, yessss..." Belle sighed as she opened the oven door. After deciding she was going to do everything she could to win Carson back, she had decided that food should definitely be part of that plan.

Her original plan of the apple pie had come back to the forefront and Belle had spent the morning creating the whole thing from scratch. After the time had gone out, she had opened the oven and was now pulling the masterpiece from the oven, her lungs filling with the sweet, warm scents of cinnamon and sugar. It was perfect.

"Now I just have to hope my meeting with Carson is as well," Belle mumbled to herself.

With the pie on a cooling rack, she took off the oven gloves and grabbed her phone. So far she hadn't had the courage to text him, but there was nothing else to take up her time now. She had another party tonight and in a couple hours would have to go to work, so meeting with Carson was now or never.

"Please say that's for us," Rich said as he came through the front door, sniffing the air.

"Touch it and you die," Belle sang out, smiling sweetly at her brother.

Rich scowled. "It's for him, isn't it?"

Belle's smile fell and she nodded. "I hope so."

Rich sighed and scratched the back of his head. "Does he know how lucky he is?"

Belle smiled. "You'll have to ask him that, but I think if I can convince him to take me back, I'll be the lucky one."

Rich smiled reluctantly. "You're sure about this? Somehow I don't see you chasing after a guy you only have a small crush on."

Belle wrung her hands together. She hadn't actually said the words out loud yet, though she'd been thinking them right before the big fight. "I think I love him, Rich," she admitted in a hoarse whisper. "And I'm just as terrified as I am excited." She pinched her lips between her teeth. "What if I'm wrong? What if I still haven't learned to pick a good one?"

Rich walked across the kitchen, pulling Belle into his chest. Her cheek squished against his nametag from work, but she didn't care, instead throwing her arms around his chest and holding tight. Rich wasn't exactly the type to show a lot of emotion and he'd been extremely careful around her after the situation with Dale.

She wasn't sure if it was because she was younger than him or if he was just giving her space, but Belle was extremely grateful for him, and it occurred to her she'd never really told him that. "Thank you," she said into his flannel shirt.

Rich leaned back. "For what?"

"For letting me crash at your house. For not telling me I was crazy when I wanted to go back to school. For not going all caveman on me when I started dating someone I had no business dating." She shrugged. "You know. For being my brother."

He grinned. "Does this mean I get the apple pie?"

Belle slapped his chest. "No. I'll make you another one tomorrow."

"Why can't you make him one tomorrow?" Rich whined.

"Because." Belle turned away and grabbed her phone off the table, working up her nerve.

"Because isn't a good reason," Rich argued.

"You're a parent," Belle said, still looking at her screen. "I'm sure you'll find yourself using it soon."

Grumbling, Rich grabbed a glass of water. "I gotta hurry and get back to the store," he said, setting down the empty glass.

"Why are you here?"

Rich scowled. "I need lunch too, ya know."

Belle grinned. "What's the matter? Sofia didn't pack one for you this morning?" Belle burst into laughter when Rich glared at her. "Let me guess... The little guy stole the show."

"Not even two and he's already taking over my wife," Rich complained.

Still laughing, Belle started to walk out of the kitchen. She needed somewhere quiet in order to send her text. "I'll only remind you one more time, touch that pie and you die!"

"Too late! My germs are all over it," Rich hollered back.

Belle smiled and shook her head. Taking a deep breath, she pulled up Carson's name. She wasn't quite brave enough to speak to him on the phone, but she could send him a text and let him have a chance to think about things before answering her.

If you have the time, I'd like to have a chance to speak to you.

Belle's thumb hesitated for a long time before pressing 'send'. It wasn't really the most elegant of sentences, but she wasn't sure what else to tell him. She didn't want to pressure him into talking to her, but she did want a chance to speak. Hopefully what little she sent gave him enough wiggle room to make his own choices.

Stuffing her phone in her pocket, she headed upstairs to get ready for work. It would help distract her while she waited for Carson to answer. It would probably take him a while to do so since they'd hadn't spoken to each other in several days and their last conversation hadn't exactly been friendly.

Just as she went to step into her room, the phone beeped and Belle froze. Her heart immediately began to pound against her chest and Belle put a hand to her stomach, which began to churn.

With a shaking hand, she reached into her pocket and pulled it out. "It's probably not even him," she told herself, trying to convince her body to calm down, but the words didn't work. Somehow she just *knew* that it was his response. But if it had happened this quick, odds were it wasn't the response Belle was going to be hoping for.

Promise me there'll be no mace involved and I'll meet you anytime, anywhere.

A broken sob broke through and Belle put a hand over her mouth. "You're too good for me, Carson Cordova," she whispered. Belle jumped slightly when she heard the front door open and realized that Sofia had arrived home with Cole. The house was about to get noisy and busy.

Lunging into her room, Belle closed the door and sat down on the edge of the bed. She didn't want an audience while she spoke to Carson.

No mace. But I do have a surprise for you.

She bit her lips while she waited, giddiness running rampant through her system.

Does this surprise involve Irish butter?

A girlish giggle broke through her lips and Belle had no way of holding back a ridiculously wide smile.

No, but it does have butter from grass fed cows.

Close enough. Name the time and place.

Belle considered her options. She could say right now, but if things went well, she'd be late to work and leaving him would be horrible, even if it was only for a few hours.

I work tonight. Can you meet me outside Harrigan's at nine thirty?

With bells on.

Belle set her phone down and ran for the shower. She might have to dress in her uniform tonight, but she definitely wanted to spend a little extra time on her makeup and hair. She was going to need all the extra help she could get.

*****

"Who put that stupid smile on your face?" Gray asked, smirking at his brother from the other side of the couch.

Carson tried to calm down and act more cool, but he just couldn't do it. The text from Belle had come out of nowhere and had saved him the trouble of trying to figure out how to start a conversation between them.

"Car..."

Carson turned his head to look at his brother. The game they were watching was still playing, but Grayson had turned the sound down. "Belle asked if we could meet."

Gray's eyebrows went up. "And?'

Carson shrugged. "And I said yes."

"Do you know what she wants?" Grayson scooted closer. "Is she hoping to patch things up?"

Carson shook his head. "I can't be sure, but it sounded promising."

"When are you planning to meet her?" Gray pushed a hand through his hair. "Don't forget we're all driving down to the movies tonight. That theatre down south is playing *It's a Wonderful Life* and Brook wanted everyone to go."

"Crap." Carson made a face. "The official party is over. Will she care if I don't go?"

Gray pursed his lips. "What do you think?"

Carson huffed and threw his head back on the couch. "What time is the showing?"

"Seven."

Carson's foot bounced. "Maybe I can just drive my own car and leave a little early. Belle's working tonight and asked me to meet her at nine-thirty."

"I think the movie is close to two hours, so yeah, you'll have to leave early to get back in time."

"We can just make sure I'm seated on the end," Carson said decidedly. "I'll sneak out when Brook's busy."

"Your funeral," Gray said.

"If it comes down to dealing with an unhappy Brook or an unhappy Belle, I'm pleasing Belle every time," Carson shot back.

Gray grinned. "Then it looks like your priorities are in the right spot." He slapped Carson's shoulder. "Brook will understand, but I'm sure she'll appreciate it if you can come for some of it."

"What is it about that movie that women love so much?" Carson grumbled. "It's old, and colorless, and about a dead guy."

"A dead guy who gets his life back." Grayson gave him a significant look. "Sounds like someone else I know."

Carson scowled. "Yeah...like you never did anything stupid when you were dating Brook."

Gray blew out a breath. "Yeah...let's not go there."

"Fine by me." Carson turned back to the television, but he couldn't concentrate on the game. His mind wouldn't leave Belle and what she might want to talk about. She had responded to his flirting. Surely that was a good sign. And if she didn't still feel like hitting him in the face with a can of mace, then maybe she'd calmed down enough to listen to reason.

The more time he had to think, the more Carson understood why Belle would have been suspicious. And Carson's angry response certainly hadn't helped anything. He should have calmly addressed her concerns instead of getting offended and angry that she apparently didn't return his strong feelings.

He knew from the beginning she was going to fall more slowly than him. Why couldn't he have remembered that when it mattered most?

"Are you going to take anything?"

Carson jumped at the comment. "What do you mean?"

"Usually a girl appreciates a gift when a guy is apologizing." Grayson stuffed a handful of popcorn into his mouth, not even looking at Carson.

"Shoot." Carson jumped to his feet. "You're right. But what do I get her?"

"Doesn't Rose run a flower shop?"

The words had barely left Gray's mouth before Carson was out of the room. He raced to his room to grab his coat and keys. Hopefully the shop wouldn't be closed yet. It was a Saturday afternoon and he had no idea when a small town like this began to roll up their carpet for the night.

After getting his things, he jogged back to the TV room. "Be back in a bit."

"Don't be late for the movie!" Gray hollered.

"I won't!" Carson shouted back. Pressing a few buttons on his GPS, Carson shot out of the driveway and let out a breath of relief when he saw the open sign on the door. He hurried in, the bell above him ringing as he stepped inside.

"Hi!" a middle aged woman said from behind the desk. She was curling ribbons for small balloon bouquets, but she set it all aside when he approached. "How can I help you today?"

"I'm looking for an arrangement for a woman friend of mine," Carson hedged.

She smiled. "Are you wanting to say anything in particular? Our owner is very into sending flowers that portray the correct message."

Carson considered his options. "Rose doesn't happen to be here, does she?" She would know exactly what Carson needed.

"No, I'm sorry. Mrs. Wamsley is off today."

Carson nodded. "That's all right." He made a face. "I, uh, need to say I'm sorry."

"Ah." The woman nodded thoughtfully. "Anything else?"

"Can flowers say, 'I was an idiot'?"

She laughed. "Not that I know of, but they can portray feelings." Her eyebrows rose. "Anything you'd like to say that way?"

Did he dare take it that far? What if Belle was only meeting in order to cut off anything between them for good? To tell him that she'd realized she should have maced him from the beginning?

Carson shook his head at himself. This was ridiculous. Where did his confidence go? Belle wouldn't have contacted him just to blow everything up in his face.

"Okay, just I'm sorry," the woman said, starting to walk away from the counter.

"Wait," Carson called out. He swallowed hard. "I'd also like to say...I love you."

The woman's smile grew. "I have just the thing."

Carson smiled back. "I'd love to see it."

"Then follow me and we'll put together something perfect."

CHAPTER 25

Belle couldn't seem to stop looking at the clock. This party has been just the same as the dozens of others they had catered over the last few weeks of December, but tonight she was extra antsy.

She wanted to make things right with Carson and she wasn't going to be able to do that until she was done here. "I think the clock is broken," she grumbled as she passed by Corey yet again.

He laughed. "That's funny. I was just thinking about how fast it was going tonight."

Belle gave him a rueful grin. "I guess perspective really does make a difference then, huh?"

"Maybe if you pretended you didn't want to see him, it would go faster?"

Belle shook her head. "If only, if only." She walked down the short hallway with laughter at her back and a tray at her shoulder. Refilling the near empty displays took much less time than she wanted it to and Belle found herself back in the makeshift kitchen, once more looking at the wall.

"A watched pot never boils," Corey reminded her. "Or in this case, a watched clock never moves."

Groaning, Belle threw herself back into work. The only way to survive this was to forget she had a date at all.

Finally, *finally*, after what seemed ages, they were cleaning up. She couldn't seem to wrap the trays fast enough, or load the vans in a quicker manner. But taking a deep breath, Belle forced herself to calm down.

The time to see Carson would come. It might come as slow as a sloth running a marathon, but it would come.

"Belle, I need you and April to help unload tonight," Mrs. Stallings announced as they slammed the back of the van doors shut.

Belle stiffened. "But I helped unload last time." She winced as soon as she said the words. They sounded like her nephew in five years, not a grown woman.

April sneered and jumped into one of the vans.

Mrs. Stallings was just as unimpressed as Belle, herself, had been. "I'll take that into consideration next time," Belle's boss said dryly. "See you at the kitchen."

Belle sighed and tugged on her ponytail. "Sorry. I'll follow you." She headed to her car, frustrated but resigned.

"Absence makes the heart grow fonder, yeah?" Corey asked as he walked away.

"One can only hope." Belle sat down and put the key in the ignition before grabbing her phone. Despite how long the night had felt, she was actually a few minutes ahead of schedule. If she hurried, she might be able to let Carson know about the change in plans.

Have to unload. Meet me at the kitchens?

Belle waited a minute, but Carson didn't respond immediately. Knowing there was little else she could do, she put the car in drive and headed out. She could only pray he got the message before driving to the office building she had worked at tonight. "It's not like it's that far though," she reminded herself. "It'll only take him a couple minutes to change course."

With that in mind, she drove back and began to help unload.

A half-hour later, Belle was on her last nerve. April wasn't fun to work with at the best of times, so with it being just the two of them doing the jobs nobody liked, the evening was not ending on a high note.

"I think that's a wrap," Belle said, wiping her hands on a towel.

April snorted and grabbed her coat and purse before shoving out the backdoor without a glance.

"Nice to work with you too," Belle grumbled as she followed. Her eyes immediately scanned the parking lot and she started to smile when she spotted a vehicle next to hers, but the smile turned into a frown when she realized it wasn't the rental Carson had been driving earlier.

The car door opened and a much smaller, more feminine body stood up. "Belle?"

Belle wasn't one to curse, but at the moment she was tempted to throw every word she knew into the cold evening air. "Emme, right?"

Emme's smile was wide as she came closer to the building and into the streetlight. "You remember me!"

Belle crossed her arms over her chest. "How could I forget?"

Emme laughed and stopped a few feet away. She clasped her hands behind her back and rocked on her heels. "I guess Carson told you that I might have...exaggerated our relationship a little bit?" She looked up from under her eyelashes.

"What's this about, Emme?" Belle said as kindly as she could manage. "I have somewhere to be."

Emme put her hands in the air. "Oh, I know. That's why I'm here." She smiled again. "Carson got delayed. His family went to see a movie and he had a flat tire on his way back." She wiggled her cell. "He said he was struggling to get messages through, but he managed to send one to my phone, asking if I would take you back to his house."

Belle scowled. "Why would he message you and not me?"

Emme shrugged. "I don't know. Maybe mine was the first number on his list?"

Belle could tell Emme was trying to put her in her place again. Now that Belle was almost completely positive that the woman was a liar, the passive aggressiveness in Emme's words was easy to pick out. "I don't believe you."

Emme frowned, looking very much like a small, confused child. "What? Why would I lie to you about something like that?"

Belle shook her head. "Why did you lie to me to begin with? I won't pretend to understand why you're trying to break Carson and me up, but it won't work."

Emme's face turned hard, the young innocent look suddenly gone. "It already has." She sneered. Slowly, she began to stalk toward Belle, who countered by backing up.

"It obviously hasn't," Belle argued. "Otherwise I wouldn't be meeting Carson tonight."

Emme's grin was smug. "Are you? Why is he late then?"

Belle felt her first true stirrings of panic. Why *was* Carson late? She had sent him a message and she was later than she should have been, so why was Carson even later? Was he not coming? Had something happened to him? Was Emme telling her the truth?

"I can see it churning in your head," Emme said, her hands going to her hips. "You're finally starting to realize, aren't you?" She leaned in and dropped her voice. "You're just not good enough." Her eyes went up and down Belle and the look of disgust left Belle feeling unworthy. "The only thing I can think of is that Carson was bored, but otherwise I can't quite figure out what he was doing with you in the first place." Emme tapped her gloved finger against her bottom lip. "You're not his type." Emme tilted her head. "In fact, are you anyone's type? Certainly not a baseball player's...right?"

Belle swallowed back the horrible words she wanted to spew back. Emme was hitting every insecurity Belle had and doing very well. *Obviously, she's had practice.* "I don't need to listen to this," Belle said, frustrated her voice was shaky. "Goodnight, Emme."

"I don't think we're quite done here, Belle."

Belle looked over her shoulder and gaped when she noticed that Emme held a small tool in her hand. Belle rushed to her car and growled. Every tire was flat. She stormed back to Emme. "What do you want?"

Emme's smile was triumphant. "Now we're ready to talk."

*****

Carson slapped his hand against the steering wheel over and over again, willing the little beater he was driving to go faster.

Somehow he had managed to get a flat tire on his expensive rental right in the middle of the biggest deadzone Carson had ever been in. After realizing the rental didn't have a spare, he'd walked to a gas station and done a very good job of utilizing every curse word he'd ever learned in multiple languages while he walked.

After calling a tow, Carson had then waited, his curse words becoming a running montage in his head rather than out loud. Now he was pushing another rental, one he'd paid an exorbitant amount for from the tow company, as fast as the tiny sedan could handle. The curse words had been exchanged with prayer as he hoped that Belle had waited for him, but considering he was going to be close to an hour late, he wasn't holding out too much hope.

It was a miracle that Ken or one of his officers hadn't pulled Carson over, considering he was one of the only cars on the road as he pulled into the parking lot of the office building Belle had sent him. The lot was empty and the building was dark.

Sighing, Carson parked and let his head fall against the steering wheel. He couldn't believe that after all this, Belle wasn't here. This was supposed to be his chance to win her back. The flowers were probably spilled all over the back seat at this point, but Carson had planned all afternoon what he was going to say and how he was going to convince Belle that he wasn't interested in anyone else, that she was the only woman for him, that Emme was a liar and a manipulator... The list went on and on. Someway, somehow, he had to get to Belle.

And now it was too late...at least for tonight.

He grumbled and picked up his phone when it buzzed. It had been going off consistently since he'd come back into cell service. He erased all the email notifications, then saw he had a text. Tapping the button, Carson's heart picked back up and he threw the phone on the seat, tearing out of the parking lot with a vengeance.

Maybe it wasn't as hopeless as he thought. "Hang on, Belle," he whispered. "We need to fix this...and I'm on my way."

The kitchen was only about two minutes away, but it felt like an eternity, but it was what he saw while he was pulling into the parking lot that truly made his heart skip a beat. "You've got to be kidding me," he growled.

Slamming on the brakes, Carson erupted from the car almost before it had locked itself into park. "What do you think you're doing?" he roared, rushing over to the women.

Emme and Belle had been having a heated discussion, but both were now facing him with differing expressions. Emme looked ticked off while Belle looked relieved.

Emme folded her arms over her chest. "Carson. What a surprise seeing you here."

He gave her a sarcastic grin. "What? Thought the flat tire would keep me from interrupting?" From the irritated expression on her face, Carson knew he had guessed right. After finding her here with Belle, he had a gut feeling that she was behind the odd occurrence.

"You slashed his tires as well?"

"As well?" Carson looked to Belle, who looked more beautiful to him than she ever had before. Man, he had missed her. But at the moment, there was something else going on. Her shoulders straightened and her dark eyes grew deeper. A strength she had been lacking before overcame her and it was like watching the first flower of spring turn toward the sun.

"How dare you," Belle seethed.

Emme jerked back, apparently offended. "Excuse me?"

"Who do you think you are?" Belle took a few steps in Emme's direction.

Emme's nose wrinkled. "I told you who I was."

Belle shook her head slowly and Carson found a slow grin creeping across his face.

"What you failed to mention was how pathetic you were."

Emme's jaw dropped. "Me? Pathetic? I'm not the one twenty pounds overweight working for pennies in a hot kitchen all day."

Carson opened his mouth to defend Belle, but she spoke first.

"And I'm not the one who followed a man *uninvited* across state lines, tried to crash his family Christmas party, approached the woman he was dating and lied to scare her off, only to then have to ruin his tires and mine, even though you don't really want Carson." Belle folded her arms over her chest. "You're after Grayson, and yet neither brother wanted you."

Carson bit the inside of his cheek. He had no idea what had come over Belle, but he loved it. She had been so beaten down when he'd found her. Though she had called him out when she thought he was Grayson, she had been slow and hesitant when it came to their relationship, despite the fact that Carson knew she liked him.

But this...this was different. Most of the time, Belle let people overlook her. She let the mean girl at work talk over her and she hid her face when catering an event. She never made the first move when it came to spending time with him, and if Carson didn't have such a strong sense of confidence, he wasn't sure they could have survived as long as they have.

Belle leaned into Emme's space. "Go home," she said softly. "All you're doing is embarrassing yourself at this point."

Emme's face hardened and she raised her hand. The sound of the slap happened before Carson even realized what was going on.

"Whoa!" he cried, lunging forward and grabbing Belle. He tucked her into his chest and almost let out a girly sigh at the contact. It felt so good to hold her. "Are you okay?" he whispered against her hair.

Belle nodded. "Hey, Car?"

"Yeah?"

"Do I have the right to charge her with destruction of property?"

He paused and leaned back. "Are you talking about the slap? You could charge her with harassment."

Belle looked up at him. "And the slashing of my tires?"

"She actually slashed them? Didn't just slow leak it?"

Belle shook her head.

"I'm right here, you know!" Emme screamed.

Carson didn't even turn. She wasn't worth looking at. "If she slashed your tires, then yes. You can do both if you want."

Belle smiled, and he could see that her right cheek was slightly puffy. He needed to get her some ice or something for it. That had to hurt and it made him angry. "Will you help me? I've never done anything like this before."

Carson gave her a tender kiss on her forehead. "Sweetheart, you've got one of California's best lawyers at your disposal. We'll hit her with anything you want."

Emme screeched and began to stomp toward them.

Carson finally turned and held up his hand. "Careful, Emme. Anything you do can only be used farther against you."

She stopped, her breathing puffing out like a bull in the cold night air. Her eyes went back and forth between Carson and Belle before she pointed a finger at him. "This isn't over."

"Belle's right. Go home. You'll be hearing from us."

Emme clenched her teeth, but stomped back to her car and got inside. The squealing of her tires was loud enough to wake the neighborhood and Carson prayed that no one called the police over it. He didn't want to deal with more tonight. He just wanted Belle.

Belle sighed once the noise was gone and looked up at him. "I'm sorry."

Carson frowned. "For what?"

"For all the trouble."

Carson shook his head and took her hand. "Come on. A talk between you and me is long overdue and it will have nothing to do with the crazy little scene we just had."

CHAPTER 26

Belle held tightly to Carson's hand as he led her to his car. She had no idea what she was going to do about her own. There was no way she could afford four new tires at the moment. She'd either have to rely on Sofia and Rich for transportation, or she'd need to borrow money. Belle had no idea which one would be worse.

"Buckle up," he said as she sat down.

Belle rolled her eyes. "Yes, Dad." Her sarcasm was cut off by Carson's mouth.

"There's nothing fatherly about my feelings for you," he whispered against her lips. "But I love you too much to risk even the slightest chance of you getting hurt. Got it?"

A fluttering sensation began in Belle's stomach and she put a hand over it, as if that would control her haywire hormones. "Got it," she whispered back.

That glorious grin of his flashed in the dim light and he closed the door before walking to the driver's seat.

Belle took a few moments to breathe deeply and pull herself together. As her head cleared from the love-induced haze Carson had created, she realized for the first time that they weren't in his fancy sports car.

Carson got in and started the engine.

"Where did you get this?" she asked, noting the worn dashboard and the unhealthy sounds from beneath the hood. Belle bit her lip. This was *not* a Carson type of vehicle. In fact, it reminded her a little of her own and it cracked her up to see her fancy lawyer driving such a dump.

"I rented it from the tow truck company," he grumbled as they pulled out onto the street. "The rental didn't have a spare."

Belle tried to hold it in, she really did, but soon a sputtering laugh was breaking through her compressed lips. She couldn't help it. It was just so opposite of the man she had fallen in love with and from the look of disgust on his face, she knew exactly how he felt about it.

"Laugh it up," Carson warned. "But at least my ride is temporary."

Belle's laughter slowly faded. "True," she said, wiping at her eye. "But don't knock mine too hard. It's paid for."

Carson chuckled. "Considering the one I've been driving is a rental, I suppose you have me there." He pulled into Grayson's driveway and Belle stiffened.

"Aren't they all going to be asleep?" she asked. "I don't want us to disturb anyone."

Carson shook his head. "They probably aren't home yet. But even if they are, there're plenty of spaces in the house where we can talk without disturbing anyone."

Belle nodded, but was still a little nervous. She just wasn't as comfortable with this level of living. *But if you stick with Carson, you'll have to get used to it.*

The thought was frightening and exciting all at once. It might be nice to not have to drive a car that wasn't held together with duct tape, but there was no way that she was going to be okay living in something this fancy all the time.

"In here." Carson ducked into a room Belle was very familiar with and she immediately felt more at ease.

It didn't matter what house a kitchen was in, it was a space that meant home.

"I'm not much of a cook." He gave her a look as if to stop whatever quip she was about to offer, and Belle grinned. "But I do make a mean hot chocolate." He began pulling open cabinets.

Belle settled herself at the bar. "How is a guy from California good at making hot chocolate?"

Carson snorted. "From spending time skiing with Gray."

Belle nodded, once again reminded of how different their lives were. Small doubts began to climb back in and Belle struggled to push them away. She had been so eager, so determined to spend time with him tonight, figuring out their relationship and apologizing for doubting him, but as much as Belle hated to admit it…Emme had been right.

Belle didn't deserve Carson. He was sweet, patient, and kind with a wicked intelligence and sense of humor. She enjoyed every single aspect of it and could finally admit to herself that she truly loved him. But what could she possibly offer in return? Belle was a too-old college student, who had a couple hundred bucks to her name. She could make a great croissant, but she couldn't keep a marriage from falling apart. What would Carson ever see in her for the long term?

"Hey."

His soft voice drew Belle from her thoughts and she pulled her eyes from the lovely granite countertop.

"What's going on in that beautiful head of yours?" He was leaning over the counter from the other side and reached out to tap her forehead.

Belle shook her head. She couldn't tell him all the junk she was now struggling with. He was too nice. He'd just assure her everything was fine.

Carson narrowed his eyes, then straightened and slapped the counter. "Come."

"Excuse me…I'm not a dog."

He smiled and held out a hand. "Isabelle, would you please join me for a moment?"

"What about the hot chocolate?" she asked, even as she stood up and took his hand.

"It'll keep." He led her out of the kitchen, but paused in the entrance to the ballroom. "Now…let's try again. What's bothering you?"

He frowned. "Is it Emme? Because I meant what I said. She won't bother us again."

Belle rolled her eyes and shook her head. "No. She's gone and that's all I care about."

"Then what is it?"

Belle shook her head again, then squeaked when Carson gave her a fierce but short kiss.

"Care to try again?" he asked, raising an eyebrow.

Belle paused, still a little off kilter. "It's no—" Another kiss cut off her words again. Belle pushed back. "Are you going to keep doing that?"

His gray eyes shot up to the ceiling before looking back at her. "As long as I have permission."

Belle looked up and groaned. "How did I not see that coming?"

He laughed and tightened his hold around her. "Sweetheart, I can do this all night." He brought their foreheads together. "What's bothering you?"

Belle let out a long breath. First things first..."I'm sorry."

He pulled back. "What? Why?"

Belle swallowed hard. "For doubting you." She couldn't look straight at him and instead focused on his shirt, where her hands were already resting against his chest. "I..." She forced herself to look up. "I was scared."

His face was solemn, but at least he wasn't pushing her away. "Of what?"

Belle's eyes closed and her head fell forward against his sternum. "Of us...of you...of the fact that I didn't belong."

*****

Carson could actually feel his heart breaking as she spoke. He'd thought he'd done such a great job of making her see things his way. He had broken down her wall, but now he realized she had needed that wall. She needed to feel like something was in her control, and he'd taken that away from her.

He sighed. "No...I'm sorry."

Belle's eyes got wide. "What? I'm the one who believed a bunch of lies and didn't give you a real chance for rebuttal."

"And I'm the one that pushed you too far, too fast, and then got angry when you didn't keep up the way I wanted you to."

Belle started to shake her head, but Carson put a stop to it with another searing kiss.

Secretly, he hoped she would continue to argue because his little mistletoe idea was paying amazing dividends.

"You can't keep doing that!" she scolded.

Carson proved her wrong.

"Carson!"

With a laugh, he simply kissed her again, then again, then again until she huffed and gave in, kissing him back. It only took seconds before the kiss grew and Carson was pulling her in as close as he could get her. She was so perfect in his arms. How could he ever let her go? Even knowing he would see her again didn't seem to be enough to assuage the hunger he was feeling. He wanted this woman in his life and he didn't want to wait to do it.

He was aware she wasn't ready to move past their current status, which had only changed in the last five minutes, but she needed to know she didn't have to doubt him. She needed to know he would always be here, however long it took for her to return his feelings.

"I love you," he whispered against her lips, moving his attention to her cheekbone, then her ear, and down to her neck.

"I love you too," she whispered back, her voice low and hoarse from their exchange.

Carson stilled before slowly moving back so he could look her in the eye. He knew he probably had a deer in the headlights look, but there was no controlling it. "What?" he squeaked.

Belle winced a little. "I love you?"

"Is that a question or a statement?"

She laughed softly and reached up to cup his face. "Carson Cordova. I've done a lot of thinking this last week and I've had a few revelations. One. You're amazing. You burst into my life and just like Sleeping Beauty, woke me up with a kiss under the mistletoe."

He grinned.

"You've been sweet, patient and kind, knowing that I was struggling and that my past had left me in a bad place." She took a shaky breath and he could feel her fingers begin to tremble against his cheeks. "I don't live in the same world as you and your fancy sports cars or not even looking at checks when you pay at a restaurant. I can barely keep up with your sharp mind, and your desire to turn everything into an argument kind of drives me crazy."

He gave her a look, but Belle just smiled.

"Heaven knows I don't deserve you...at all." She squeezed his face a little when he tried to shake it. "But heaven also knows that I want to. I love you."

"Belle," Carson said, his voice thick with emotion. "You know...the funny thing is...I was desperate to be seen as myself, but I chased the woman who thought I *was* someone else."

Belle gave a watery laugh.

"Sweetheart, you're beautiful." He kissed the tip of her nose. "Inside and out and whether or not you have two nickels to rub together doesn't mean a thing." He kissed her cheek. "And we're not in two separate worlds. No one can keep up with my sarcasm the way you do." He kissed her other cheek. "And no one is able to shut up my devil's advocate side faster than you." He kissed right between her eyebrows. "But the best thing about you is that you're a fighter. You're loyal and hardworking. You don't seek the limelight, but you aren't afraid to jump in with both feet either."

Belle sniffled and Carson took one hand off her back in order to wipe a stray tear.

"I love you," he continued. "I love you for who you are and who you're trying to become. But most of all, I love you because you see me for who *I* am. Not because I'm related to someone famous, or because I have deep pockets. But as just plain Carson Cordova. Argumentative, bubble pushing, opinionated me."

Belle shook her head. "There's nothing plain about you."

"After our mutual confessions, what do you say to putting the last ugly week behind us and just choosing to move forward? No secrets this time?"

Belle pressed her lips together. "What about when you go back to California?"

Carson shrugged. "I don't know. But I'm pretty sure two intelligent people like us can figure it out." He ducked his head to look her straight in the eye. "What do you say?"

"I—"

Carson cut her off with another kiss.

"Car—"

And another. She'd catch on eventually.

Laughing, Belle shook her head, finally figuring out what he was looking for. "Yes!" she cried, leaving a playful slap on his shoulder.

"That's my girl," he said before turning the short playful kisses into something more tender.

"Yes, yes, I am," Belle managed to get out before giving in fully and letting the magic of the mistletoe above them lead them along.

Sometime later they were back in the kitchen, but the mood had changed. Carson couldn't seem to stop smiling and he found himself working hard to catch Belle's eye every time he moved through the room.

Her soft and shy smile made him want to drop the two mugs he was working on and carry her away to some cabin deep in the woods so they wouldn't be disturbed for the foreseeable future, and he could have her all to himself.

Her question about California was nagging in the back of his brain. While he didn't mind jumping into the deep end, there was no way Belle would be ready to marry him... But maybe she would be ready for something else.

Carson handed her a mug, then sipped his own.

"Mmm..." Belle tilted her head back with her eyes closed, savoring the taste. "You're right. You're really good at this."

He grinned behind his mug. "I aim to please." The look she gave him told Carson she was more than pleased.

Forget the hot chocolate. There were more important things in life.

He set down his mug and took hers away.

"Hey!"

Taking her hand, Carson led her to the TV room.

"What are we doing?" Belle asked.

"Turning on a Christmas movie that we're not going to watch."

"Uh..." Belle gave him a look.

Carson shrugged as he tugged her down beside him on the sofa. "I figured it gave me a good excuse as to why my brother is going to find me holding and making out with you whenever he and Brook get home."

"Carson!"

That was the last word Belle got out before the movie started and Carson pulled her onto his lap, proceeding to do just as he'd promised. If Grayson and Brook found them, they were smart enough to walk away without disturbing the busy couple, who probably wouldn't have noticed them anyway.

CHAPTER 27

Belle rubbed her sweaty hand against her jean clad thigh. Christmas at the Cordova home had been picture perfect. The food, the fire in the fireplace, the tree and wrapped presents. Everything looked like it came out of a holiday movie and Belle had been terrified to touch a single thing, despite the fact that Brook and several of Carson's friends had given her gifts.

Belle felt horrible that she had been unable to give gifts in return, though she had shown up with a large tray of her pain au chocolates. It was all she'd been able to think of that she could afford that would cover everyone.

Everyone except Carson.

She had a special gift for him that wasn't worth much monetarily, but it meant a lot to her, and she hoped that Carson would understand its meaning. Her apple pie had been forgotten in the car the night of their reunion, but this time she had something else planned.

"Come with me," he whispered, squeezing the hand he held and rising from the couch.

Belle left behind the noisy room without a single protest. She needed a break from the hubbub, even though everyone was lovely. All the children had come with their parents this time and the noise level, which had been high with the adults, was now three times as high. It was a noise Belle knew well, since Cole had screamed all morning as he played with his new truck set. She had no idea that truck noises were so high or so piercing.

"Where are we going?" she whispered, tripping along happily in Carson's wake.

Carson turned to grin at her. "I have something for you."

Belle tugged him to a stop. "You didn't...buy me anything, did you?"

Carson pulled her into walking again. "If I did?"

She shook her head, even though his focus wasn't on her. "Carson, you already gave me something." She had loved the box full of baking supplies. They were all much better quality than she would be able to afford for herself for several years. The fact that he had another gift for her only made her more nervous. There was no way she could compete with that.

He shrugged. "It's a boyfriend's privilege to do what he wants with gifts."

Belle couldn't help but smile at the word *boyfriend*. Mostly in her mind, she had been referring to him as the man she was dating, but boyfriend had such a nice, more permanent ring to it. And the fact that he was the one who said it first gave her all the feels. "In that case, I guess I should admit that I have something for you too."

Carson's grin widened. "Reaaaally? That sounds interesting." One eyebrow quirked. "Does it have anything to do with mistletoe?"

Belle laughed and slapped his arm. "Is that all you think about?"

He tapped his chin. "Yes. Yes, it is." He laughed when she smacked him again. "Can you blame me?" He jerked her toward him and kissed her temple. "Any guy dating someone like you wouldn't be able to help themselves."

Belle actually felt herself melt inside. This man was too good to be true. How did he always seem to know exactly what to say? Emme had been perfect at hitting Belle's insecurities and Carson seemed just as perfect at putting them to rest.

The longer they went in their marriage, the less Belle's ex-husband had paid attention to her. She had come away from their divorce feeling frumpy, old, and worn. Carson had helped her feel young, beautiful, and powerful, and it was a heady sensation.

"Okay, let's go in here."

Belle followed him inside a small study sized room. After closing the door behind her, she turned and gasped. This was no random room. Small Christmas lights had been hung across the ceiling, creating a warm glow that matched the fire in the fireplace. Flower arrangements filled with holiday decor and colors were strewn throughout the room. All in all, it was a stunning, cozy getaway from the rest of the world, and Belle loved it.

Carson came up behind her and wrapped his arms around her from behind. "What do you think?"

"It's beautiful," she breathed, her eyes still wandering all around the room. "Where in the world did you get flowers like that at this time of year?"

She felt him chuckle. "Let's just say I know someone."

Belle spun. "Oh...the redhead. Right? Rose? She's a florist."

Carson tapped the side of his nose. "Nothing gets past you."

Belle rolled her eyes. "You're ridiculous."

"And you're just as oblivious as usual."

She frowned, then followed his finger to the hanging mistletoe just above their heads. Belle laughed. "You planned for everything."

"Of course." Carson bent his head and took the next several minutes to let Belle know just how he felt about her.

Once she was out of breath and struggling not to jerk him closer, he pulled back and let go of her. When Carson pushed a hand through his hair and blew out a breath, she knew he was just as affected as she was. That feeling of power resonated inside of her again.

"Is it warm in here?" he asked, clearing his throat when his voice came out funny. "Maybe I shouldn't have lit the fire."

Belle smiled. "Come sit with me and I'll give you your gift." Once they were settled on the couch, Belle pulled a small envelope from her back pocket. Her fingers shook and the paper crackled. There was nothing pretty or holiday-ish about her gift, but it represented something she hadn't trusted with another person...ever.

Carson's warm hand landed on hers. "Breathe, sweetheart. It's okay. You don't have to give it to me."

Belle shook her head, still struggling to meet his eyes. "I *want* to give it to you." She finally forced her eyes up. "But sometimes taking a leap of faith is hard."

He waited, just watching to see what she would do.

Taking a deep breath, Belle put the envelope in his hand, but her throat was too tight to get words out.

Carson looked between her and the small white rectangle several times before he shifted so he could more easily open it. He pulled out the folded bundle of papers and unfolded them.

Belle chewed her bottom lip as she waited for him to understand. She needed him to figure it out because she was too terrified to say it.

Carson was frowning as he lifted the first page and looked at the second. "Is this...?" His eyes widened and he jerked his head toward Belle before going back to the papers. He frantically moved through all of them, his lips moving slightly as he read a few words from each page.

Finally, after what seemed like an eternity, he carefully folded the papers and put them back in the envelope. They were then slipped into the pocket on his shirt before he turned to Belle. "I've never treasured something more. Thank you."

Belle nodded. "I love you," she said, her shaky voice barely audible. "Thank you for finding me."

Carson cupped her face and left the sweetest butterfly kiss on her forehead. "Thank you for trusting me," he said against her skin.

*****

Carson knew if his brother was here, Gray would tease Carson about the fact that his eyes were filled with wet emotions men didn't usually like to admit to. But who could blame him? Belle had given him copies of her recipes. The very thing she held onto as if her life, or livelihood, depended on. She had given it to *him*. She had given her trust to *him*.

Out of all the men in the world who could have caught her eye, it was Carson. The man who had lived in a shadow since he was a young boy. He had never felt so empowered or so tall. The woman he loved with all of himself trusted him with all of her.

He cleared his throat, trying to keep the tears out of his voice. "I, uh...have something for you as well." He reached across the coffee table and grabbed a black binder. He couldn't help but chuckle. Neither of them had taken the initiative to make their gifts overly attractive. Perhaps it had to do with the reasons behind them. Now that he had seen her gift, he knew they had both attempted to give gifts of the heart, rather than gifts for fun. He'd take a crinkled envelope anyday.

He handed her the binder and Belle gave him an amused look. "Light reading?"

He grinned back. "Just open it."

She did, her unmanicured fingers carefully resting against the first page. She studied it for a minute, then looked up at him with a furrowed brow. "I don't understand."

Carson leaned forward. "These are buildings for rent."

"Buildings?" she squeaked. "For what?"

Carson took a fortifying breath. This was where things might get a little sticky. But after receiving her gift, he prayed she understood. "Belle, I can't stand the idea of going back down to California and leaving you behind."

Her big brown eyes filled with tears. "I know it's going to be horrible."

He nodded. "Agreed. Which is why I did some research." He pointed to the first page. "This building has cheap rent and probably a little more square footage than you want, but it's in a place with a lot of foot traffic." He flipped the page. "This one might be a little small, but with a good remodeling, I think it would be functional for your first few years at first." He flipped another page. "This one is one of my favorites. It's newer and would take minimal work to have it set up for you. It's in a great neighborhood and close to an elementary school." He grimaced. "The downside is the rent reflects all that."

"Wait, wait, wait..." Belle put up her hand and shook her head. "These are all...places to open my bakery?"

He nodded slowly. "Yes."

She stared. "These aren't in Oregon, are they?"

He shook his head, still moving slowly.

"In California?"

Carson's heart was about to pound right up his throat, he was so worried. Asking her to move to California was a big deal, but he honestly knew he'd have to quit his job otherwise. The idea of being separated from her for an extended amount of time made him sick to his stomach. He couldn't do it and there was no way she was ready to say yes across the altar.

"You want me to move to California." It was a statement, not a question, but he answered anyway.

"I'm asking you to consider it."

"And where would I live?"

Carson flipped to another section of the binder. "These are all places that are available right now." He scrunched his nose. "Although, it all moves fast enough in Cali that I can't guarantee they will be available a week from now, but as of yesterday, they were all open."

Belle nodded, her eyes glued to the page.

He held his breath. Was she upset? Did she think he'd crossed a line? Was she ready to run like before? He couldn't see her eyes, so he couldn't read her emotions. Not knowing was making him crazy.

"Is there one that's your favorite?"

The question caught him off guard, but he quickly recovered. Carson flipped a few pages in and tapped on a picture. "This one."

Her brown eyes met his. "And why is that?"

Carson forced himself to stay calm. "Because this one happens to be right next to me."

Her eyebrows shot up. "So we'd be neighbors?"

He nodded. "Yes."

"That would be a big move." Her face still showed no emotion.

Carson swallowed. "It is...and it's only the first one."

"First one?"

"I'm asking you to move to California to be my neighbor, because when the time is right...I'm going to ask you to not live next to me, but to live with me." He was having a heart attack. Carson was positive the pounding against his chest could be heard throughout the entire mansion he was sitting in.

Her eyes refilled with tears. "You want to marry me?"

"When you're ready."

"What if I'm not ready for another year? Or five years? Or ten?"

Carson smiled and shook his head. He took the binder and set it aside, taking her hands in his own. "Mistletoe doesn't lie," he quipped, making her laugh through her emotions. "I knew from our first kiss that you were going to be the one for me." He squeezed her fingers. "That's not going to change. I'll wait for you however long it takes, no matter what. One, five, ten...one hundred..." He shook his head. "I don't care." He brought his forehead to hers. "You're worth waiting for."

Belle broke down as her arms went around him. She cried into the crook of his neck and Carson wrapped his arms around her, rubbing her back and letting her come to grips with all of it. He knew he'd thrown a lot at her, but if there was any chance of him getting his dreams and helping Belle get hers, this was the path he saw. And so far, she hadn't run away or told him to leave, so he was hoping this was a good cry, not a bad one.

Finally, Belle pulled back and wiped her eyes. "I'm going to need a really big loan," she said.

He nodded. "I have some contacts at the bank. I think we can figure it out."

"You realize this is crazy, right?" Belle laughed softly. "Just picking up and moving to California only a month after meeting you?"

"Well, I'm no Grayson Cordova, but I'm hoping I'm worth enough to help you make your decision."

Belle scowled. "I would think you'd know by now that I'm not into Grayson. I'm into you." She put her palms on his cheeks. "I'm terrified inside that someday you'll change your mind about me, but I want, so, so, badly, to believe this is all going to work out. That's why I gave you my recipes. That's why I admitted that I love you." She kissed him much shorter than he wanted. "And since those recipes are headed to California, I suppose it makes sense for me to be too."

Carson couldn't help the whoop that flew from his mouth. He jumped to his feet and pulled Belle up with him, picking her up and spinning her in a circle. "We'll get it all figured out," he assured her quickly. "Your building will have the best of everything. That kitchen stuff you love so much? All of it. Everything you need, we'll make sure you have."

Belle put her fingers on his lips, effectively stopping his rambling. "All I want right now is for you to kiss me under the mistletoe."

Carson smiled and tucked her tighter against his chest. "We don't need the mistletoe anymore," he teased, rubbing his nose against hers. "We've used it enough that we have mistletoe permission anytime we want."

"Is that your excuse for just kissing me all the time?"

He tapped the side of his nose. "One smart cookie."

She laughed. "That never gets old."

"Nope." Carson brought their mouths close together. "It never will." And then he gave her a kiss that no mistletoe could ever keep up with.

EPILOGUE

Belle wiped her hands on her apron and went to answer the door. "Hey, you," she said, opening the door farther to let Carson inside.

"Hey, yourself," Carson responded. His arms were full, but he leaned in for a quick kiss as he crossed her threshold. Stopping after Belle closed the door, he closed his eyes and took in a long breath. "Smells good in here." He moaned.

Belle laughed and smacked his shoulder. "No eating the cookies. I made them for the tree." She pointed to the artificial tree she had set up in the corner just the night before. It was amazing how far she had come during this last year. Carson had opened her eyes to a world she had forgotten and Belle had never been happier.

The last year had been spent renting an apartment she really couldn't afford, building a business from the ground up, hiring two new employees for said business and of course, dating her too-handsome neighbor.

She was happier than she had ever been, though a small part of her was beginning to wonder if she and Carson would ever move to the next level. She loved Carson with everything in her, but he seemed content to keep living next door to each other, rather than becoming a single household.

Belle wasn't ready to broach the subject, but she struggled sometimes, worrying that she just wasn't enough to tempt him to make the leap from attached to married.

"Carson!" She hurried over and tried to wrestle the cookie from his hands. She'd been so caught up in all her thoughts that he had gotten to the table and snatched one without her noticing. "Those are for the tree!"

Carson laughed and maneuvered her so that his arms were now wrapped around her instead of leaning over the table. "Now whatcha gonna do? Hm?"

Belle put her hands on his shoulders and tried to look coy. "I don't know..." She tilted her head. "Maybe I'll use some of those self defense moves I learned in class last week."

"Our future children will thank you not to do that," Carson said with a wince.

Belle stilled. "What?" she breathed.

Carson nuzzled her neck. "What, what?"

"Carson." She grabbed his face and forced him to stand still. "You said *our children.*"

He raised his eyebrows. "Yeah."

"We'd have to be married to have children," Belle pointed out, feeling as if they were somehow talking in circles with each other. How could he just throw out a line like that as if it were no big deal? Didn't he understand women's feelings at all?

Carson smirked. "Yeah."

Belle waited. "Yeah? That's all you're gonna say?"

He laughed then, a great big belly laugh. Belle stepped back as he bent over, resting his hands on his knees. "You should see your face," he said through his gasping breaths.

Belle put her hands on her hips. "I'm starting to think you should just take those cookie supplies and go home."

Carson straightened and shook his head, reaching out to grab her waist when she tried to walk away. "Hold on," he said, his humor finally fading. "You aren't letting me finish."

"Finish what? Laughing at me?" Belle argued. She didn't like what was happening with this conversation. Marriage was a sacred thing to her. She had gone into hers with stars in her eyes and the ending of it had nearly broken her. How dare he joke about something like that!

He shook his head, his smile still a mile wide. "No. Enjoying you." Carson leaned down for a short but fierce kiss.

Belle pushed him back. "I don't like joking about things like children and marriage," she said softly.

"I'm not joking," Carson insisted.

"That would suggest you've proposed, which you haven't," Belle snapped right back.

Carson sighed and began to dig into his pocket. "I guess I did things out of order, huh?"

Belle's frustration fled. "What do you mean?"

"I mean, usually a guy gives the girl a ring, *then* asks, but I put the cart before the horse." Carson stepped back, holding the very ring box he had been referring to. "Are you ready this time? I want to make sure we do it right."

Belle's bottom lip began to tremble. "Are you for real?" she asked. "Don't toy with me, Carson Cordova."

All the amusement in the situation finally faded from his face. "Isabelle Kerr, I've never been more serious." He brushed a tear from her cheek. "I know I tease a lot. I can't seem to help it. I've told you how much I enjoy breaking the rules in my private life since my professional one is so shaped by them, but right now, I suppose it's time to do it right."

He got down on one knee and Belle felt her heart begin to pound in her chest. She couldn't believe this was real. After all this time, was she really going to get the man of her dreams permanently?

"Isabelle," Carson said in a low tone. "You are my perfect woman."

A snort of laughter broke through her tears.

"You're feisty, full of life, the best baker I've ever met, and so beautiful it takes my breath away every time I see you."

The tears doubled.

"I know I'm not always easy to get along with, I know being part of the Cordova family isn't all it's cracked up to be, I know you've just spent the last year building your independent self, but I'm asking all the same...Belle, love of my life, verbal sparring partner extraordinaire, miracle worker with flour and yeast, will you please allow me to be your partner? Will you make room in that wonderfully self sustaining world of yours to allow me to walk with you? Not in front and not behind, but *with* you? Holding your hand? Stealing kisses along the way? And enjoying everything life throws at us together?"

Belle had no words. Now she knew. She knew exactly why Carson had waited a full year to ask to marry her, and it only made her love him more. How could she possibly turn down a man who had put her own needs ahead of his own? One that was the exact opposite of her ex-husband who only took and never gave?

Carson had given her everything. Her life was only as good as it was because he had encouraged her in it and then stood back and watched her grow. She owed him everything, but even more, she *wanted* to give him everything.

"I love you," she rasped through her tears. "And it would be the greatest honor imaginable to be at your side. Not because you're related to a famous movie star, or because you have a good career, but because you're you. Argumentative, teasing, supportive, you." She laughed a little, wiping at her cheeks. "And no more pretending to be your brother stuff. I don't want to share you with Hollywood. I want you all for myself."

Carson jumped to his feet and put the beautiful solitaire on her left hand. "I think that's the most perfect plan I've ever heard." He gave her a soft, lingering kiss. "Thank you."

Belle grabbed his shirt and pulled him closer. "Don't get all gentle on me now, Cordova. I know exactly what type of man lurks beneath that calm facade."

"Brace yourself," Carson warned with a wink. "I might be a little excited at the moment."

"Oh good," Belle breathed as he leaned in. "That makes two of us."

And there were. Two of them. Two with the same ideas for the future and two who would move forward together to create a family and a home of their own. Belle would never have suspected that an unexpected mistletoe kiss would lead to all this, the miracle that being part of a pair would make her even stronger than being by herself.

Don't Miss Jude's Story!

Look for the next book in the series

"Her Unexpected Gift"

www.ingramcontent.com/pod-product-compliance
Lightning Source LLC
Chambersburg PA
CBHW070923190726
48292CB00004B/1080

9 781956 176179